THE WIRE DEVILS

Also Published by the
University of Minnesota Press

The Boomer: A Story of the Rails by Harry Bedwell

THE
WIRE DEVILS

Frank L. Packard

Introduction by Robert MacDougall

University of Minnesota Press
Minneapolis
London

Originally published in 1918 by the Copp, Clark Company, Ltd., Toronto, and the George H. Doran Company, New York

First University of Minnesota Press edition, 2013

Published by the University of Minnesota Press
111 Third Avenue South, Suite 290
Minneapolis, MN 55401-2520
http://www.upress.umn.edu

LIBRARY OF CONGRESS CATALOGING-IN-PUBLICATION DATA
Packard, Frank L. (Frank Lucius), 1877–1942.
The wire devils / Frank L. Packard ; introduction by Robert MacDougall.
First University of Minnesota Press edition.
ISBN 978-0-8166-8456-4 (pb : alk. paper)
I. Title.
PS3531.A2154W57 2013
813'.52 — DC23   2013000522

Printed in the United States of America on acid-free paper

The University of Minnesota is an equal-opportunity educator and employer.

20 19 18 17 16 15 14 13   10 9 8 7 6 5 4 3 2 1

CONTENTS

— INTRODUCTION —

Robert MacDougall

Industrial America was born, according to Henry Adams, in May 1844. On the twenty-fourth day of that month, Samuel Morse demonstrated his telegraph to a gathering of dignitaries in the Supreme Court chambers of the U.S. Capitol. Using the code that bears his name, Morse tapped out four words from the Bible's Book of Numbers: WHAT HATH GOD WROUGHT. His message traveled to Baltimore on an iron wire strung along the right-of-way of the Baltimore and Ohio Railroad. There, an associate received the message and sent it back to Washington. Henry Adams wasn't present—he was six years old at the time—but looking back six decades later, Adams declared this the moment that everything changed. "The old universe was thrown into the ash-heap," he wrote, "and a new one created."[1]

Many people think of Samuel Morse as the telegraph's inventor, but it would be more precise to say that he designed the first electrical telegraph system that became practical and widespread. As usually happens in the history of technology, Morse's breakthrough combined and refined several existing ideas. His demonstration of May 24, 1844, is similarly misremembered as the first telegraph message. In fact, it was not even the first message sent along the Washington–Baltimore line, which had been in operation for several weeks. We remember "what hath God wrought" as the first telegraph message because of the aptness and resonance of that famous phrase.

Morse's message captured the wonder and anxiety evoked by this amazing new technology, which turned words into lightning and flung them around the earth at incomprehensible speed. The steam engine and the railroad provoked similar responses in nineteenth-century Americans—a powerful brew of awe, excitement, and sometimes fear that historians have called the "technological sublime."[2] Together, these new engines of power, transportation, and communication transformed the nineteenth-century United States. Or, to be more clear about who was acting on whom, nineteenth-century Americans seized these technologies and used them to transform their world.

Writing his memoirs at the start of the twentieth century, Henry Adams felt the America he lived in was unrecognizable as the country of his youth. *The Education of Henry Adams,* published in 1918, was his somber attempt to come to terms with a world transformed by railroads, telegraphs, and industrialization. "The American boy of 1854," Adams believed, "stood nearer the year 1 than to the year 1900."[3] Historians who study this period have returned again and again to Adams's *Education* as a classic document of the anxieties produced by technological change. But other books from this era offer different portraits of the same phenomenon. One such source, published in the same year as *The Education of Henry Adams,* is Frank L. Packard's novel *The Wire Devils.* Packard's potboiler is less erudite than Adams's memoir, to put it mildly. But *The Wire Devils* is just as telling, hugely entertaining, and perhaps a more representative artifact of the technological sublime. It also has more fight scenes.

Frank Lucius Packard was born in 1877 to American parents in Montreal, Quebec, and he crossed back and forth between Canada and the United States throughout his life. In the consolidation of industrial America, 1877 was an eventful year. Historian Robert Bruce called it "the year of violence."[4] Railway construction was rebounding after several years of panic and depression. The railroad and telegraph lobbies played something of a kingmaker's role in resolving the deadlocked election of the previous year. The compromise they brokered put Rutherford Hayes in the White House and removed federal troops from the post–Civil War South, effectively ending Reconstruction. The Western Union Telegraph Company entered the telephone business in 1877, in competition with the newly formed Bell Telephone Company. This was also the year of the Great Railroad Strike, America's first truly national confrontation between capital and labor. And in the West, the U.S. Army brought the Black Hills War against the Lakota and Cheyenne to a violent

conclusion after the Battle of the Little Big Horn
one year before. Packard grew up in the golden age
of railroading, an era of nation-building and heroic
feats of engineering but also of violent conflict and
corruption.

Packard graduated from Montreal's McGill
University in 1897 and became a civil engineer for
the Canadian Pacific Railway, where he took notes
and observed details that would fuel his future literary career. He began writing professionally around
1902. Within a few years, he was able to move to New
York City and write full-time, selling stories of railroad adventure to magazines such as *Munsey's* and
the *Century*. Packard married in 1910 and took his
bride on a one-year tour of the American and Canadian West in search of material for his stories. They
then settled in Lachine, Quebec, where, over the
next three decades, Packard would write dozens of
popular novels, short stories, screenplays, and serials.
Readers of railroad fiction remember him for a series
of short stories collected in three volumes: *On the
Iron at Big Cloud* (1911), *The Night Operator* (1919),
and *Running Special* (1925). Frank Donovan Jr., the
chief chronicler of American railroad literature, considered these stories the acme of their genre and rated
Packard second only to Frank Hamilton Spearman,
the dean of America's literary railroad school.[5]

Outside the railroad genre, Packard was best
known for his creation Jimmie Dale, the Gray Seal.
The star of three novels, two collections of stories,
and at least one movie serial, Jimmie Dale was a gen-

tleman thief turned good, an audacious cat burglar and safecracker who used his talents to fight crime. Packard's depictions of underworld New York were vivid and convincing for the time, and his thrillers formed a sort of bridge between the dime novels of the 1800s and the grittier pulp fiction of the 1930s and beyond. Few elements of the Jimmie Dale adventures were entirely original, but Packard brought them all together: the wealthy playboy, the secret identity, the gadget-filled hideout, the flamboyant nom de guerre— updated for a twentieth-century milieu. The blue-print he offered for future dual-identity crime fighters proved so ingenious that all the masked avengers and caped crusaders to follow (the Shadow, the Spider, Zorro, Batman, and the rest) could be said to owe a debt to Jimmie Dale.[6]

Packard's railroad fiction and his crime thrill-ers came together in the book you now hold in your hands. First published in 1918, *The Wire Devils* fea-tures an outlaw hero not unlike Jimmie Dale, but transports him from New York City to the railroads of the West. We never learn just where the fictional city of Selkirk is located (there is a real Selkirk in Manitoba, Canada, but *The Wire Devils* is plainly set in the United States), but it seems there must be an express train there from Sing Sing prison, so frequently do the hoodlums of the Bowery and the Lower East Side ride the rails to Selkirk. In trans-planting the gangs of New York to the booming railroads and telegraph lines of the West, Packard creates a hybrid western and gangland thriller, set in a crisply drawn world of train robberies and railroad detectives, tapped wires and secret codes.

The Wire Devils is perhaps the foremost example of what I have elsewhere called wire thrillers, a string of novels from the late nineteenth and early twentieth centuries that used the railroad, telegraph, and telephone as a backdrop for adventure.[7] Like the novels of Clive Cussler or Tom Clancy, these were the high-tech thrillers of their day. Loaded with railroad slang and technical jargon, the wire thrillers offered fast-paced narratives driven by then cutting-edge technologies. They portrayed the business of telegraphy and the railroads as an exciting demimonde of crime and derring-do. Other examples of the genre include Arthur Stringer's *The Wire Tappers* (1906) and *Phantom Wires* (1907), Franklin Pitt's *Brothers of the Thin Wire* (1915), and Frederick Van Rensselaer Dey's marvelously titled *Fighting Electric Fiends; Or, Bob Ferret among the Wire Tappers* (1898). *The Wire Devils* is probably the best of the breed, both on its own terms as a thriller and as an artifact of the excitement and anxiety that once surrounded the telegraph and railroad.

What makes *The Wire Devils* worth reading nearly a century after it was written? At least three good reasons present themselves to me. First, the book is a valuable document of the railroad and the telegraph at the zenith of their influence on American life. It was written to entertain, not to become historical evidence or a piece of industrial sociology, but Packard had been a real railroad man. He knew and cared about how things worked, and he strove to get the details right. In reading the novel, we are treated to frequent, enthusiastic descriptions of how the railroad and telegraph operated, both independently and together. The titular crooks in *The Wire Devils* earn their name by hijacking a railroad's telegraph lines. The book contains much discussion of how this could be done, what the railroad detectives might do to trace the intruders on their network, and how the criminals thwart those efforts. Wires are cut, tapped, and traced. Messages are coded and cracked, forged and intercepted. *The Wire Devils* is a primer of sorts on the intertwined machinery of a railroad and its telegraph, showing how those networks of commerce and information might be manipulated or misused.

Pulp historian Robert Sampson pointed out the trickery in Packard's apparent realism. "The sense of reality that fills his work is slickly deceptive," Sampson wrote. "The vivid descriptions" contain "brazen sleight-of-hand."[8] But this was praise, not criticism. *The Wire Devils* is a thriller and cannot honestly be called realistic. Packard's protagonist, the Hawk, has an astonishing knack for finding convenient trapdoors and for overhearing only the most significant snatches of conversation. The novel's gang of crooks is "an organised criminal league as dangerous and powerful as has ever existed in this country," yet it seems to contain only about six members. Packard's goal as a thriller writer was not true realism but mimesis: feels real–ism, if you like. The more melodramatic aspects of his story are grounded and supported by his careful depiction of the technologies involved. If we are convinced by Packard's descriptions of telegraph sounders, taps, and junctions, we can be carried along by the engine of his story, and we are less likely to be derailed by its more preposterous twists and turns.

Besides describing how the railroad and telegraph were used, *The Wire Devils* captured something harder for historians to reconstruct: what ordinary people thought and especially how they felt about the new technological systems that were reordering their world. This is a question historians always want to ask and can almost never answer. What did it *feel* like? What did it feel like to live through the transportation and communication revolutions of the late nineteenth and early twentieth centuries? What did it feel like to live in a vast nation suddenly made small by railroad lines and telegraph wires? The light it sheds on these questions is another reason *The Wire Devils* remains well worth reading today.

The Education of Henry Adams documented the unease of one brilliant but idiosyncratic intellectual as he looked back in melancholy on a lifetime of technological change. But Adams spoke truly only for Henry Adams. Many of his countrymen rushed to embrace the march of progress. They may have feared the telegraph, but they loved it even more. As Perry Miller memorably put it, Americans "flung themselves into the technological torrent. . . . They shouted with glee in the midst of the cataract, and cried to each other as they went headlong down the chute that here was their destiny, here was the tide that would sweep them toward the unending vistas of prosperity."[9] What makes *The Wire Devils* and other thrillers in this genre such useful documents for historians is that they capture both the gloom and the glee, the anxiety but also the excitement surrounding the telegraph and other new devices. That very contrast, that alternating current of fascination and unease, electrifies the technological thriller. It makes the wire thrillers rich sources for reconstructing how Americans once felt about the technologies that they employed to reshape their world.

Few developments seemed more novel or remarkable in the late nineteenth and early twentieth centuries than the new technologies of transportation and communication. In the decades after the Civil War, railroad construction linked the far-flung corners of the United States with thousands of miles of track. The telegraph traveled with those rails, stitching together a new national grid of commerce and information. The first transcontinental telegraph linked the East Coast and the West Coast in 1861. And the telephone, born one year before Frank Packard in 1876, would make the wire a mass medium, eventually connecting nearly every home and life to these new networks of communication and exchange. Such changes were both exciting and scary, as moments of true change always are. Thrillers like *The Wire Devils* explored and exploited this ambivalence.

The changes embodied by the railroad and telegraph were not only technical in nature; they were
economic and political, too. Their rails and wires
formed the nerves and arteries of a new economic
order. In particular, the railroad and telegraph made it
possible for American businesses to grow to unprece-
dented size. Originally organized as local and regional
undertakings, American railroads used the telegraph
to expand their own operations over great distances,
amassing mountains of capital and armies of employ-
ees. Other industries followed in their tracks. The
investment mechanisms that provided funds for railroad construction in the 1870s and 1880s bankrolled
an extraordinary wave of corporate mergers and
consolidations in the subsequent decades. The trans-
formation was profound. An economy of local, family-
oriented firms rapidly gave way to one dominated
by large, nation-spanning corporations. Face-to-face
transactions were eclipsed in importance by long-
distance commerce. Big business, in both an economic
and a geographic sense, had arrived.

Economic and financial fiction became very popular in the late nineteenth and early twentieth centuries, as writers and readers struggled to understand
the transformations through which they lived. *The
Wire Devils* is not explicitly about such matters, but
the new economy is everywhere in the background
of the novel. The railroad and the telegraph are depicted in *The Wire Devils* as booming networks of
commerce and crime. A surprising amount of hard
currency rides the rails around Selkirk City. Cash

boxes and payrolls, along with gold, diamonds, and even a vial of radium, all make tempting targets for the Wire Devils and the Hawk. The railroad and the telegraph were not just a setting or plot device for Frank Packard. As high-tech networks carrying money, goods, and information, they gave him a concrete way to depict criminal and commercial transactions that would otherwise be difficult to portray. They were the new economy made visible. The anxiety and excitement that *The Wire Devils* explores were provoked not only by new technologies but also by this deeper economic change.

"It is a well-known fact that no other section of the population avail themselves more readily and speedily of the triumphs of science than the criminal class," police inspector John Bonfield told the *Chicago Herald* in 1888. "The educated criminal skims the cream from every new invention, if he can make use of it." Bonfield went on to recount the tale of a Chicago millionaire he dubbed "George Maxwell," one of the first people in the city to install a private telephone line between his office and his home. Working at his office, Maxwell was telephoned from his own home by a man who claimed to have bound and gagged his wife and servants and demanded twenty thousand dollars to spare their lives. The helpless millionaire paid the ransom to a waiting confederate, then rushed home, only to find his household undisturbed and his wife perfectly unharmed. She told him that a well-dressed gentleman had visited and, finding Maxwell absent, had asked permission to call him on his private phone. After making the call, he went away, remarking that the telephone was "a very useful invention—it facilitated business so much."[10]

Bonfield claimed this story was true; the magazine that retold his account dubbed it "an interesting fairy tale."[11] True or not, Bonfield's story was in keeping with sensational fictions of crime over the wires that became popular at this time. In *The Four Just Men,* a 1909 potboiler by Edgar Wallace, a cabinet minister is murdered by telegraph, electrocuted over the wires. In Arthur Stringer's 1906 thriller *The Wire Tappers,* a millionaire speculator uses access to a private telegraph line to predict and manipulate the worldwide price of cotton, instigating a bubble and then a massive panic on the stock exchange. And in *The Wire Devils,* of course, the criminals not only listen in to secret messages on the telegraph, they hijack the entire network, using it to transmit their own illicit plans and instructions—until an even more cunning operator turns their tools against them. All of these stories explore the criminal potential of the telegraph and the often blurry line between legitimate commerce and crime.

Besides crime and commerce, *The Wire Devils* is full of codes, ciphers, and secret messages. These are standard conventions of the thriller genre, but they also reflected preoccupations of Packard's time. Knowing the code (Morse code in particular, as well as other secret languages, like technical jargon and criminal slang) marks the heroes of the wire thrillers and their adversaries as members of a technological elect, party to secret struggles behind the mundane surface of the world. Wire thrillers almost always featured scenes in which their heroes or villains used Morse code to communicate under the nose of some unsuspecting quarry, flashing sunlight on a mirror or tapping out dots and dashes along a drainpipe. *The Wire Devils* takes this trope one step further: every time the Hawk decrypts a message, Packard spells out each step in full, as if inviting us to get out our cipher pads and play along.

The telegraph was made for codes and ciphers. Every telegraph message must be transmitted in a code of dots and dashes, and from its early days people took further steps to encrypt their messages. Commercial codebooks were widely available; these were dictionaries assigning code words to hundreds of possible phrases and messages. In one such book, for example, COQUARUM meant "engagement broken off," while GNAPHALIO meant "please send a supply of light clothing."[12] This served both economy and privacy: replacing a long sentence with a single code word made a telegram cheaper to send, and those seeking greater security could create custom codes or use a genuine substitution cipher, like the one employed in *The Wire Devils*. Telegraph companies tried to limit the use of codes and ciphers because they meant less revenue for each message and because it was more difficult to accurately transmit strings of coded gibberish than regular English words. But every effort the industry made to control the practice only pushed their customers to produce more devious codes.

The Wire Devils also depicts a world of counterfeits and counterfeiters, where nothing is as it seems.
Its pages feature phony bills, phony crooks, phony
identities, and more. This too reflected the economic
and cultural upheavals of Packard's day. Counterfeit money had been ubiquitous in nineteenth-
century America, especially before the adoption of a
single government currency in 1863. In the 1850s, it
was estimated that a staggering one-third of all the
banknotes in the United States were fake. After the
1860s, standardized bills and the energetic efforts of
the U.S. Secret Service (a subplot in *The Wire Devils*)
greatly reduced the amount of counterfeit money
in circulation, but the crime remained widespread.
Counterfeiting also had a symbolic significance that
continued to resonate well into the twentieth century. The phony banknote, like the grifter who passed
it, symbolized the perils of an increasingly mobile,
anonymous society, where people and money traveled
faster and farther than traditional ties of reputation
and honest dealing.

Historians Thomas Haskell and Stephen Kern
have both written about a "crisis of causation" in late
nineteenth-century America. Technologies like the
railroad and the telegraph gave new power to their
users, but they also increased the ability of distant
people and events to affect those users' lives. As rails
and wires shrank the nation, it became harder and
harder to imagine ordinary individuals as the masters
of their fates. Local sources of meaning and order,
like the family, the parish, and the small town, were

"drained of causal potency," in Haskell's words, becoming "merely the final links in long chains of causation that stretched off into a murky distance."[13] The small seemed threatened by the big, the local by the national, in every part of American life.

Such fears were vividly expressed in the popular culture of the day. Turn-of-the-century journalists and cartoonists loved to depict corporations and the technological systems they operated as giant octopuses, many-headed hydras, or spiders spinning giant webs. Long, sinuous tentacles and webs were natural symbols for the rails and wires of technological networks and soon became symbols of corporate power more broadly. The apotheosis of this imagery was probably Frank Norris's 1901 novel *The Octopus,* which depicted the fictional Southern Pacific railroad as a colossal, tentacled, blood-sucking monster. The same kinds of metaphor were extremely common in *The Wire Devils* and its ilk. The Hawk calls his nemesis "the Master Spider," his minions are "little spiders," and the telegraph network is a "web" in which he ensnares his prey. Norris's style was more literary than Packard's, although his more lurid descriptions of the railroad as octopus easily outpulped the pulps. But both authors were drawn to these metaphors by the challenge of describing technological systems and illustrating economic change. Norris conceived *The Octopus* as the first book of an epic trilogy that would capture what he called "the New Movement, the New Finance, the reorganization of capital, the amalgamation of powers, the consolidation of enormous enterprises."[14] Packard's aim was just to tell a good story, but *The Wire Devils* is set in the same milieu. Depictions of corporations as monstrous spiders or grasping octopuses expressed something Americans feared to be true about the way their economy had changed.

What distinguishes Norris's Octopus from Packard's Master Spider is that, in *The Wire Devils,* the Spider is a single man. Clever as he is, the Hawk is cleverer. And once the Spider (also known, considerably less ominously, as the Ladybird) has been brought to justice, the conspiracy is over. In Norris's novel, by contrast, nobody commands or controls the Octopus. It is a symbol of impersonal economic forces; it serves only its shareholders, and it runs on its own steam. Stephen Kern's history of causality in fiction specifically cites *The Octopus* to mark a shift toward more complex models of interdependence, where there are no convenient villains to unmask and thus no easy answers.[15] But in the wire thrillers there is always a man behind the curtain. The changes unleashed by new technology may be frightening and far-reaching, but in the end they are nothing that an intrepid man of action cannot solve.

This is the catharsis offered by a good thriller. It tells us that our worst fears are true but then puts everything right. It whips up our anxieties and then resolves them in the simplest way. *The Wire Devils* draws considerable power from the idea that gangsters have taken over the telegraph. This lets Packard indulge in the frightening notion of a criminal railroad without suggesting, as *The Octopus* surely does, that the railroads were criminal in and of themselves. At the opposite pole of the battery powering *The Wire Devils* is the Hawk, a seeming criminal who is really (and if you have read any thrillers in your life, I do not think I am spoiling the surprise) on the side of law and order. The clever construction of *The Wire Devils* lets its readers root for an outlaw against the tendrils and tentacles of the railroad for nineteen of twenty chapters. Only its final pages restore the proper order of things, so that the good guys really are good guys, the bad guys really are bad guys, and the railroad and the telegraph are redeemed.

This brings us to the third and best reason to dust off this century-old thriller. After all this time, *The Wire Devils* remains a good story, well told. Yes, the structure is formulaic, and yes, we have had one hundred years to become familiar with that structure since Packard's day. But the formula became a formula because it works, especially when executed well. And Packard does just that. The high-tech thriller is not a genre that typically improves with age. In 1918, *The Wire Devils* was "torn from the headlines." It would have seemed marvelously up-to-date. Today the cutting-edge technologies it lovingly describes are dusty museum pieces. It is a testament to Packard's skills as a writer that the book still works at all—and it does. The writing is crisp and fast-paced. The gangster slang is a hoot. The escapes are still close, and the double-crosses are still clever. There is little of the moralizing and almost none of the racism or jingoism that modern readers of old pulps must often try to ignore. The book is so relentlessly focused on action and forward motion that it avoids the sodden passages into which other novels from the period often sank. We know where the tracks of this railroad go, but that doesn't prevent us from enjoying the ride.

In the history of the thriller, just as in the history of technology, wholly new inventions are far less common than clever adaptations and imitations. But clever adaptation is nothing to sneeze at. It takes skill and ingenuity to copy and improve a complex machine, recombining and streamlining its parts. Frank Packard did not invent the high-tech thriller, but *The Wire Devils* is a sturdy and ingenious example of its construction, merging elements from dime novels and story papers, more serious naturalist fiction, and Packard's own experience as a railroad man. Its machinery may creak in a few places, but even those moments have their charms. The truth is that nearly one hundred years after its writing, the thing still goes like a runaway train.

NOTES

1. Henry Adams, *The Education of Henry Adams: An Autobiography* (Boston: Houghton & Mifflin, 1918), 5.

2. Leo Marx, *The Machine in the Garden: Technology and the Pastoral Idea in America* (New York: Oxford University Press, 1964), 195–207. For further discussion, see David E. Nye, *American Technological Sublime* (Cambridge, Mass.: MIT Press, 1994).

3. Adams, *Education,* 53.

4. Robert V. Bruce, *1877: Year of Violence* (Indianapolis: Bobbs-Merrill, 1959).

5. Frank P. Donovan, *The Railroad in Literature* (Boston: Railway & Locomotive Historical Society, 1940), 21–25.

6. Robert Sampson, *Yesterday's Faces,* vol. 1, *Glory Figures* (Bowling Green, Ohio: Bowling Green University Popular Press, 1983), 132–62. For the lowdown on Jimmie Dale and other matters, I am indebted to Jess Nevins, two-fisted librarian and world authority on the pulps of yesteryear.

7. Robert MacDougall, "The Wire Devils: Pulp Thrillers, the Telephone, and Action at a Distance in the Wiring of a Nation," *American Quarterly* 57 (September 2006): 715–41.

8. Sampson, *Yesterday's Faces,* 1:128–29.

9. Perry Miller, "The Responsibility of Mind in a Civilization of Machines," *American Scholar* 31 (Winter 1961–62): 51–69, 55.

10. "Heavy Swindling by Telephone," *Electrical Review,* August 11, 1888, 8.

11. Ibid.

12. Tom Standage, *The Victorian Internet* (New York: Berkley Books, 1998), 112.

13. Thomas L. Haskell, *The Emergence of Professional Social Science: The American Social Science Association and the Nineteenth-Century Crisis of Authority* (Champaign: University of Illinois Press, 1977), 15, 40; Stephen Kern, *A Cultural History of Causality: Science, Murder Novels, and Systems of Thought* (Princeton, N.J.: Princeton University Press, 2004).

14. Frank Norris, *The Octopus: A Story of California* (New York: Doubleday & Company, 1901), 99.

15. Kern, *A Cultural History of Causality,* 208–10.

THE WIRE DEVILS

The Wire Devils

—I—

THE SECRET CODE

TWO switch lights twinkled; one at the east, and one at the west end of the siding. For the rest all was blackness. Half way between the switch lights, snuggled close against the single-tracked main line, the station, little more than a shanty and too insignificant to boast a night operator, loomed up shadowy and indistinct. Away to the westward, like jagged points sticking up into the night and standing out in relief against the skyline, the Rockies reared their peaks. And the spell of the brooding mountains seemed to lie over all the desolate, butte-broken surrounding country—for all was utter silence.

And then there came a sound, low at first, like a strange muttering from somewhere to the westward.

9

It died away, grew louder, was hushed again—and broke into a sustained roar. Came then the quick, short gasps of the exhaust—it was a freight, and a heavy one. And suddenly, from up the track, circling an intervening butte, an electric headlight cut streaming through the black. It touched the little station in a queerly inquisitive way in the sweep of its arc, lingered an instant over the platform, then swung to the right of way, and held there, the metals glistening like polished silver ribbons under the flood of light.

Straining, panting at its load, reddening the sky as the fire-box door was flung open, the big ten-wheeler stormed by, coughing the sparks heavenward from its stack. The roar in the still night grew deafening, as boxcar, flat and gondola, lurching, swaying, clanking, groaning, an endless string, tugging at one another, grinding their flanges, screaming as they took up the axle play, staggered with a din infernal past the lonely and unlighted station.

The roar sank into a gradually diminishing murmur. The tail-lights winked like mischievous little red eyes in the distance—and vanished.

All was stillness and that brooding silence again.

And then a man's form, like a black shadow in the darkness, rose from the trackside, and crept to the platform, and along the platform to the station door.

The man bent forward, and the round, white ray of a pocket flashlight played upon the lock. He examined the lock for an instant appraisingly, then drew a bunch of skeleton keys from his pocket, and, selecting one of the number without hesitation, unlocked the door, stepped inside, and closed the door behind him.

The flashlight swept in a circle around the interior of the little station. There were but two rooms—the small waiting room which he had entered, and in which he now stood; and, partitioned off from this, the door open, a still smaller inner room, the agent's office. He moved at once into the latter, and his flashlight, swiftly now, searched around the walls and held upon the clock. It was six minutes to ten.

"Pretty close work!" muttered the man. "Six minutes to wait."

The ray travelled now over the operator's table, and from the table to the switchboard. He reached out, "cut in" the office circuit, listened for an instant as the sounder began to chatter—then the ray swept over the table again. Under a newspaper, that the day man had apparently flung down at haphazard on leaving the office, he found a pad of telegraph blanks, from which, evidently wary of the consequences of using a pad with its resultant tell-tale impressions on the under sheets, he tore off a sheet and laid it down ready to hand before him.

This done, he nodded complacently, sat down in the operator's chair, tilted the chair back, put his feet up on the table, and coolly picked up the newspaper. It was the evening edition of the Selkirk City *Journal*, that had presumably been tossed off at the station by a charitable train crew of some late afternoon train out from the city. He held the paper in one hand, the flashlight in the other, scanned the page, which happened to be an inner one, cursorily, turned it over, and suddenly leaned forward a little in his seat. He was staring at the headline at the top right-hand corner of the front page.

NOTORIOUS CRIMINAL RELEASED FROM SING SING

POLICE ARE WARNED THAT MAN MAY BE IN THIS VICINITY

HARRY MAUL, ALIAS THE HAWK, KNOWN TO BE IN THE WEST

The telegraph sounder chattered volubly for an instant, as though to challenge and silence the raucous ticking of the clock, and ended in a splutter of wrath, as it were, at the futility of its attempt. The clock ticked on. There was no other sound. And then the man spoke aloud.

"That's me," he said. "The Hawk." The paper rattled in his hand. There was a twisted smile on his lips in the darkness. "I guess I'm pretty well known."

The Hawk's eyes fixed on the text, and he began to read:

"It is reported that Harry Maul, better known to the police as the Hawk, safe-breaker, forger and thief, one of the cleverest 'gentleman' crooks in the country, who is at large again after a five-years' penitentiary term, is somewhere in the West.

"The crime wave that has recently been sweeping over Selkirk City and its vicinity, and particularly the daring and, in too many cases, successful outrages with which the railroad officials and detectives have been called upon to cope of late, may, as a very plausible theory, have lured the Hawk here as to a promising field in which to resume his criminal operations. Certain it is that, while we have been the victims of a band of mysterious desperadoes for some time past, the last week or so has seen a very marked increase in the number of crimes that have been committed—a significant coincidence with the Hawk's release from Sing Sing.

"A twenty-thousand-dollar diamond necklace was stolen from a private car two nights ago; there was an express car robbery on Monday of this week; and a sleeping car was thoroughly and systematically looted the night before. True, it is mere conjecture to connect the Hawk with these in any way, since the gang that has been operating in this neighbourhood has proved itself quite capable of all and more than this without any outside and highly specialised assistance, and it would appear is in no whit inferior in resource and devilish ingenuity to the best, or worst, that Sing Sing has to offer in the shape of this so-called Hawk; but, out of conjecture, one question naturally suggests itself.

Granting the presence of the Hawk, is he here as a rival of the criminals of whose existence we are already only too well aware, or is he one of them through old-time associations before Sing Sing put a temporary check upon his activities?"

There was more—a virulent outpouring of wrath at the intolerable extent to which the community, its life and property, was being endangered, and a promise of summary vengeance upon the criminals if caught.

"Quite so!" murmured the Hawk, lowering his feet slowly to the floor. "I guess it wouldn't be healthy to get caught around these parts. I have a feeling that it would be the nearest telegraph pole instead of a trial!"

He tossed the newspaper back on the table. The sounder, spasmodic in its chatter, for the moment was still. All was silence, profound, absolute. Then the clock struck, loud, resonant, smashing through the silence, startling. And at the same instant the sounder broke into a quick tattoo. The Hawk snatched a pencil from his pocket, and jerked his body forward—then relaxed again.

"Stray stuff," he muttered. "Got in ahead of him. We'll get it in a minute now."

Pencil poised in his hand, the flashlight playing on the blank sheet of paper before him, the Hawk waited. The sounder ceased—and almost instantly broke again, rattling sharply through the room. The

Hawk nodded, as his pencil began to travel across the paper.

" 'mtlky'—stroke at five.   Two-three-one to-night," he said aloud.

Without pause, without hesitation, without the slightest indication of spacing to break its continuity, the sounder rattled on—and finally, as abruptly as it had begun, it stopped.

On the sheet of paper the Hawk had written this:

mtlkyeqodktrpcvkqlmtpkpwrtrgtftuqcyqtnttsghv
ukopgfkxtikukqprelcnrcatocuvgdatfgumttlvgpvjf
qwucpmtfkpuckjihgvqptkijvrsawvpxodttdgtqprg
qplqosd

He reached out for the pad, tore off another sheet, and in two parallel columns set down the letters of the alphabet, one column transposed. There was a faint smile on his lips, as he turned again to the cipher and began to write in another line of letters under the original message.

"I wonder what Poe and his predominant 'e' would do with this!" he chuckled.   " 'Combi'—stroke two. Key letter—stroke three." He frowned the next instant.   "What's this!   Ah—stroke three, instead of one." He completed the transposition, stared at the several lines which were now scattered with vertically crossed-out letters, whistled low under his breath, and a grim look settled on his face.

The message now read:

ṃ/lk/combi/natio/z/ninup/perdrṇ/awerl/seftsi/
dediv/ision/e/alpay/mastedardesk/tenth/ousan
ṃ/dinsa/eton/ightps/utnum/beron/eonjo/b

Mechanically, he separated words and sentences,
and, eliminating the superfluous letters, wrote out the
translation at the bottom of the sheet:

> "Combination in upper drawer left side divi-
> sional paymaster ('s) desk. Ten thousand in
> safe to-night. Put Number One on job."

The Hawk stood up, "plugged out" the station circuit, and, gathering up the two sheets of paper he
had used, put them in his pocket; then, leaving the
door of the operator's room open behind him, as he
had found it, he stepped out from the station to the
platform, and, with his skeleton key, relocked the
station door. He stood for a moment staring up
and down the track. The switchlights blinked back
at him confidentially. He listened. The eastbound
freight, from which he had jumped some twenty
minutes before, would cross Extra No. 83, the westbound way freight, at Elkton, seven miles away, but
there was no sound of the latter as yet.

He turned then, and, jumping from the platform
to the track, swung into a dog-trot along the roadbed. The Hawk smiled contentedly to himself. It
was all timed to a nicety! A mile or so to the west,
the right of way rose in a stiff grade that the way
freight would be able to negotiate at no better speed

than the pace at which a man could crawl. He could make the distance readily, board her there, and the way freight would get him to Selkirk—and the divisional paymaster's office!—by about midnight.

He ran on, the swing and ease of a trained athlete in his stride. And, as he ran, he took the sheets of paper from his pocket, and, tearing them into small fragments, scattered the pieces at intervals here and there.

He reached the foot of the grade, and paused to look back along the track, as suddenly from behind him came the hoarse scream of an engine whistle. That was the way freight now, whistling perfunctorily for the deserted station! He had made the grade in plenty of time, though the nearer to the top he could get the better, for the freight, requiring all the initial impetus it could attain, would hit the foot of the grade wide open.

The Hawk broke into a run again, glancing constantly back over his shoulder as he sped on up the grade. And then, when he was well on toward the summit, opening the night like a blazing disk as it rounded a curve, he caught the gleam of the headlight. It grew larger and larger, until, beginning to fling a luminous pathway up the track that, gradually lengthening, crept nearer and nearer to him, he swerved suddenly, plunged down the embankment, and, well away from the trackside, dropped flat upon the ground.

The engine, slowed, was grunting heavily on the incline as it strained by the spot where he lay; there was the glimmer of the front-end brakeman's lamp from the top of one of the forward cars—and, with a quick, appraising glance to measure the length of the train, the Hawk, on hands and knees, crawled forward, and up the embankment, and, in the shadow of the rolling cars themselves, stood up. There would be sharp eyes watching from the cupola of the caboose. He laughed a little. And not only the train crew there, perhaps! The railroad detectives, at their wits' ends, had acquired the habit of late of turning up in the most unexpected places!

A boxcar rolled by him, another, and still another —but the Hawk's eyes were fixed a little further along toward the rear on an open space, where, in the darkness, a flat car gave the appearance of a break in the train. The flat car came abreast of him. He caught the iron foot-rung, jumped, and, with a powerful, muscular swing, flung himself aboard.

The car was loaded with some kind of carriage, or wagon, tarpaulin-covered. The Hawk crawled in under the tarpaulin, and lay down upon his back, pillowing his head on a piece of timber that blocked the carriage wheels.

The train topped the grade, gained speed, and roared on through the night. Occasionally, during what was close to a two-hours' run, it stopped at intermediate stations, and the Hawk peered furtively out from under the tarpaulin to locate the surroundings, with which he appeared to be intimately familiar; and once, nearing the end of the run, as the faint-suffused glow from the city's lights in the distance showed under the shadows of the towering peaks, he spoke aloud.

"Ten thousand dollars," remarked the Hawk pleasantly. "Nice picking for a few hours' work—ten thousand dollars!"

THE TEN-DOLLAR COUNTERFEIT NOTE

THE Hawk crawled out from under the tarpaulin and dropped to the ground, as the freight, slowing down, began to patter in over the spur switches of the Selkirk yard. He darted, bent low, across several spurs to escape the possibility of observation from the freight's caboose; then began to make his way toward the roundhouse ahead of him. He would have to pass around behind the roundhouse in order to get up opposite the station and the divisional offices. The Hawk glanced sharply about him as he moved along. He dodged here and there like some queer, irresponsible phantom flitting amongst the low, myriad red, green and purple lights that dotted the yard; and he carefully avoided those other lights, the white lights of the yardsmen, now bobbing as the men ran up and down, now swinging from the footboard of a passing switcher, that seemed to be unusually ubiquitous —for the Hawk was secretive, and for certain good and valid reasons was possessed of an earnest desire that no stranger should be reported prowling around the railroad yard that night.

He reached the roundhouse, stepped close up

against the wall to take advantage of the security
afforded by the shadows, and began to circle the
building. The Hawk was treading silently now.
Halfway around the building he halted abruptly,
his head cocked suddenly in a listening attitude
toward a small, open and lighted window on a
level with his shoulders, and in order to pass which
he had just been on the point of stooping down.

"I think," said the Hawk softly to himself, "I
think this sounds as though it interested me."

He crept cautiously forward, and from the edge
of the window glanced inside. It was the turner's
"cubbyhole," or office. The door was closed, and
two men were standing there, talking earnestly. The
Hawk's face, dimly outlined now in the window light,
smooth-shaven, square-jawed, the eyes and forehead
hidden by the brim of the slouch hat that was pulled
forward almost to the bridge of his nose, set with
a curious and significant smile. It was not a bad
place for a private conference! He had thought he
had recognised the voice—and he had not been mistaken. The big, heavy-built, thin-lipped, pugnacious-
faced man was MacVightie, the head of the railroad's
detective force; the other, a smaller man, with alert
grey eyes, his forehead furrowed anxiously, whose
clenched hand rested on the table, was Lanson, the
division superintendent.

"I don't know, damn it, MacVightie!" Lanson was
saying savagely. "I don't know what to think, or
believe—I only know that a Pullman hold-up one
night, a twenty-thousand-dollar necklace stolen the

next, an express car looted, and several other little pleasant episodes all jammed one on top of the other, means hell to pay out here and nothing to pay it with, unless we can do something almighty quick!"

"Any more of those messages?" inquired Mac-Vightie—there was an ominous abstraction in his tones.

"Yes—to-night."

"Make anything of it?"

"No," said Lanson; "and I think it's about time to put a kink in that little business, whether they mean anything or not. This cat-and-mouse game we've been playing isn't——"

"We'll get back to that in a minute," interrupted MacVightie quietly. "Here's a little something else that may possibly fit into the combination." He reached into his pocket, took out his pocketbook, opened it, and handed the division superintendent a crisp new ten-dollar note.

The Hawk's lips thinned instantly, and he swore sharply under his breath.

"What's this?" asked Lanson, in surprise.

"Phony!" said MacVightie laconically.

"Counterfeit!" Lanson turned the note over in his hands, staring at first one side and then the other. "Are you sure? I'd take it any time."

"You'd have lots of company with you"—there was a sudden rasp in the detective's voice. "Pretty good one, isn't it? The East is being flooded with them. Two of them showed up in the banks here in the city yesterday, and one to-day."

Lanson frowned perplexedly.

"I don't get you, MacVightie," he said.

"Suppose they were being struck off around here," suggested MacVightie curtly. "I don't say they are, but suppose it were so. They'd likely be shoved out as far away from this locality as possible, wouldn't they—back East, say. They're so good that a jag of them got by before they began to be detected— and now suppose we assume that they're beginning to sift back around the country."

"Well?"

"Well"—MacVightie caught the superintendent up quickly—"I didn't say I could prove it; but, coupled with the fact that I happen to know that the police have traced the work back to somewhere west of Chicago, I've got a hunch that the gang that is operating around here and the crowd that is turning out the phony money is the same outfit. The Lord knows"—he smiled bitterly—"they're clever enough! And to go back to those messages now. If there was anything in them at all, anything more than some irresponsible idiot tampering with a key somewhere, we were face to face, not with a mere gang of train robbers, but with an organised criminal league as dangerous and powerful as has ever existed in this country—and that's what made me hesitate. We couldn't afford to take any chances, to start out after a mare's nest, and we had to make as nearly sure of our ground as possible before we played a card. We went on the principle that if it was only somebody playing the goat, he'd get tired of it before long if no one paid any attention to him; if it meant any-thing more than that, he'd keep on." MacVightie's pugnacious face screwed up into a savage grimace. "Well, maybe this counterfeiting idea has had some-thing to do with deciding me, but, anyway, I'm satis-fied now. He *has* kept on. And I'm satisfied now that those messages are a cipher code that the gang is using, and that our cat-and-mouse play, as you call it, instead of being abortive, is exactly what's going to land our men for us. That's one thing I came to tell you to-night—that I'm ready now to take the gloves off on this wire game."

Lanson smashed his fist down on the table top.

"Good!" he exclaimed grimly. "I'd like to make things hot for somebody, and it'll at least be easy enough to catch whoever is using the wire."

MacVightie shook his head.

"Oh, no; it won't!" he said evenly. "I didn't mean to give you that impression, and don't you make the mistake of under-estimating the brains we're up against, Lanson. I'm no expert on telegraphy, that's your end of it, but I know they wouldn't sit in on any game where they didn't hold trumps up their sleeves. Get me? Now let's see what it looks like. As I understand it, these messages, no matter from what point on the division they are sent, would be heard on every sounder on the line—that's right, isn't it?"

"Yes—sure! Of course!" agreed Lanson.

"And it might be an operator working with them

as an inside man; or, with the necessary outfit, the wire could be tapped at any point, couldn't it?"

"Yes," said Lanson; "but the minute he starts in, we could begin to 'ground' him out."

"Go on!" invited MacVightie. "I'm listening."

"We could tell whether he was working east or west of any given point," explained the superintendent; "and, with the operators instructed beforehand, practically narrow him down to, say, between two stations."

The Hawk, as he, too, listened, permitted an amused smile to flicker across his lips.

"Um!" said MacVightie. "And would he be aware that this 'grounding' process was going on?"

"Yes—naturally," admitted Lanson. "We can't prevent that."

MacVightie shook his head again.

"That doesn't sound good to me," he said slowly. "All he'd have to do would be to beat it then—and the next time start in fifty miles away, and you'd have to begin all over again. And, besides, who's *receiving* the messages? You can't put any tabs on that. Every sounder from Selkirk City to Rainy River registers them, and all a man's got to do is *listen*. You see, Lanson, it's not so easy—eh?"

Lanson frowned.

"Well, what do you suggest?" he asked uncomfortably. "We can stop it."

"But we don't *want* to stop it!" returned MacVightie. "We could have done that from the first. What we want is our man now. And it strikes me that the first thing to do is to find out whether one of our own operators is in on this or not. Unless the line is tapped somewhere, it's a cinch that a station key is being used, isn't it? Send some linemen that you can trust over the division. If they find anything at all, they'll find the spot where the messages are coming from, won't they? If they find nothing, we'll know we've got to look nearer home—amongst our own men."

Lanson, in his turn, shook his head.

"Not necessarily," he objected. "We've a number of small stations where there's no night operator. They might have got into one of those. The messages all come through at night."

"Well, I'll call the turn there!" responded Mac-Vightie, with a short laugh. "See that I get a list of those stations in the morning, and I'll detail men to take care of that end of it."

The Hawk drew back a little, shifting his strained position—the amused smile was no longer on his lips.

"And as for that 'ground' business," went on Mac-Vightie, "go slow with it till you get your linemen's report. Don't do any more than try it out with some operator you can absolutely depend upon, say, about halfway down the line. You say you would be able to tell whether the messages were coming from east or west of that point; that'll cut the division in half for us as far as our search is concerned, and that's worth taking a chance on. But don't overdo it, Lanson. We don't want to throw any scare into him—yet."

"All right," agreed Lanson. "I'll start things moving to-night. Martin, at Bald Creek, will be the best man, I guess. I'll send a letter down to him on No. 8."

"And warn him to make no reports by *wire*," cautioned MacVightie.

"All right—yes, naturally," agreed the superintendent again. Then, after a short pause, anxiously: "Anything turned up at all, MacVightie? Any clue to that necklace? The governor's wife is making a holler that's reached from here to the road's directors down in Wall Street."

"Damn it," growled MacVightie. "I'm well enough aware of it—but the necklace isn't any more important than any one of the other affairs, is it? No; there's nothing—not a blamed thing!"

"Well, what about this Sing Sing convict, the Hawk, that the papers are featuring to-night?" Lanson asked. "Anything in that?"

"I don't know—maybe," McVightie answered viciously. "He's only one more, anyway. This gang was operating before he was released—and it's likely enough, if they're old pals of his, that he's come out here to give them a hand. The New York police say he went to Chicago immediately after his release, two weeks ago. The Chicago police reported him there, and then he disappeared; then Denver spotted him a few days later—and that's the last that's been seen of him. You can make what you like of that. He's certainly been hitting a pretty straight trail west. He wasn't stopped, of course, because he isn't 'wanted' at present; he's only a man with a bad record, and labelled dangerous. We were warned to look out for him, that's all."

"Got his description?" inquired Lanson.

"Yes"—MacVightie's laugh was a short bark. "Medium height, broad-shouldered, muscular, black hair, black eyes, straight nose, good-looking, and gentlemanly in appearance and manner, dresses well, age twenty-four to twenty-six, no distinctive marks or disfigurement."

"There's probably not more than twenty-five thousand men in Selkirk City who would answer to every detail of that!" Lanson commented sarcastically.

"Exactly!" admitted MacVightie. "And that's——"

The Hawk was creeping forward again in the shadows of the roundhouse.

"Yes, I guess it interested me," muttered the Hawk; "I guess it did. I guess I'm playing in luck to-night."

— III —

FROM the roundhouse it was only a few yards to the rear of the long, low-lying freight sheds and, unobserved, the Hawk gained this new shelter. He stole quickly along to the further end of the sheds; and there, crouched down again in the shadows, halted to make a critical survey of his surroundings.

Just in front of him, divided only by a sort of driveway for the convenience of the teamsters, was the end wall of the station, and, in the end wall— the window of the divisional paymaster's office. The Hawk glanced to his left. The street upon which the station fronted, an ill-savoured section of the city, was dark, dimly lighted, and deserted; the only sign of life being the lighted windows of a saloon on the corner of a narrow lane that bisected the block of somewhat disreputable, tumble-down wooden structures that faced the station. To his right, on the other side of the freight shed, the railroad yard had narrowed down to the station tracks and a single spur alongside the shed. There was no one in sight in either direction.

The Hawk's eyes strayed back to the paymaster's

window. The station, like its surrounding neigh-
bours, was an old wooden building; and, being low
and only two-storied, the second-story window offered inviting possibilities. From the sill of the lower
window, a man who was at all agile had the upper
window at his mercy. Against this mode of attack,
however, was the risk of being seen by any one who
might pass along the street, or by any one who might
chance upon the end of the station platform.

"What's the use!" decided the Hawk, with an
abrupt shrug of his shoulders. "Play safe. There's
a better way."

The Hawk crept across the driveway, reached the
street side of the station, peered cautiously around
the corner of the building, and, satisfied that he was
unobserved, edged down along the building for a
short distance, paused in a doorway, glanced quickly
about him again—and then the door opened and
closed, and he was standing in a murky passageway,
that was lighted only by a single incandescent far
back by a stair well.

He stood motionless, listening. From above,
through the stillness, came the faint drumming of a
telegraph key. There should be no one upstairs now
but the dispatcher, whose room was at the opposite
end of the building from the paymaster's office—
and, possibly, with the dispatcher, a call boy or two.
And the hallway above, he could see, was dark.

Moving stealthily forward, as noiseless as a cat
in his tread, the Hawk took a mask from his pocket,
slipped it over his face, and began to mount the

stairs. He gained the landing—and halted again. It was pitch black here, since even the door of the dispatcher's room, where there would be a light, was closed.

And then once more the Hawk moved forward— and an instant later, the paymaster's door at the extreme end of the corridor, under the deft persuasion of his skeleton keys, had closed behind him.

It was not quite so dark here. The lights from the platform and the yard filtered in through the window in a filmy sort of way; but it was too dark to distinguish objects in anything more than grotesque, shapeless outlines.

The Hawk produced his flashlight, and turned it upon the lock he had just picked. It was a spring lock, opened readily from the inside by the mere turning of the doorhandle. He tried it carefully, assuring himself that it could not be opened from the corridor without a key—and then his light swept around the room. It played in its circuit upon the paymaster's flat-topped desk against the wall, and upon a large safe in the corner, near the window, whose polished nickel dial sent back an answering flash under the darting ray; but the Hawk, for the moment, appeared to be interested in neither desk nor safe. The flashlight was holding in a kind of dogged inquisitiveness upon another door close to the window, and directly opposite the safe.

He stepped without a sound across the room, and, reaching this door, snapped off his flashlight. He tried the door cautiously, found it unlocked, and very softly opened it the space of an inch. He listened attentively. There was no sound. He pushed the door open, switched on his flashlight again, and stepped through the doorway. It appeared to be a clerks' office—for the paymaster's staff, presumably. The Hawk seemed to possess a peculiar penchant for doors. The only thing in the room that apparently held any interest for him now was the door that opened, like the paymaster's, upon the corridor. He slipped quickly across the room, and, as before, examined the lock. Like the other, it was a spring lock; and, like the other, he tested it to make sure it was locked on the outside.

"Ten thousand dollars," confided the Hawk to the lock, "isn't to be picked up every night; and we can't afford to take any chances, you know."

He began to retrace his steps toward the paymaster's office, but now, obviously, with more attention to the details of his surroundings, for his flashlight kept dancing quick, jerky flashes in all directions about him.

"Ah!" The exclamation, low-breathed, came suddenly. "I thought there ought to be something like this around here!"

From beside a desk, he stooped and picked up an empty pay satchel; then, returning at once to the other office, but leaving the connecting door just ajar, he dropped the pay bag in front of the safe, and went silently over to the desk—a mouse running across the floor would have made more commotion than the Hawk had made since his entry into the station.

". . . Upper drawer, left side," he muttered. "Locked, of course—ah!" A tiny key, selected from its fellow outlaws, was inserted in the lock—and the Hawk pulled out the drawer, and began to rummage through its contents.

From the back of the drawer, after perhaps a minute's search, he picked up a card, and with a nod of satisfaction began to study it.

" 'Left—two right; eighty-seven, one quarter—left; three . . . ' " The Hawk's eyes travelled swiftly over the combination. He read it over again. "Thank you!" murmured the Hawk whimsically—and dropped the card back in the drawer, and locked the drawer.

A moment more, and the white beam of the flashlight was playing on the face of the safe, and the silence of the room was broken by the faint, musical, metallic whirring of the dial. Bent forward, a crouching form in the darkness, the Hawk worked swiftly, a sure, deft accuracy in every movement of his fingers. With a low thud, as he turned the handle, the heavy bolt shot back in its grooves, and the ponderous door swung open. And now the flashlight's ray flooded the interior of the safe, and the Hawk laughed low—before him, lying on the bottom of the safe, neatly banded as they had come from the bank, were a dozen or fifteen little packages of banknotes.

The Hawk dropped on his knees, and reached for

the pay bag. Ten thousand dollars was not so bulky, after all—if the denominations of the notes were large enough. He riffled one package through his fingers—twenties! Gold, yellow-back twenties! There was a sort of beatific smile on the Hawk's lips. He dropped the package into the bag.

Tens, and twenties, and fives—the light, in a curiously caressing way, was lingering on the little fortune as it lay there on the bottom of the safe. There was only a pile or two of ones, and the rest was—*what was that!*

The smile vanished from the Hawk's lips, and, in a rigid, tense, strained attitude, he hung there, motionless. What was that—that dull, rasping, sound! It was like some one clawing at the wall outside. The *window!*

With a single motion, as though stirred to life by some galvanic shock, the Hawk's hand shot out and swept the packages of banknotes into the bag. He snapped off his flashlight. The room was in darkness.

That sound again! And now a creak! The window was being opened. Something black was bulking there on the sill outside—and something queerly white, a man's face, was pressed against the pane, peering in.

The Hawk glanced sharply around him. Inch by inch he was pushing the safe door shut. He could not reach the door leading to the clerks' office, for he would have to pass by the window, and—he shrank back quickly, the safe door closed but still unlocked, and crouched low in the corner against the wall. The window slid up to the top, and with a soft *pad*, like some animal alighting on the floor, the man had sprung into the room.

The Hawk's fingers crept into his pocket and out again, tight-closed now upon an automatic pistol. The other's flashlight winked, went out, then shot across the room, locating the desk—and once more all was darkness.

There was not a sound now, save the short, hurried breathing of the other, panting from the exertion of his climb. Then the man's step squeaked faintly crossing the room—and the Hawk, a few inches at a time, began to edge along the wall away from the neighbourhood of the safe.

Then the man's flashlight gleamed again, lighting up the top of the desk. There was a sharp, ripping sound, as of the tearing of wood under pressure, and the upper drawer, forced open by a steel jimmy, was pulled out.

"Birds of a feather!" said the Hawk grimly to himself. "Number One, of the Wire Devils! I didn't beat him to it by as much margin as I thought I would!"

The Hawk shifted his automatic to the hand that was clutching the pay bag, and, with the other hand, began to feel in wide sweeps over the wall above his head. The electric-light switch, he had noticed in that first quick glance when he had entered the room, a glance that had seemed to notice nothing, and yet in which nothing had escaped the sharp, trained eyes, was somewhere about here.

"Dangerous—for both of us—if it's seen outside," communed the Hawk with himself again. "But when he finds the safe unlocked, and the goods gone, there'll be trouble. If he gets a flashlight on me, he's got me where he wants me. Ah—here it is!" The Hawk's fingers touched the switch. He lowered the pay bag cautiously to the floor between his feet, his automatic free in his hand again.

There was a rustling of papers in the drawer; then the man's hand, holding a card, was outlined as though thrown upon a screen, as, with his other hand, he focused his flashlight upon it. Then the flashlight swung an arc over the opposite wall, and pointed a pathway to the safe, as the man turned abruptly and stepped back across the room.

The Hawk, one hand raised to the switch on the wall, his automatic outflung a little in the other, tense, like an animal in leash, watched the other's movements.

The dark-outlined form was in shadowy relief against the light, that played now upon the glistening knob and dial of the safe. The man gave a preliminary, tentative twist at the handle. Came a quick, dismayed, hissing sound, like the sharp intake of breath. The safe door was wrenched open with a jerk. There was a low, angry cry now. The man sprang back, and as though involuntarily, in a sort of uncertain, panic-struck search, his flashlight shot along the wall—and fell full upon the Hawk.

The Hawk's finger pressed the switch. The room was ablaze with light. With a startled, furious oath, the man's hand was sweeping significantly toward his pocket.

"No, you don't!" snarled the Hawk, covering the other. "No, you don't! Cut that out!" His eyes, behind the mask, narrowed suddenly. "Hello!" he sneered. "It's 'Butcher' Rose—I might have known from the way you opened that drawer!"

It was a moment before the man answered.

"Blast you!" he whispered finally. "You gave me a bit of a start, you did! I thought at first you were a 'bull'!" His eyes fastened on the pay bag at the Hawk's feet. The top gaped open, disclosing the banknotes inside. The man raised his eyes to the Hawk's, and a cunning look came over his thin, hatchet-like face. "Caught with the goods this time, eh?" he jerked out.

The Hawk smiled unpleasantly.

"Yes," he said. "The nest's empty. What is it they used to tell us in the nursery?—it's the early bird that grabs the worm. How long you been out in these parts, Butcher?"

"Look here," said the Butcher ingratiatingly, ignoring the question, "I guess it's a case of split— eh?"

"You've got a nerve!" ejaculated the Hawk coolly.

"Well, put that light out, then, and we'll talk it over," suggested the Butcher. "If it's seen from outside, we'll both get caught."

"I'd rather take a chance on that, than a chance

on you," replied the Hawk curtly. "There's nothing to talk over. I've got the coin, and you've got a frost—all you've got to do now is beat it."

Sharp, little, black, ferret eyes the Butcher had, and they roamed around the room now in an apparently aimless fashion—only to come back and fix hungrily on the bag of banknotes again. A sullen look came into his face, and the jaw muscles twitched ominously.

"So you're the Hawk they're talking about, eh?" he said, trying to speak smoothly. "Well, there's no use of us quarrelling. If you know me, we must be old pals. Take off that mask, and let's have a look at you. There ain't any reason why we can't be pals again."

"Nix!" said the Hawk softly. "Nothing doing, Butcher! It suits me pretty well the way it is. I've made it a rule all my life to play a lone hand, and the more I see of the raw work that guys like you try to get away with, the more I pat myself on the back. Savvy? Why, say, even a drag-worker on Canal Street wouldn't show his face to a self-respecting crook for a month, he'd be so ashamed, if he took a crowbar to a desk drawer the way you did, you poor boob!"

The Butcher's face flushed, and he scowled.

"You're looking for trouble, ain't you!" he said hoarsely. "Well, mabbe you'll get it—and mabbe you'll get more than you're looking for. How'd you get wise to this game to-night?"

"It's the way I make my living—getting wise.

How'd you suppose?" queried the Hawk insolently.

The Butcher was chewing at his lips angrily; his eyes, closed to slits, searched the Hawk's masked face.

"This is the second time!" he said, between his teeth. "You pinched that necklace, and——"

"O-ho!" exclaimed the Hawk, with a grin. "So *you* were after that, too, were you?"

The Butcher's flush deepened.

"That's none of your damned business!" he gritted. "And if I thought——" He bit his lips quickly.

"Go on!" invited the Hawk sweetly. "Don't mind me. If you thought—what?"

"You've had the luck with you," mumbled the Butcher, half to himself. "It can't be anything else, there's no chance of a leak. But I'm going to tell you something—your luck's going to get a hole kicked in it. I'll tell you something more. There's a few of us that have picked out this little stamping ground for ourselves, and we ain't fond of trespassers. Get that? It ain't going to be healthy for you to linger around here over more than one train!"

"Are the rest of 'em all like you?" inquired the Hawk maliciously.

"You'll find out quicker than you'll want to, perhaps!" the Butcher retorted furiously.

"All right!" said the Hawk. "And now I'll tell you a little something. I don't know who are in this gang of yours, but you might take them a little message from me. If they're finding it crowded out here, they'd better move on to somewhere where competition isn't so likely to put them out of business through lack of brains, because I'm kind of figuring on hanging around until it gets time to open my château down at Palm Beach and stick my feet up on the sofa for a well-earned rest. Do you stumble to that? And"—the Hawk was drawling now—"I might say, Butcher, that I don't like you. My fingers are crossed on that trespassing gag. It don't go! I don't scare for any half-baked outfit of near-crooks! I stick here as long as there's anything worth sticking for."

The Butcher's eyes seemed to be fascinated by the pay bag—they were on it again. He choked a little, swallowing hard; and, attempting a change of front, forced a smile.

"Well, don't get sore!" he said, in a whining tone. "Mabbe I was only trying to chuck a bluff, and got called. But, say, how'd you like to break in here to-night like I did, and find another fellow'd got all the swag? Say, it's damned rough, ain't it? Say, it's fierce! And, look here, I'm in on it now, anyhow. I know who took it. I'm going to keep my mouth shut, ain't I? You ain't going to leave me out in the cold, are you? All I ask is a split."

"It's not much!" said the Hawk, in a velvet voice. "It hardly seems enough. You're too modest, Butcher. Why don't you ask for the whole of it? You might as well—you'd stand just as much chance of getting it!"

The smile faded from the Butcher's lips, and his face became contorted with rage again. He raised his fist and shook it at the Hawk. He cursed in abandon, his lips livid, beside himself with passion.

"You'll get yours for this!" He choked, in his fury, over his words. "You think you're slick! I'll show you what you're up against inside of twenty-four hours! You'll crawl for this, d'ye hear, blast you—you'll *crawl!*—you'll——"

The Hawk's automatic, dangling nonchalantly in his hand, swung suddenly upward to a level with the other's eyes.

"That's enough, you cheap skate!"—there was a cold, menacing ring in the Hawk's voice now. "I've heard enough from you. You and your hot-air crowd of moth-eaten lags! If you, or any of you, run foul of me again, you won't get off so easy! Tell 'em that! Tell 'em the Hawk said so! And you beat it! And beat it—*now!*" He caught up the pay bag, and advanced a step.

The Butcher retreated sullenly.

"Get out of that window!" ordered the Hawk evenly. "And take a last tip from me. If you try to plant me, if you let a peep out of you while I'm making my own getaway, I'll *get* you for it, Butcher, if it's the last thing I ever do. Go on, now! Step quicker!"

Still sullenly, mumbling, his mouth working, the Butcher retreated backward toward the window. The Hawk, his lips like a thin straight line just showing under the mask, followed grimly, step by step. And then, suddenly, both men halted, and their eyes met and held each other's in a long tense gaze.

From outside in the corridor came the sound of voices and footsteps. The footsteps drew nearer; the voices grew louder. The Hawk shot a glance toward the door. He drew in his breath sharply. No, there was no fanlight, the light would not show in the hall. That was the superintendent's voice. That letter Lanson was going to send down on No. 8! The other, probably, was MacVightie. Yes; it *was* MacVightie—he caught the detective's gruff tones now. The door on the opposite side of the corridor from the paymaster's room opened.

The Butcher licked his lips.

"Me for the window, and for it quick!" he muttered under his breath.

He turned, and, his back to the Hawk now, tiptoed to the window, turned again sideways, as though to throw one leg over the sill—and his right hand, hidden, suddenly lifted the side of his coat.

It came quick, quick as the winking of an eye. Racketing through room and building, like the detonation of a cannon in the silence, came the roar of a revolver shot, as the Butcher fired through his coat pocket. Mechanically, the Hawk staggered backward; and then, the quick, keen brain working like lightning, he reeled, dropped the pay bag, and clutched wildly at his side. He was not hit. The Butcher had missed. So that was the man's game! Clever enough! They'd break in here at the sound of the shot, and find him dead or wounded on the floor!

The Butcher, a devil's triumph in his face now,

came leaping back from the window, and, stooping, snatched at the pay bag.

"I'd put another in you to make sure," whispered the Butcher fiercely; "only they'll get you anyway, you——"

The Hawk straightened, his arm streaked outward from his side, his pistol butt crashed on the Butcher's skull, and he was upon the other like a flash, his free hand at the Butcher's throat.

From the room opposite came startled cries; across the corridor came the rush of feet—then the doorhandle was tried, the door shaken violently.

The Butcher was struggling but feebly, making only a pitiful effort to loosen the Hawk's clutch upon his throat, hanging almost limply in the Hawk's arms, half dazed by the blow upon his head. White to the lips with passion, the Hawk whipped his hand into the other's pocket, whipped out the other's revolver, and flung the man away from him. And then, as the Butcher reeled and lurched backward to the window, and, clawing frantically at the sill, attempted to work his way out, the Hawk ran silently back, picked up the pay bag, and, jumping to the window again, caught the Butcher roughly by the collar of the coat.

The Butcher, white, haggard-faced with fear, moaned.

"For God's sake!" he pleaded piteously. "Let me go! Let me go! For God's sake, let me go—they'll get me!"

There was a terrific crash upon the door, as of

some heavy body hurled against it. The Hawk laughed mirthlessly.

"If I let you go, you'd break your neck!"—the Hawk's words were coming through clenched teeth. "Don't worry, Butcher! They'll not get you. I don't want *them* to get you. I want to get you myself for this. Some day, Butcher, some day *I'll* do the getting!" He pushed the Butcher's feet over the sill. "Feel with your toes for the window casing beneath! Quick!" He leaned out, gripping at the Butcher's collar, lowering the man—his lips were close against the Butcher's ear. "Some day—for this—you yellow cur—you and me, Butcher—remember—*some day!*"

A crash again upon the door! The Butcher's feet were on the lower sill; but here the man lost his hold, and toppled to the ground. The Hawk glanced backward into the room. The door was yielding now. He looked out of the window again. The Butcher had regained his feet, and was swaying against the wall, holding to it, making his way slowly, weakly toward the corner.

The Hawk threw one leg over the sill. With a rip and tear, the door smashed inward, sagging from its lower hinge. Came a hoarse yell. MacVightie was plunging through the doorway.

Instantly the Hawk, hugging the pay bag, drew back his leg, and dove into the clerk's room through the door which he had left ajar. There would have been no use in letting the Butcher go at all if he led the chase through the window—the man was barely crawling away. Across the room, light enough now from the open doorway behind him to point the way, raced the Hawk. He reached the corridor door, as MacVightie lunged through the connecting door in pursuit.

MacVightie's voice rose in a bellow of warning: "Look out there, Lanson! The next door—quick!"

But the Hawk was the quicker. He tore the door open, and dashed through, just eluding the superintendent and another man—the dispatcher probably, attracted by the row—as they sprang forward from the paymaster's door.

Running like a deer, the Hawk made for the stairway. It was lighter now in the hall. The dispatcher's door along at the farther end was open. At the head of the stairs, a call boy, wide-eyed, gaped, open-mouthed. The Hawk brushed the boy aside incontinently, and, taking the stairs three and four at a time, leaped downward, MacVightie's bull-like roar echoing behind him, the top stairs creaking under the detective's rush.

The street door opened outward, and as the Hawk reached it, and, wrenching at the knob, pushed it open, there was a flash, the report of a revolver shot—and, with a venomous *spat*, the bullet buried itself in the door jamb, not an inch from his head, it seemed, for the wind of the bullet was on his cheek.

Cries sounded now from the railroad yard; but the street in front of him, deserted, was still undisturbed. He was across it in a twinkling, and, passing the saloon that was now closed, darted into the lane.

He flung a glance over his shoulder—and his lips set hard. MacVightie, big man though he was, was no mean antagonist in a race. The detective, quicker in initiative, quicker on his feet, had outdistanced both Lanson and the dispatcher, and was already halfway across the street.

Again MacVightie fired.

On the Hawk ran. If he could reach the next corner—providing there was no one about the street —there was a way, a risky way, but still a way, his best chance of escape. The cheap combination lodging house and saloon, that was just around the corner, was where he had a room. Yes, it was his *one* chance! He must get to cover somewhere without an instant's delay. With MacVightie firing now, emptying his revolver up the lane, with the yells and shouts growing constantly in volume from farther back toward the station, it was only a question of minutes before the whole neighbourhood would be aroused.

Again he glanced behind him. It was very dark in the lane. He was grimly conscious that it was the blackness, and not MacVightie's poor marksmanship, that had saved him so far. That flash of the other's revolver was perhaps fifty yards away. He had gained a little, then! If there was any one around the corner, the plan of reaching his room would not serve him, and he would still have to run for it. Well, he would see in an instant—it was only two yards more—a yard—now!

Without slackening his pace, at top speed he swung from the lane—and, with a gasp of relief at sight of an empty street, slipped into a doorway just beyond the now dark entrance to a saloon that occupied most of the ground floor of a dirty and squalid three-story building.

The door gave on a narrow flight of stairs, and up these the Hawk sprang swiftly and with scarcely a sound. And now, as he ran, he pulled his mask from his face and thrust it into the pay bag; a pocketbook from his inside coat pocket followed the mask, and, with the pocketbook, the flashlight, and the two pistols, his own and the Butcher's. He opened a door at the head of the landing, and stepped into a room, leaving the door partly open.

He was not safe yet—far from it! He did not under-estimate MacVightie. It would be obvious to MacVightie that he was not far enough ahead to have disappeared in any but one way—into some building within a very few yards of the lane! And the presumption, at least, would be that this was the one.

The Hawk worked now with almost incredible speed. He switched on the light, ran to the window that opened on the rear of the building, felt with one hand along the sill outside, lifted the pay bag out of the window, let go of it, and turned instantly back into the room. He hung up his hat on a wall peg, and tearing off his jacket, flung it haphazardly upon the bed. There was a small table against the wall near the foot of the bed. The Hawk opened a drawer, snatched up a pack of cards, and sat down at the table.

The street door opened and closed. A quick, heavy tread sounded on the stairs.

In his shirt sleeves, his back to the door, the Hawk was coolly playing solitaire.

"I guess I'd better be smoking," murmured the Hawk. "Maybe I'm breathing a little hard."

He picked up a pipe from the table, lighted a match—and, half the deck of cards in one hand, the lighted match in the other, swung around in his chair with a startled jerk.

The door slammed back against the wall. Mac-Vightie had unceremoniously kicked it wide open. MacVightie was standing on the threshold.

The Hawk, in a sort of surprised gasp, sucked the flame of the match down into the bowl of his pipe, and stared at MacVightie through a curtain of tobacco smoke. The detective's eyes travelled sharply from the Hawk around the room, came back to the Hawk, narrowed, and, stepping into the room, he shut the door with equal lack of ceremony behind him.

"Say, you got a gall!" ejaculated the Hawk.

"You bet your life I have!" flung out MacVightie. "Now then, my bucko, what are you doing here?"

"Say," said the Hawk, as though obsessed with but a single idea, "say, you got a gall! You got a gall, busting into a fellow's room and asking him what he's doing there! Say, maybe you might answer the same question yourself—eh? What are *you* doing here?"

"Your room, is it?" snapped MacVightie.

"Sure, it's my room!" replied the Hawk, a little tartly.

"How long you been here?"

" 'Bout a week"—the Hawk was growing ungracious.

"Boarding here?"

"Yes."

"Where'd you come from?" MacVightie was clipping off his words. "What do you do for a living?"

"Say," said the Hawk politely, "you go to hell!"

MacVightie stepped forward toward the Hawk with an ominous scowl; and, throwing back the lapel of his coat, tapped grimly with his forefinger on a shield that decorated his vest.

The Hawk whistled low.

"O-ho!" said the Hawk, with sudden cordiality. "Well, why didn't you say so before?"

"I'm saying it now!" snarled MacVightie. "Well, where do you come from?"

"Chicago," said the Hawk.

"What's your business?"—MacVightie's eyes were roving sharply again around the room.

"Barkeep—when I can get a job," answered the Hawk; and then, insinuatingly: "And, say, I'm looking for one now, and if you can put me on to anything I'd——"

"I guess you've got to show me!" growled Mac-Vightie, uncompromisingly.

"Look here," ventured the Hawk, "what's up?"

"I'm waiting!" prompted MacVightie significantly.

"Oh, all right!" The Hawk flared up a little. "If you love your grouch, keep on hugging it tight!" He jerked his hand toward the coat that was lying on the bed. "I must have lost the letter the pastor of my church gave me, but there's a couple there from the guys back in Chicago that I worked for, and there's my union card with them. Help yourself!"

MacVightie picked up the coat brusquely, shoved his hand into the inside pocket, brought out several letters, and began to read them.

The Hawk shuffled the half deck of cards in his hand monotonously.

There was a puzzled frown on MacVightie's face, as he finally tossed the letters down on the bed.

"Satisfied?" inquired the Hawk pleasantly.

MacVightie's frown deepened.

"Yes, as far as that goes," he said tersely; and then, evenly, his eyes boring into the Hawk: "About five minutes ago a man ran into this house from the street. What's become of him?"

The Hawk started in amazement—and slowly shook his head.

"I guess you've got the wrong dope, ain't you?" he suggested earnestly.

"Don't try that game!" cautioned MacVightie grimly. "And don't lie! He had to come up these stairs, your door was partly open, and he couldn't have passed without you knowing it."

"That's what I'm saying," agreed the Hawk, even more earnestly. "That's why I'm saying you must have got the wrong dope. Of course, he couldn't have got by without me hearing him! That's a cinch! And, I'm telling you straight, he didn't."

"Didn't he?" MacVightie's smile was thin. "Then he came in *here*—into this room."

"In here?" echoed the Hawk weakly. His gaze wandered helplessly around the room. "Well, all you've got to do is look."

"I'm going to!" announced MacVightie curtly— and with a sudden jerk he yanked the single bed out from the wall. He peered behind and beneath it; then, stepping over to a cretonne curtain in the corner that served as wardrobe, he pulled it roughly aside.

There were no other places of possible concealment. MacVightie chewed at his under lip, and eyed the Hawk speculatively.

The Hawk's eyes were still travelling bewilderedly about the room, as though he still expected to find something.

"Are you dead sure he came into this house," he inquired heavily, as though the problem were entirely beyond him.

MacVightie hesitated.

"Well—no," he acknowledged, after a moment. "I guess you're straight all right, and I'll admit I didn't see him come in; but I'd have pretty near taken an oath on it."

"Then I guess he must have ducked somewhere else," submitted the Hawk sapiently. "There wasn't no one went by that door—I'm giving it to you on the level."

MacVightie's reluctant smile was a wry grimace.

"Yes, I reckon it's my mistake." His voice lost its snarl, and his fingers groped down into his vest pocket. "Here, have a cigar," he invited placatingly.

"Why, say—thanks"—the Hawk beamed radiantly. "Say, I——"

"All right, young fellow"—with a wave of his hand, MacVightie moved to the door. "All right, young fellow. No harm done, eh? Good-night!"

The door closed. The footsteps without grew fainter, and died away.

The Hawk, staring at the door, apostrophised the doorknob.

"Well, say, what do you know about that!" he said numbly. "I wonder what's up?"

He rose from his chair after a moment as though moved by a sort of subconscious impulse, mechanically pushed his bed back against the wall, and returned to his chair.

He dug out his pipe abstractedly, filled it, and lighted it. He gathered up the cards, shuffled them, and began to lay them out again on the table—and paused, and drummed with his fingers on the table top.

"They're after some guy that's ducked his nut somewhere around here," he decided aloud. "I wonder what's up?"

The Hawk spread out his remaining cards—and swept them away from him into an indiscriminate heap.

"Aw, to blazes with cards!" he ejaculated impatiently.

He put his feet up on the table, and sucked steadily at his pipe.

"It's a cinch he never went by that door," the Hawk assured the toe of his boot. "I guess he handed that 'bull' one, all right, all right."

The minutes passed. The Hawk, engrossed, continued to suck on his pipe. Then from far down the stairs there came a faint creak, and an instant later the outer door closed softly.

The Hawk's feet came down from the table, and the Hawk smiled—grimly.

"Tut, tut!" chided the Hawk. "That treadmill diminuendo on the top step and the keyhole stunt is pretty raw, Mr. MacVightie—pretty raw! You forgot the front door, Mr. MacVightie—I don't seem to remember having heard it open or close until just now!"

The back of the Hawk's chair, as he pushed it well away from the table and stood up, curiously enough now intercepted itself between the keyhole and the interior of the room. He stepped to the door, and slipped the bolt quietly into place; then, going to the window, he reached out, and, from where it hung upon a nail driven into the sill, picked up the pay bag.

"That's a pretty old gag, too," observed the Hawk almost apologetically. "I was lucky to get by with it."

The Hawk's attention was now directed to his trunk, that was between the table and the foot of the bed. He lifted the lid back against the wall, and removed an ingeniously fashioned false top, in the shape of a tray, that fitted innocently into the curvature of the lid. The Hawk stared at a magnificent diamond necklace that glittered and gleamed on the bottom of the tray, as its thousand facets caught the light—and grinned.

"If you'd only known, eh—Mr. MacVightie!" he murmured.

From the pay bag the Hawk took out the packages of banknotes, the flashlight, the mask, the two pistols, and packed them neatly away in the tray. The only article left in the bag was his pocketbook. He opened this, disclosing a number of crisp, new ten-dollar bills. He held one of them up to the light for a moment, studying it admiringly.

"I guess these won't be much more good around here, according to that little conversation between MacVightie and the superintendent," he muttered— and, with a shrug of his shoulders, tossed the entire number into the tray.

He fitted the false top back into the lid, and closed

the trunk. There remained the empty pay bag. He frowned at it for an instant; then, picking it up, he tucked it under the mattress of his bed.

"I'll get rid of that in the morning"—he nodded his head, as he turned down the bed covers.

The Hawk began to undress, and at intervals voiced snatches of his thoughts aloud.

"Pretty close shave," said the Hawk, "pretty close. . . . Ten thousand dollars is some haul. . . . All right as long as they don't find out I've got the key to their cipher. . . . And so Butcher Rose is one of the gang, eh? . . . Number One—Butcher Rose. . . . Guess he got away all right—from Mac-Vightie. . . . He nearly did me. . . . Pretty close shave. . . ."

The Hawk turned out the light, and got into bed.

"I guess I played in luck to-night," said the Hawk softly, and for the second time that night. "Yes, I guess I did."

— IV —

AT BALD CREEK STATION

IT was twenty-four hours later.

A half mile away, along a road that showed like a grey thread in the night, twinkled a few lights from the little cluster of houses that made the town of Bald Creek. At the rear of the station itself, in the shadow of the walls, it was inky black.

There was stillness! Then the chattering of a telegraph instrument—and, coincident with this, low, scarcely audible, a sound like the gnawing of a rat.

The chattering of the instrument ceased; and, coincident again, the low, gnawing sound ceased— and, crouched against a rear window, the Hawk chuckled a little grimly to himself. Within, and diagonally across from the window, an otherwise dark interior was traversed by a dull ray of light that filtered in through the open connecting door of the operator's room beyond. Inside there were Lanson, the division superintendent, and Martin, the trusted Bald Creek operator; while at any minute now, MacVightie would be up on No. 12. They were preparing to spring their trap for the Wire Devils to-night! The Hawk was quite well-informed on this point, for the very simple reason that the Hawk himself had not been entirely idle during those twenty-four hours that were just past!

Again the sounder broke into a splutter; but this time the gnawing sound was not resumed—the window fastenings were loosened now.

Came then the distant rumble of an approaching train; the rumble deepening into a roar; the roar disintegrating itself into its component sounds, the wheel trucks beating at the rail joints, the bark of the exhaust; then the scream of the brakeshoes biting at the wheel tires; the hiss of steam—and in the mimic pandemonium, the Hawk raised the window, and crawled in over the sill.

And again the Hawk chuckled to himself. Up and down the line to-night, at all stations where there were no night operators, the road's detectives stood guard over the telegraph instruments. It had been MacVightie's plan, originated the night before. It was very clever of MacVightie—if somewhat abortive! Also, quite irrelevant of course, and quite apart from that little matter of ten thousand dollars which he, the Hawk, had taken from the paymaster's safe last night, MacVightie to-night was likely to be in no very pleasant mood!

The engine without, blowing from a full head of steam, drowned out all other sounds. The Hawk picked his way across the room to a position near the connecting door, and composedly seated himself upon the floor behind a number of piled-up boxes and parcels. With a grin of acknowledgment to the escaping steam, he coolly moved two of the parcels a few inches to right and left, thus providing himself with an excellent view into the operator's room. From one pocket he took an exceedingly small flashlight, and from another a notebook, and from his hip pocket his automatic pistol. This latter he transferred to his right-hand coat pocket. Bunching the bottom of his coat over his hand, he flashed on the tiny ray, found a convenient ledge formed by one of the boxes, and upon this laid down his notebook. The first page, as he opened the book, contained a neatly drawn sketch of the interior of Bald Creek station. He turned this over, leaving the book open at a blank page, and switched off his light.

The door from the platform opened and closed, as the train pulled out again, a man stepped into the operator's room—and in the darkness the Hawk smiled appreciatively. It was MacVightie, and MacVightie's thin lips were drawn tighter than usual, and the brim of the slouch hat, though pulled far forward, did not hide the scowl upon MacVightie's countenance.

"Well, you're here all right, Lanson, eh?" he flung out brusquely. "Nothing yet, by any chance, of course?"

Lanson, from a chair at the operator's elbow, nodded a greeting.

"Not yet," he said.

MacVightie was glancing sharply around him.

"Martin," he ordered abruptly, "close those two ticket wickets!"

The operator rose obediently, and pulled down the little windows that opened, one on each side of the office, on the men's and women's waiting rooms.

"What's that door there?" demanded MacVightie, pointing toward the rear room.

"Just a place I had partitioned off for stores and small express stuff," Martin answered. "There's no back entrance."

"All right, then," said MacVightie. He pulled up a chair for himself on the other side of the operator, as Martin returned to his seat. "You know what you're here for, Martin—what you've to do? Mr. Lanson has told you?"

"Yes," Martin replied. "I'm to test out for east or west, if there's any of that monkeying on the wire to-night."

"Show me how it's done," directed MacVightie tersely.

The operator reached over to the switchboard and picked up a key-plug.

"I've only got to plug this in—here—or here. Those are my ground wires east and west. The main batteries are west of us at Selkirk, you know. If I ground out everything east, for instance, and he's working to the east of us the sounder'll stop because I've cut him off from the main batteries, and we'll hear nothing unless I adjust the relay down to get the weak circuit from the local batteries. If he's working west of us the sounder will be much stronger because the main batteries at Selkirk, with the eastern half of the division cut out, will be working on a shorter circuit."

"I see." MacVightie frowned. "And he'd know it—so Mr. Lanson told me last night."

"Yes; he'd know it," said Martin. "The same as we would."

"Well, you can do it pretty quick, can't you?" suggested MacVightie. "Sort of accidentally like! We don't want to throw a scare into him. You'd know almost instantly whether he was east or west, wouldn't you? That's all that's necessary—*to-night!* Then let him go ahead again. We'll have found out what we want to know." He turned to Lanson, his voice rasping suddenly. "Did you see the *Journal* on the 'Crime Wave' this afternoon?"

Lanson's alert, grey eyes took on an angry glint.

"No; I didn't see it, but I suppose it's the old story. I wish they'd cut it out! It hurts the road, and it doesn't get them anywhere."

"Perhaps not," said MacVightie, with a thin smile; "but it gets *me!* Yes, it's about the same—all except the last of it. Big headlines: 'Ten thousand dollars stolen from paymaster's safe last night—What is being done to stop this reign of assassination, theft, outrage, crime?—Has the clue afforded by the Hawk's release from Sing Sing been thoroughly investigated?' And then a list of the crimes committed in the last ten days—two murders, one in the compartment of that sleeping car; the theft of the diamond necklace; the express robbery; and so on through the list, ending up with last night. Then a nasty shot at the local police; and, finally, prefacing the remark with the statement that the crimes were all connected with the railroad, a thinly veiled hint that I am either a boy on a man's job, or else asleep, in either of which cases I ought to be—well, you understand?" MacVightie's fist came down with a crash on the operator's table.

Lanson, with a worried look, nodded his head.

"Damn it!" said MacVightie. "I——" He stopped abruptly, and laid his hand on the operator's sleeve. "Look here, Martin," he said evenly, "you're the one man that Mr. Lanson has picked out of the division, you're the one man outside of Mr. Lanson and myself who has any inkling that these secret messages coming over our wires have anything to do with these crimes—you understand that, don't you? This is pretty serious business. The newspaper didn't exaggerate any. We're up against a gang of crooks, cleverly organised, who will stop at nothing. Murder appears to be a pastime with them! Do you get me—Martin?"

For a long second the two men looked each other steadily in the eyes.

"Yes," said Martin simply.

"All right!" said MacVightie. "I just want you to realise the necessity of keeping anything you may hear, or anything that may happen here to-night, under your hat." He turned to Lanson again, the scowl heavy upon his face once more. "I was going to say that I know who the man is that slipped through my fingers last night."

"You—*what!*" Lanson leaned sharply forward in his chair. "But he got away! You said he——"

"It was the Hawk"—MacVightie bit off the words.

"The Hawk?"

"The Hawk!"

"But how do you know?" demanded Lanson incredulously. "You said yourself that he had left no clue to his identity. How do you know?"

MacVightie reached into his pocket, took out his pocketbook, and from the pocketbook passed a new, crisp ten-dollar banknote to Lanson.

"What's this?" inquired Lanson. "The counterfeit ten-dollar bill you showed me last night?"

"No—another one," MacVightie answered curtly. "Look on the other side."

Lanson turned the banknote over, stared at it, and whistled suddenly under his breath.

"'With the compliments of the Hawk!'" he read aloud. He stared now at MacVightie. "Perhaps it's a fake, inspired by that newspaper article yesterday evening," he suggested.

"It's no fake," declared MacVightie grimly. "The Hawk wrote that there all right—it was inside the *pay bag* in which the ten thousand was carried away from the paymaster's office last night."

"You mean—you recovered the bag?" cried Lanson eagerly. "Where? When?"

The Hawk, watching MacVightie's face, grinned wickedly. MacVightie's jaws were clamped belligerently, and upon MacVightie's cheeks was an angry flush.

"Oh, yes, I 'recovered' it!" MacVightie snapped. "He's got his nerve with him! The bag was found reposing in full view on the baggage counter at Selkirk this afternoon—addressed to me. Nobody knows how it got there. But"—MacVightie's fist came down again upon the operator's table—"this time he's overplayed his hand. We knew he had been released from Sing Sing, and that he had come West, but it was only surmise that he was actually around here—now we *know*. In the second place, it's pretty good evidence that he's in with the gang that's flooded the country with those counterfeit tens, and you'll remember I told you last night I had a hunch it was the same gang that was operating out here— well, two and two make four!"

"You think he's——?" Lanson swept his hand suggestively toward the telegraph instruments.

"Yes—and the leader of 'em, now he's out here on the ground!" returned MacVightie gruffly.

The Hawk had taken a pencil from his pocket, and was scribbling aimlessly at the top of the page in his notebook.

"Sure!" confided the Hawk to himself. "I thought maybe you'd dope it out like that."

There was silence for a moment in the office, save for the intermittent clicking of the sounder, to which the Hawk now gave his attention. His pencil still made aimless markings on the top of the page—it was only routine business going over the wire. Then

Lanson moved uncomfortably in his chair, and the chair legs squeaked on the bare floor.

MacVightie spoke again:

"Well," he said bluntly, "you've got all of my end of it, except that I've placed men in hiding at every station on the line where there are no night operators. What about you? Started your outside line inspection?"

"Yes," Lanson answered. "I've had three men out with section crews working from different points. But it's slow business making an inspection that's careful enough to be of any use, and even then it's a pretty tall order to call the turn on anything when there's already so many legitimate splices and repairs on the wires."

"Well—any results?" asked MacVightie.

Lanson shook his head.

"We found what we thought was a new splice in one place, but it turned out to have been made by one of our own men two weeks ago, only he had forgotten to report it."

MacVightie's eyes narrowed.

"One of our *own* men—eh?" he repeated curtly. "Who was it?"

"Nothing doing there!" Lanson shook his head again, emphatically this time. "It was Calhoun."

"Calhoun—eh?" observed MacVightie softly.

Lanson bridled slightly.

"What's the matter with Calhoun?" he inquired testily. "Got anything against him?"

"Never heard of him before," said MacVightie,

with a short laugh. "But I'll take pains to make his acquaintance."

"Then you might as well spare yourself the trouble," advised Lanson. "I can tell you beforehand that he carries a good record on this division, and that he's one of the best linemen we've got."

"I daresay," admitted MacVightie coolly. "But amongst other things we're looking for *good* linemen to-night—who forget to make reports. You needn't get touchy, Lanson, because one of your men's names comes up. You can make up your mind to it there's an inside end to this, and——"

The tiny ray of the Hawk's flashlight shot suddenly upon the notebook's open page, as the sounder broke into a sharp tattoo.

" 'wtaz'—stroke at four," he muttered, as he began to write. "Three—one—two. They've changed the code to-night—'qxpetlk——' "

There was a sharp exclamation from the other room.

"Listen! There he is now!" Martin cried.

Chairs were pushed back—the three men were on their feet.

"What's he sending?" questioned MacVightie instantly.

The Hawk scowled at the disturbance, as, over their voices, he concentrated his attention upon the sounder. He wrote steadily on:

". . . huwkmuhhdtlqgvh. . . ."

"Same as usual," Martin replied. "Just a jumble of letters."

"Well then, get ready to throw that ground, or whatever you call it, into him!" ordered MacVightie tensely.

"I'm ready," said Martin.

"All right then—*now!*"

The Hawk nodded to himself, as his pencil unflaggingly noted down letter after letter. The sounder was very perceptibly stronger.

"West!" Martin cried out. "You noticed the difference in strength, didn't you? He's somewhere between here and Selkirk. That's——"

The sounder had suddenly ceased.

"But he's stopped," said MacVightie; "and you said if he stopped——"

"That's nothing to do with it!" Martin interposed hurriedly. "The wire isn't grounded now."

"He's taken to cover, I guess," said Lanson. "I was afraid he would scare, no matter how——" He broke off abruptly. "Wait! What's that!"

The sounder was clicking again; but the sharp, quick tattoo was gone, and in its place, as though indeed it drawled, the sending came in leisurely, deliberate fashion.

The Hawk's pencil resumed its labours—and then, with a queer smile, the Hawk scratched out what he had just written. It was no longer code—it was in exceedingly plain English.

Martin was reading directly from the sounder:

" 'Try—that—game—just—once — more— and—the—division— goes —up—in—the—air

—and—a—train—or—two—maybe—to—a—
place—that — Mister — MacVightie — will—
some—day—honour — with—his — presence.
That's—quite—plain—isn't—it? If—you—
think — this — is — a—bluff—call—it. Now
—keep—off—the—wire—or—have—it — cut.
Suit—yourselves.' "

"Well, of all the infernal nerve!" exploded Mac-
Vightie furiously.

"And the worst of it," said Lanson shortly, "is
that he's got us where he wants us!"

Once more the sounder broke into the old quick
tattoo. The Hawk was writing steadily again.
There was silence now between the three in the office.

A minute, two, three went by—the sounder
ceased—the Hawk closed his notebook. Then in its
leisurely drawl the sounder broke again; and again
Martin read aloud:

" 'Pleasant — evening — isn't—it? Ask—
MacVightie — if — he—has—seen—anything
—of—the—Hawk. Good-night.' "

But this time there was only a menacing smile
on MacVightie's lips.

"He's west of here, you say?" he shot at Martin.

"Yes," said Martin briefly.

"And that splice of Calhoun's, Lanson? Where
was that?"

Lanson, drumming with his fingers on the edge of the operator's table, looked up with a frown.

"Nothing but coincidence," he said tersely. "Yes, it was west of here—pretty near Selkirk." He moved toward the door. "There's nothing more we can do here to-night. I'm going back on No. 17. Let's get out on the platform until she shows up."

The Hawk very carefully replaced his notebook, his flashlight and his pencil in his pockets, and, as MacVightie and the superintendent went out of the door, he retreated softly back to the rear window. The window being up, he quite as noiselessly slipped out over the sill. He debated a moment about the window, and decided that if any significance were attached to the fact that it was found open, Mac-Vightie, for instance, was fully entitled to make the most of the significance! Then, the rattle of a wagon sounding from the direction of the road, the Hawk moved along to the end of the station, and waited.

The wagon, in the light of its own smoky oil lamps, proved to be the town hotel bus. There were evidently other passengers for Selkirk besides himself and the two officials, as several people alighted from the bus. In view of this fact the Hawk calmly lighted a cigarette, though the glow of the match exposed his face only to the blank wall of the station, and walked around to the front platform.

He located MacVightie and Lanson; and, thereafter, at a safe distance, did not lose sight of them. MacVightie's memory for faces would hardly be over-rated if credited with being able to bridge a matter of some twenty-four hours, particularly as MacVightie had evidenced unusual interest in the occupant of the room on the first landing over a certain ill-favoured saloon the night before! The Hawk, therefore, was unostentatiously attentive to MacVightie's movements; so much so that, when No. 17 pulled in and MacVightie and Lanson boarded the chair car at the rear of the train, the Hawk, when No. 17 pulled out, quite logically boarded the smoking car at the forward end.

The Hawk chose the most uncomfortable seat in the car—the rear seat with stiff, upright, unyielding back, that was built against the wash-room—and, settling himself down, produced his notebook and pencil. The water-cooler could be quite confidentially trusted not to peer over his shoulder!

On the second page of the notebook—the first having been devoted to the sketch of Bald Creek Station—the Hawk, as he had taken it from the sounder, had written this:

"wtazqxpetlkhuwkmuhhdtlqgvhmmpyhqltvddf
rmnluvponfkhomovfdhgvkerkmmawrqfljkwte
dvsoedtdqqhmgfdoifkrxqkuvwruhgsruwmtdoo
ommtlqhvksolfoghvklstrvrzqmqxpemkhurqjkh
hvdbfvkdzcmnvohrtpqghutzklwkjhkdqmmogv
pdlqlfxoquhgpifthglxgpkhlmfjkwhttwbhvdpqg
kdrllueomosdfnhtashqkjvlyhtgmwdlomruhgegf
orwmpqkhvwtzrwkmmrxvddgiqggrqoodusnvrx
wmfkriuhkvhuymthixqljtgwrqpxpehhouwkdmd
gwsxwsvdexmuoohwtjqlqklmp"

The Hawk tore out a page from the back of the notebook, and set down the letters of the alphabet in a column. Opposite these he painstakingly set down another column of letters. After that the Hawk worked slowly. It was not quite so simple as it looked—not merely the substitution of letters in a different order of rotation. Nor, apparently, from the Hawk's observations as he muttered to himself, were all messages to be deciphered alike—the code appeared to possess within itself an elasticity for variation.

"At four . . . key letter changed . . . stroke!" muttered the Hawk. "N-u-m-b . . . pass three . . . e-r-t-h . . . stroke one. . . ."

The Hawk's notebook, closed, was reposing idly on the window ledge and the Hawk was lighting another cigarette, as the conductor came down the aisle. The Hawk presented the return stub of a ticket to Selkirk. The conductor punched it, and passed on—and the Hawk picked up his notebook again.

Again he was interrupted—and again. The water-cooler, after all, was not proving an unmixed blessing. It seemed as though every man in the car were possessed of an inordinate thirst. They were well on toward Selkirk when the Hawk finally completed the deciphering of the message.

It now ran:

"ψ¼½numbⱦⱦkerthⱳreeaⱦⱦndseⱳⱳpveniⱦsaacⱳ kirspⱷⱷchelⱳlscaⱨgshboⱪⱳⱳxtonⱦightⱦⱷaspldⱦ

annendcal∤∤houn∤∤∤∤tore∤port∤∤alll∤∤∤∤lines∤p
lic∅∅eshi∤∤∤sownn∤nnumb∤∤keron∤∤hesay∤shaw∅∤
ksle∤∤∤nder∤whit∤∤ehann∤∤∅dsma∤nicu∅∅redm∤∤∤
ediugmhei∤∤∤ghte∤∤wyesa∤ndha∤∤irbl∤∅∕acke∤xp
en∤∕sive∤∕∤tail∤ored∅∅clot∤∤∅hest∤wothn∤∤ou
sa∅∅∕nddo∅llars∤∕sout∤∕∤kofre∤servn∤efun∤∕∤dto
n∤umbe∤∕rtha∤∕d∅tput∕sabu∤∕ullet∤∕∤inhi∤∤m"

He arranged the scattered letters into words, and the words into sentences:

"Number Three and Seven Isaac Kirschell(')s cash box to-night as planned. Calhoun to report all line splices his own. Number One says Hawk slender white hands, manicured, medium height, eyes and hair black, expensive tailored clothes. Two thousand dollars out of reserve fund to Number that puts a bullet in him."

The Hawk inspected his hands, and smiled whimsically. Number One was the Butcher. He had not given the Butcher credit for being so observant! Presently he stared out of the window.

"Wonder how much of a haul I can make to-night?" he murmured. "Regular El Dorado—having 'em work it all up and handing it to you on a gold platter. Pretty soft! Hope they won't get discouraged and quit picking the chestnuts out of the fire for me—while there's any chestnuts left!"

And then the Hawk frowned suddenly. The chestnuts appeared to be only partially picked for him to-night. What was the game—as planned? **There must** have been a previous message that had got by him. His frown deepened. There was no way of remedying that. To hope to intercept them all was to expect too much. There was no way whereby he could spend twenty-four hours out of twenty-four in touch with a sounder. He shrugged his shoulders philosophically after a moment. Perhaps it was just as well. They credited him with playing a lone hand, believing that his and their depredations were clashing with one another simply by virtue of the fact that their mutual pursuits were of a competitive criminal nature, that was all. If it happened with *too* much regularity, they might begin to suspect that he had the key to their cipher, and then—the Hawk did not care to contemplate that eventuality. There would be no more chestnuts!

The Hawk read the first part of the message over again. Who was Isaac Kirschell? The name seemed to be familiar. The Hawk studied the toe of a neatly-fitting and carefully polished shoe thoughtfully. When he looked up again, he nodded. He remembered now. He had lunched the day before in a restaurant that occupied a portion of the ground floor of an office building, the corridor of which ran through from street to street. In going out, he had passed along the corridor and had seen the name on the door panels of two of the offices.

He resumed the study of his boot toe. It was not a very vital matter. A moment spent in consulting the city directory would have supplied the information in any case. He nodded again. MacVightie was unquestionably right. Some one on the inside, some railroader, and probably more than one, was in on the game with the Wire Devils—and it was perhaps as well for this Calhoun that MacVightie, already suspicious, was not likewise possessed of the key to the cipher! Also, Lanson had been right. It was no easy task to locate a new splice on a wire that was already scarred with countless repairs. Still, if Lanson's men went at it systematically and narrowed down the radius of operations, it was not impossible that they might stumble upon a clue—if Calhoun did not placidly inform them that it was but another of his own making! But even then, granted that the wire was found to have been tapped in a certain place one night, that was no reason why it should not, as Mr. MacVightie had already suggested, be tapped fifty miles away the next! The Hawk grinned. Mr. Lanson and his associates, backed even by Mr. MacVightie, were confronted with a problem of considerable difficulty!

"I wonder," communed the Hawk with himself, "who's the spider that spun the web; and I wonder how many little spiders he's got running around on it?"

He perused the message once more; but this time he appeared to be concerned mainly with the latter portion. He read it over several times: "Two thousand dollars to the Number that puts a bullet in him."

"Nobody seems to like me," complained the Hawk

softly. "MacVightie doesn't; and the Butcher's crowd seem peeved. Two thousand dollars for my hide! I guess if I stick around here long enough maybe it'll get exciting—for somebody!"

The Hawk tore up the message, the sheet on which he had deciphered it, the sketch of Bald Creek station, tore all three into small fragments, opened the window a little, and let the pieces flutter out into the night. He closed the window, returned the note-book, innocent of everything now but its blank pages, to his pocket—and, pulling his slouch hat down over his eyes, appeared to doze.

IN WHICH A CASH BOX DISAPPEARS

TWENTY minutes later, as No. 17 pulled into Selkirk, the Hawk, his erstwhile drowsiness little in evidence, dropped to the platform while the train was still in motion, and before MacVightie and Lanson in the rear car, it might be fairly assumed, had thought of leaving their seats. The Hawk was interested in MacVightie for the balance of the night only to the extent of keeping out of MacVightie's sight—his attention was centered now on the office of one Isaac Kirschell, and the possibilities that lay in the said Isaac Kirschell's cash box.

He glanced at the illuminated dial of the tower clock. It was eighteen minutes after ten.

"That's the worst of getting the dope a long way down the line," he muttered, as he hurried through the station and out to the street. "But I had to get a look at MacVightie's cards to-night." He struck off toward the downtown business section of the city at a brisk pace. "It ought to be all right though to-night—more than enough time to get in ahead of them—they're not likely to pull any break in that locality until well after midnight. Wonder what

Kirschell's got in his cash box that's so valuable? I
suppose they *know,* or they wouldn't be after it!
They don't hunt small game, but"——the Hawk sighed
lugubriously——"there's no chance of any such luck
as last night again. Ten thousand dollars in cash!
Some haul! Yes, I guess maybe they're peeved!"

The Hawk, arrived at his destination, surveyed
the office building from the opposite side of the
street. The restaurant on the ground floor was
dark, but a lighted window here and there on the
floors above indicated that some of the tenants were
working late. It was therefore fairly safe to presume that the entrance door, though closed, was
unlocked. The Hawk crossed the street unconcerned-
ly, and tried the door. It opened under his hand——
but noiselessly, and to the extent only of a bare inch,
in view of the possibility of a janitor being somewhere about. Detecting no sound from within, however, the Hawk pushed the door a little further open,
and was confronted with a dimly lighted vestibule,
and a long, still more dimly lighted corridor beyond.
There was no one in sight. He slipped inside——and,
quick and silent now in his movements, darted across
the vestibule and into the corridor.

Halfway along the corridor, he halted before a
door, on whose glass panel he could just make out
the words "Isaac Kirschell," and, beneath the name,
in smaller letters, the intimation that the entrance
was next door. The Hawk's decision was taken in
the time it required to produce from his pocket a
key-ring equipped with an extensive assortment of

skeleton keys. If by any chance he should be disturbed and had entered by the designated office door, his escape would be cut off; if, on the other hand, he entered by this unused door, and left it unlocked behind him, he would still be quite comfortably the master of the situation in almost any emergency.

The door seemed to offer unusual difficulties. Even when unlocked, it stuck. The Hawk worked at it by the sense of touch alone, his eyes busy with sharp glances up and down the corridor. Finally, succeeding in opening it a little way, it was only to find it blocked by some obstruction within. He scowled. A desk, probably, close against it! The door was certainly never used. He would have to enter by the other one, after all, and—no! He had reached his arm inside. It was only a coat-stand, or something of the sort. He lifted it aside, stepped in, and closed the door behind him.

The Hawk's flashlight—not the diminutive little affair that had served him for his notebook—began to circle his surroundings inquisitively. He was in a small, plainly furnished private office. There was a desk, two chairs, and a filing cabinet. Also there were two doors. The Hawk opened the one at his left, and peered out. It gave on what was presumably the general office; and at the upper end was a partition with the name, "Mr. Kirschell," upon the door. He looked at the panel of the door he had just opened. It bore no name.

"This belongs to Kirschell's secretary probably," he decided. "The other door from here opens, of

course, into Kirschell's private office. Wonder what
Mr. Isaac Kirschell's business is?"

He closed the door leading into the outer office,
and moved across the room to the second door that
already stood wide open, and almost directly faced
what he had taken for granted was the secretary's
desk. He stepped over the threshold. Mr. Kirschell's sanctum was somewhat more elaborately furnished. Apart from a rather expensive flat-topped
desk in the centre of the room, there was a massive
safe, new and of modern design, a heavy rug upon
the floor, and several very comfortable leather-up-
holstered chairs. A washstand, the metal taps highly
polished, and a mahogany towel rack occupied the
far corner. The Hawk inspected the safe with the
eye of a connoisseur, scowled unhappily by way of
expressing his opinion of it, and turned to the desk.
He opened a drawer, and picked up a sheet of business stationery. The letterhead read:

ISAAC KIRSCHELL
LOANS, MORTGAGES & GENERAL EXCHANGE

"Ho, ho!" observed the Hawk. "Sort of a glori-
fied pawnbroker, eh? I——"

The sheet of paper was shot back into the drawer,
the flashlight was out—and on the instant the Hawk
was back in the other office, and crouched on the floor
behind the desk. Some one had halted outside in
the corridor before the main office door, and now
a key was turned in the lock. The door was opened

and closed, footsteps crossed the general office, paused for a moment outside Mr. Kirschell's door, then the lights in Mr. Kirschell's room went on, a man entered, tossed his hat on a chair, and sat down at the desk. It was obviously Mr. Kirschell himself.

Through the wide opening between the ends of the desk that sheltered him, the Hawk, flat on the floor, took stock of the other. The man was rather small in stature, with a thin, palish face, sharp, restless, very small black eyes, and he was extremely well dressed—the Hawk noted the dainty little boutonnière in the lapel of the man's coat, and smiled queerly. From Mr. Kirschell's face he glanced at the face of Mr. Kirschell's safe, then back at Mr. Kirschell again—and fingered his automatic in the pocket of his coat.

The Hawk, however, made no further movement—Mr. Kirschell's actions suggested that it would be unwise. The man, though apparently occupied with some mail which he had taken from his pocket, kept glancing impatiently at his watch. It was quite evident that he was expecting some one every moment. The Hawk frowned perplexedly. The message that night, even when deciphered, left much, too much, to the imagination! It was quite possible that Mr. Kirschell was to be relieved of his cash box with more address and finesse than by the bald expedient of ruining Mr. Kirschell's safe! This appointment, for instance, might—and then the Hawk smiled queerly again.

The corridor door had opened and closed for the second time. A heavy step traversed the outer office, and a man, hat in hand, in cheap store clothes, stood before Mr. Krischell's desk.

"Mentioned in dispatches!" said the Hawk very softly to himself. "I guess that's Calhoun. So that's the game—eh?"

"You're late, Mr. Calhoun!" Kirschell greeted the other sharply. "Five minutes late! I have put myself to considerable inconvenience to give you this appointment."

Calhoun's hair was tossed, there was a smudge across his cheek, and his hands were grimy, as though he had just come from work. He was a big man, powerfully shouldered. His grey eyes were not friendly as they met Kirschell's.

"I couldn't help it," he said shortly. "I've been up the line all day. I told you I couldn't get here until about this time."

"Well, all right, all right!" said Kirschell impatiently. "But, now that you are here, are you prepared to settle?"

"I can give you a small payment on account, that's the best I can do," Calhoun answered.

Kirschell tilted back in his swivel chair, and frowned as he tapped the edge of his desk with a paper cutter.

"How much?" he demanded coldly.

"Forty dollars"—Calhoun's hand went tentatively toward his pocket.

"Forty dollars!" There was derision in Kirschell's voice, an uninviting smile on Kirschell's lips. "That's hardly more than the interest!"

"Yes," said Calhoun, snarling suddenly, "at the thieving rates you, and the bloodsuckers like you, charge."

Kirschell's uninviting smile deepened.

"Considering the security, the rate is very moderate," he said evenly. "Now, see here, Calhoun, I told you plainly enough this thing had to be settled to-day. You don't want to run away with the impression that I'm a second Marakof, to be staved off all the time. I bought your note from the pawnbroker's estate because the executors didn't like the look of it, and weren't any too sure they could collect it. Well, I can! I'm new out here, but I'm not new at my business. Excuses with me don't take the place of cash. I hold your note for five hundred dollars, which is past due, to say nothing of six months' interest besides—and you come here to-night and offer me forty dollars!"

"I would have paid Marakof," said Calhoun, in a low voice; "and I'll pay you as fast as I can. You know what I'm up against—I told you when you first got after me, as soon as you got that note. My brother got into trouble back East. What would you have done? That five hundred kept him out of the 'pen.' He's only a kid. Damn it, don't play the shark! Marakof renewed the note—why can't you?"

"Because I don't do business that way," said Kirschell curtly.

Calhoun's voice grew hard.

"How much did you pay for that note, anyway?"

Kirschell shrugged his shoulders.

"I didn't say I wasn't taking *any* risk with you," he replied tersely. "That's the profit on my risk. And as far as you are concerned—it's none of your business!"

Calhoun shrugged his shoulders in turn, and, taking a small roll of bills from his pocket, smoothed them out between his fingers.

"I got a wife, and I got kids," said Calhoun slowly. "And I'm doing the best I can. Do you want this forty, or not?"

"It depends," said Kirschell, tapping again with his paper cutter. "How about the rest?"

"I'll pay you what I can every month," Calhoun answered.

"How much?"—bluntly.

"What I can!" returned Calhoun defiantly.

The two men eyed each other for a moment—and then Kirschell tossed the paper cutter down on the desk.

"Well, all right!" he decided ungraciously. "I'll take a chance for a month—and see how you live up to it. Hand it over, and I'll give you a receipt."

Calhoun shook his head.

"I don't trust the man who don't trust me," he said gruffly. "I don't want that kind of a receipt. You'll indorse the payment on the back of the note, Mr. Kirschell, if you want this forty."

"What?" inquired Kirschell, staring.

"You heard what I said," said Calhoun coolly. "I'm in the hands of a shark, and I know it. That's plain talk, isn't it?"

"But," Kirschell flared up angrily, "I——"

Calhoun calmly returned the money to his pocket.

"Suit yourself!" he suggested indifferently. "I ain't asking for anything more than I have a right to."

"Very well, my man!" said Kirschell icily. "If our dealings are to be on this basis, I hope you will remember that the basis is of your own choosing." He swung around in his chair, and, rising, walked over to the safe.

And then, for the first time, the Hawk moved. He edged silently back along the floor until far enough away from the doorway to be fully protected by the darkness of the room, and stood up. Kirschell was swinging the heavy door of the safe open. The cash box was to be produced! Lying down, the Hawk could not hope to see its contents if it were opened on the desk; standing up, he might be able to form a very good idea of how tempting its contents would prove to be.

Kirschell took a black-enamelled steel box from the safe, and returned to the desk. He opened this with a key, threw back the cover—and the Hawk stuck his tongue in his cheek. A few papers lay on the top—otherwise it was crammed to overflowing with banknotes. Kirschell selected one of the papers, and picked up a pen in frigid silence.

But the Hawk was no longer watching **the**

scene. His head was cocked to one side, in a curious, bird-like, listening attitude. He could have sworn he had heard the outer office door being stealthily opened. And now Calhoun was speaking—rapidly, his voice raised noticeably in a louder tone than any he had previously employed.

"I ain't looking for trouble, Mr. Kirschell," he stated hurriedly, as though relenting, "and I don't want you to think I am, but——"

There was a sharp cry from Kirschell. The room was in darkness. Came a quick step running in from the outer office, no longer stealthy now—the crash of a toppling chair—a gasping moan in Kirschell's voice—the thud of a falling body—a tense whisper: "All right, I've got it!"—then the steps running back across the outer office—the closing of the corridor door—and silence.

The Hawk, grim-lipped, had backed up against the wall of the room.

Calhoun's voice rose hoarsely:

"Good God, what's happened! Where's the electric-light switch?"

Kirschell answered him faintly:

"At—at the side of the door—just—-outside the partition."

The lights went on again, and the Hawk leaned intently forward. Calhoun was standing now in the doorway between the outer and the private office, his eyes fixed on Kirschell. The swivel chair had been overturned; and Kirschell, a great crimson stream running down his cheek from above his temple, was struggling to his knees, clutching at the edge of the desk for support. The cash box was gone.

Kirschell's eyes swept the top of the desk haggardly, as though hoping against hope. He gained his feet, lurching unsteadily. A crimson drop splashed to the desk.

"My chair!" he cried out weakly. "Help me!"

Calhoun stepped forward mechanically, and picked up the chair. Kirschell dropped into it.

"You're hurt!" Calhoun said huskily. "You're badly hurt!"

"Yes," Kirschell answered; "but it—can wait. The police first—there was—three thousand dollars—in my cash box." With an effort he reached out across the desk for the telephone, pulled it toward him—and, on the point of lifting the receiver from the hook, slowly drew back his hand. A strange look settled on his face, a sort of dawning, though puzzled comprehension; and then, swaying in his chair, his lips thinned. He drew his hand still further back until it hovered over the handle of the desk's middle drawer. His eyes, on Calhoun, were narrowing.

"You devil!" he rasped out suddenly. "This is your work! I was a fool that I did not see it at first!"

Calhoun's face went white.

"What do you mean?" he said thickly.

"What I say!" Kirschell's voice was ominously clear now, though he sat none too steadily in his chair.

"Then you lie!" said Calhoun fiercely. "You lie —and if you weren't hurt, I'd——"

"No, you wouldn't!"—Kirschell had whipped the drawer open, and, snatching out a revolver, was covering Calhoun. He laughed a little—bitterly. "I'm not so bad that I can't take care of myself. It was pretty clever, I'll give you credit for that. You almost fooled me."

"Damn you!" snarled Calhoun. "Do you mean to say I've got your cash box?"

"Oh, no," said Kirschell. "I can *see* you haven't. I don't even know which of you two struck me. But I do know that you and the man who *has* my cash box worked up this plant together."

Calhoun stepped forward threateningly—only to retreat again before the lifted muzzle of the revolver.

"You're a fool!" he snarled. "You've nothing on me!"

"That's for the police to decide," returned Kirschell evenly. "It would have been a pleasant way of disposing of that note, wouldn't it—if you hadn't under-rated me! And your pal for his share, I daresay, was to take his chance on whatever there might be in the cash box! Why did you say you couldn't come until *night*, when I gave you until to-day as the last day in which to settle? Why did you insist on my indorsing the payment on the note, which necessitated my opening the safe and taking out the cash box in which you knew the note was kept, for you saw me put it there a week ago, when you first came here? And just after I was knocked down I heard your accomplice whisper: *'All right, I've got it.'* It's possible the police might form the same opinion I have as to *whom* those words were addressed!"

Calhoun's face had grown whiter.

"It's a lie!" he said scarcely above a whisper. "It's a lie! I had nothing to do with it!"

"I want my three thousand dollars!" Kirschell's lips were set. He held a red-stained handkerchief to his cheek. "If I call the police now they'll get *you*—but it's your accomplice that's got my money. And it's my money that I want! I'll give you half an hour to go to him, and bring the money back here —and leave the police out of it. If you're not here in that time, I put it up to the police. Half an hour is time enough for you to find your pal; and it's not time enough for you to attempt to leave the city— and get very far!" Kirschell laid his watch on the desk. "You'd better go—I mean half an hour from *now.*"

Calhoun hung hesitant for a moment, staring at the muzzle of Kirschell's revolver. He made as though to say something—and instead, abruptly, with a short, jarring laugh, turned on his heel, and passed out of the room.

The Hawk was already edging his way along the wall toward the corridor door.

"Three thousand dollars!"—the Hawk rolled the words like so many dainty morsels on his tongue, as he communed with himself. "I guess it's my play to stick to Mr. Calhoun!"

— VI —

SOME OF THE LITTLE SPIDERS

THE Hawk reached the door, as Calhoun stepped into the corridor from the general office and passed by outside, evidently making for the main entrance of the building. He opened the door cautiously the width of a crack—and held it in that position. A man's voice, low, guarded, from the corridor, but from the opposite direction to that taken by Calhoun, reached him.

"Here! Calhoun! Here!"

Calhoun halted. There was silence for an instant, then Calhoun retraced his steps and passed by the door again. There were a few hurried words in a whisper, which the Hawk could not catch; and then the footsteps of both men retreated along the corridor.

The Hawk opened the door wider, and peered out. The two men were well down the corridor now; and now, as they passed the single incandescent that lighted that end of the hall, Calhoun's companion reached up and turned it out.

"Why, say—thanks!" murmured the Hawk, and stepped out into the corridor himself.

It was now quite dark at that end, and the men had disappeared. The Hawk moved silently and swiftly along, keeping close to the wall. Presently he caught the sound of their voices again, and nodded to himself. He remembered that in going out this way yesterday he had noticed that the corridor, for some architectural reason, made a sharp, right-angled jut just before it gave on the side-street entrance. He stepped now across to the other side of the corridor, and stole forward to a position where he could look diagonally past the projecting angle of the jut. The two men, standing there, showed plainly in the light from a street arc that shone into the entrance-way through the large plate-glass square over the door. The Hawk, quite secure from observation, nestled back against the wall—and an ominous smile settled on the Hawk's lips. The face of Calhoun's companion was covered with a mask.

"There's nothing to be leery about here," the man was saying. "There's no one goes out or comes in this way at night. Well, it's a nice mess, eh? So the old Shylock called the turn on you, did he?"

There seemed to be a helpless note in Calhoun's voice. He passed his hand heavily across his eyes.

"What's the meaning of this?" he cried out. "What do you know about what happened in there?"

"Nothing much," said the other coolly. "Except that I'm the guy that pinched the swag, and hit Kirschell that welt on the head."

"*You!*" Calhoun involuntarily stepped back.

"Yes, sure—me!" The man shrugged his shoulders. "Me and a pal who was outside. He's away now putting the cash box where it won't come to any harm—savvy? He'll be back pretty soon."

The Hawk's lips moved.

"Number Three and Number Seven," whispered the Hawk gently.

"I—I don't understand," said Calhoun dazedly. "Then why are you telling me this. And why are you staying here? And how did you know that Kirschell accused me of being in it?"

"That's another one that's easy," announced the man evenly. "Because it was part of the game to *make* him think so."

Calhoun seemed to stiffen up.

"What! You mean, you——"

"You're getting it!" said the other shortly. "But you'd better wait until you get it all before you start spitting your teeth out! Mabbe you've heard of a little interference with the telegraph wires, and a few small jobs pulled off around here where some inno-cent parties accidentally got croaked? Ah—you have, eh! Well, that's where you come in, Calhoun. We want you—and when we want anything, we get it! See? We knew about that note, and we've been expecting the railroad crowd to wake up some time, and we had you picked out to place our bets on against them. They woke up to-day and began to nose over the line. It ain't likely to do them much good, but there's a chance—and we ain't taking chances. We don't want much from you, Calhoun, just a little thing, and it'll bring you more money than you ever saw in your life before and without you running any risk. All you've got to do is stand for anything in the shape of a splice or tap on the line that they're suspicious of—you can say it's a repair job of your own, see?"

An angry flush was tinging Calhoun's cheeks.

"Is that all?" he burst out passionately. "Well, I'll see you damned first!"

"Will you?" returned the other calmly. "All right, my bucko! It's your funeral. Take your choice. That—or twenty years in the penitentiary. You're in cold on this. Think it over a bit. For instance, how did you come to make the break of wanting Kirschell to indorse the payment on the back of the note, which made him open his safe?"

"How do you know I did?" Calhoun flashed back sharply.

"Mabbe I'm only guessing at it," said the man nonchalantly; "and mabbe I was back in the outside room when you did. But, say, you don't happen to remember, do you, a little talk you had with a stranger up the line to-day? And how the conversation got around to loan sharks, and how he told about a trick they had of giving receipts that were phony, and how he beat one of them to it by making the shark indorse on the paper itself? Kind of sunk in, and you bit—eh, Calhoun? We don't do things by halves. We happen to *need* you. And what do you think I made the break of whispering so Kirschell would hear me for?"

The color was ebbing from Calhoun's face.

"It's not proof!" The defiant ring in his voice was forced. "I——"

"It's enough to make Kirschell believe it, and that's all we wanted for a starter. We'll take care of the rest!" stated the man grimly. "What did he say to you?"

Calhoun answered mechanically:

"He said if I didn't return in half an hour with the cash box, he'd notify the police."

"Oh, ho!" The man's lips widened in a grin under the edge of his mask. "So he's going to wait here, eh? Well, so much the better! It'll save us a trip to his house. Now, see here, Calhoun, let this sink in!" He put his hand in his pocket and drew out a slip of paper. "Here's your note. It was on the desk where Kirschell was writing on it, and I pinched it when I pinched the cash box. We didn't figure we were going to make the haul we did to-night—we were after you. But there's *some* money in that cash box, as you saw for yourself. Here's the idea: Kirschell's read a thing or two about what's going on around here—enough to make him know that there ain't much our gang'll stop at. If you say you're with us, me and my pal 'll go in there and throw the fear of God into him. Do you get it? He'll think himself lucky to get off by keeping his mouth shut about to-night when he finds out who he's up against. Also you get the note back, and a share of the cash—and more to come later on."

"No!" Calhoun cried out. "No! I'm no thief!"

"All right!" agreed the other indifferently.

"That's one side of it. Here's the other: Kirschell certainly believes you took it. He's a shark all right, and he thinks more of his money than he does of anything else, or he wouldn't have given you the chance he did. But when you don't show back there with the coin, he'll take the only other hope he's got of getting his money and turn on the police tap—see? What are you going to do then? Make a break for it, or let 'em get you? Well, it doesn't matter which. This note and a chunk of the cash gets mailed to-night—and the police get tipped off to watch your mail in the morning. Kind of reasonable, isn't it? Your pal, not being able to find you, and not tumbling to the fact that the police have got you until too late, comes across with your share like an honest little man! I think you said something about proof, Calhoun? And I think I told you before that we didn't do things by halves. How about that on top of Kirschell's story—do you think it would cinch a jury, or do you think they'd believe any little fairy story you might tell them, say, about meeting me? Does it look any more like twenty years than it did?"

There was a sudden agony in Calhoun's face.

"My God!" he whispered. "You—you wouldn't do that?"

The man made no answer. He still held the note in his hand—but in the other now he carelessly dangled a revolver.

"You wouldn't! You wouldn't!" Calhoun's voice

was broken now. "I've a wife and children, and——my God, what am I to do!"

"That half-hour Kirschell gave you is slipping along," suggested the other uncompromisingly. "Here's the note, and there's easy money waiting for you."

Calhoun turned on the other like a man demented.

"Do you think I'd touch that cash! Or touch that note—I *owe* it! I may not have been able to pay it —but I owe it!"

"Oh, well, suit yourself as to that, too!" said the man cynically. "It's the other thing *we* want. What's the wife and the kids you're talking about going to do if you go up for twenty years?"

Calhoun, with a miserable cry, buried his face in his hands.

There was silence—a minute dragged by.

"Well?" prompted the man curtly.

Calhoun dropped his hands, met the other's eyes for an instant—and turned his head away.

"Ah, I thought you would!" said the man calmly. "My pal ought to be back by now, and as soon as he comes we'll go in there and hand Kirschell his little jolt, and——" He stopped. There was a light rapping on the entrance door. "Here he is now! We'll——"

The Hawk was retreating back along the corridor. Again he opened the door of what he had designated to himself as the secretary's office, and for the second time that night stepped silently into the room, closing the door behind him. The sound of run ning water came from Kirschell's private office, but there was no other sound—the Hawk made none as he once more gained his place of vantage behind the desk.   Kirschell was bending over the wash-bowl, his back turned, bathing his temple and face, and now, straightening up, he bound a towel tightly around his head.

The Hawk watched the proceedings impassively, his head, in that bird-like, listening attitude, cocked on one shoulder toward the outer door.   Steps were coming along the corridor.   But this time Kirschell, too, heard them—for he turned, and, as the corridor door opened, started toward his desk.   He reached it and sat down, as Calhoun entered the room.

"Ah, ha!" snapped Kirschell triumphantly.   "So you've thought better of it, have you?   I imagined you would!   Well, where's the——"   The words seemed to freeze on his lips; there was a sudden terror in his face.   "What—what does this mean?" he faltered.

Two masked men, the one who had been with Calhoun in the corridor, and a taller, more heavily built man, had stepped in behind Calhoun, and were advancing toward the desk.

The short man pointed a revolver at Kirschell's head.

"Calhoun says he keeps a gun in the middle drawer of the desk," he grunted to his companion.   "Get it!"

The other, leaning over, pulled the drawer open,

and, appropriating Kirschell's revolver, stuck it in his pocket.

Kirschell's tongue circled his lips. He looked wildly from one to the other.

"We just dropped in to make a confession, Mr. Kirschell," said the short man, with an ugly jeer. "We don't like to see an innocent man suffer—understand? I'm the one that lifted your cash box, you measly shark—me and my pal there. I heard you trying to stick it on Calhoun. We ain't asking any favours for ourselves, and when we get through with you, you can tell the police it was us, and that we're part of the crowd that's been making things lively around these parts—you've been reading the papers, ain't you?—but you open your mouth about Calhoun, you put him in bad when he had nothing to do with it, and inside of twenty-four hours you'll be found in a dark alley somewhere with a bullet through you! Get me? You know who you're up against now, and you've got fair warning!"

Kirschell was huddled in his chair. His little black eyes were no longer restless—they were fixed in a sort of terrified fascination on the speaker.

"Yes." He licked his lips again. "Yes, I—I understand," he mumbled.

From his pocket the Hawk took a mask, which he slipped over his face; and from his pocket he took his automatic.

"I don't think he believes you," sneered the second masked man, with a wicked grin. "Perhaps mabbe we'd better twist his windpipe a little, just to show him in a friendly way that there ain't any mistake about it—eh?"

"No, no!" Kirschell's voice was full of fear. "No, no! I believe—I——" His words ended in a choked scream.

The man's hands had shot swiftly out, and closed on Kirschell's throat. He was shaking, twisting, and turning Kirschell's head from side to side. His companion laughed brutally. Came a series of guttural moans from Kirschell—and Kirschell's body began to slip limply down in his chair.

Calhoun had gone white to the lips.

"Stop it! My God, stop it!" he burst out frantically. "You promised me you wouldn't do him any harm."

"You mind your own business!" snarled the man with the revolver. "We know how to handle his breed. Give him enough to hold him for a while, Jim! We——"

"Drop that revolver! *Drop it!*" The Hawk was standing in the doorway.

There was a startled oath from the leader of the two men as he whirled around, a gasp as he faced the Hawk's automatic—and his weapon clattered to the floor. The other, in a stunned way, still hung over Kirschell, but his hands had relaxed their hold on Kirschell's throat.

"Thank you!" drawled the Hawk. "I must say I agree with Mr. Calhoun. It's not a pleasant sight to watch a man being throttled." His voice rang suddenly cold. "You, there!" His automatic indicated the man beside Kirschell. "Stand back at the end of the desk, and put up your hands!"

Calhoun had not moved. He was staring numbly at the Hawk. Kirschell, making guttural sounds, was clawing at his throat.

"Mr. Calhoun," requested the Hawk coolly, "as I happen to know that you have little reason to love either of these two gentlemen, will you be good enough to pick up that revolver and hand it to me?"

Calhoun stooped mechanically, and extended it to the Hawk.

"And now our friend over there with his hands up, Mr. Calhoun," purred the Hawk. "You will find two in his pockets—his own, and Mr. Kirschell's. Mr. Kirschell, I am sure, is already fairly well convinced that you are in no way connected with the robbery of his cash box, and I am equally sure that in no way could you better dispel any lingering doubts he might still entertain than by helping to draw these gentlemen's teeth."

Calhoun laughed a little grimly now.

"I don't know who you are," he said, his lips set, as he started toward the man; "but I guess you're right. I'd like to see them get what's coming to them."

"Quite so!" said the Hawk pleasantly. He accepted the two remaining revolvers from Calhoun; and from his pocket produced his skeleton keys. He handed them to Calhoun, designating one of the keys on the ring. "One more request, Mr. Calhoun," he said. "I entered by the door that opens

on the corridor from this other office here. Will
you please lock it; and, on your way back, also lock
this connecting door through which I have just come
in—the key of the latter, I noticed, is in the lock."

Calhoun nodded, took the keys, and stepped quickly from the room. Kirschell, evidently not seriously hurt from the handling he had received, though
still choking a little and clearing his throat with
short coughs, was regarding the Hawk with a ques-
tioning stare. The eyes of the other two men were
on the Hawk's revolver. The shorter of the two
suddenly raised a clenched fist.

"The Hawk!" he flashed out furiously. "You
cursed snitch! You'll wish you were dead before
we're through with you!"

"So the Butcher told me last night." The Hawk
smiled plaintively. "Move a little closer together,
you two—yes, like that, at the far end of the desk
beside each other. Thank you! You are much easier
to cover that way."

Calhoun returned, locking the connecting door behind him, and handed the door key, together with
the key-ring, back to the Hawk.

The Hawk moved forward to the desk. He was
alert, quick, ominous now. The drawl, the pleas-
antry was gone.

"Out there in the hall," he said coldly, "I heard
Mr. Calhoun refuse to take back his note—from a
thief. You"—his revolver muzzle jerked toward
the short man—"hand it out!"

The man reached viciously into his pocket, and tossed the note on the desk.

The Hawk pushed it toward Kirschell.

"Mr. Kirschell," he said quietly, "you no doubt had good reasons for it, but you have none the less falsely accused Mr. Calhoun. Furthermore, Mr. Calhoun has been instrumental in laying these two who have confessed by the heels. Under the circumstances, if you are the man I think you are, you will tear that up."

Kirschell fingered the note for an instant. He looked from Calhoun to the Hawk, and back at Calhoun again.

"Yes," he said abruptly—and tore it into several pieces. "I suppose I could hardly do less. You are quite right! And, Mr. Calhoun, I—I apologise to you."

A flush spread over Calhoun's face. He swallowed hard, and his lips quivered slightly.

"Mr. Kirschell," he stammered, "I—I——"

"That's all right!" interposed the Hawk whimsically. "Don't start any mutual admiration society. I dislike embarrassing situations; and besides, Mr. Calhoun"—his eyes travelled from one to the other of the two masked men—"I think you had better go now."

"Go?" repeated Calhoun, somewhat bewilderedly.

"Yes," supplemented the Hawk. "As far as you are concerned, you are clear and out of this now. Stay out of it, and say nothing—that's the best thing you can do."

"Well, that suits me," said Calhoun with a wry smile, "if Mr. Kirschell——"

"Exactly! I see!" approved the Hawk. "It does you credit. But Mr. Kirschell and I are quite capable of settling with these two; and you can thank Mr. Kirschell further to-morrow if you like—when I'm not here! Now—if you please!"

Calhoun turned, and walked to the door. His footsteps echoed back from the general office. Then the corridor door closed behind him.

The Hawk addressed the two masked men.

"Last night," remarked the Hawk gently, "it was the Butcher, and to-night it is—pardon me"—he was close in front of the two now, and, with a jerk, snatched the masks from their faces—"Whitie Jim, and the Bantam! Well, I might have known from the Butcher! You're all out of the same kind of cocoons! The poor old simp at the head of your gang is sure stuck with a moth-eaten lot! He's sure collected a bunch of left-overs! Why, say, back there in New York, where a *real* crook couldn't keep the grin off his face every time he met you, even the police had you passed up as harmless cripples!"

"You go to blazes!" growled the Bantam, with an oath. "You'll sing through the other side of your mouth for this yet!"

"You are not nice to me, Bantam," said the Hawk, in a pained voice. "You don't appreciate what I'm doing for you. It was a piker game you tried to hand Calhoun; but, even at that, I wouldn't have queered it if it would have helped you work out a few more

little deals, so that I could skim the cream off them.
But it wouldn't! I don't see what you gain by inter-
fering with the telegraph lines, but I'll let you in on
something. I've been keeping an eye on MacVightie
because MacVightie's been keeping an eye on me,
and I overheard him talking to the superintendent
to-night. MacVightie's got an idea that Calhoun's
fooling with the wires now. See where you would
have been? If Calhoun had ever got started on the
real thing, some of you would have been nipped—
and, say, there's nothing like that going to happen
if I can help it! You and your crowd are too valuable to me to take any chances of your getting in
wrong anywhere. I'm not wringing the neck of the
goose that lays my golden eggs! Tell that to the
guy that's supposed to have the brains of your outfit, will you? And you might add that I don't want
any thanks. I'm getting well paid."

"You'll get paid, curse you!" The Bantam's voice
was hoarse with fury. "You butted in once too
often last night. The Butcher warned you. There
ain't any more warnings. You've got the drop on
us here to-night, but——"

"It's getting late," said the Hawk wearily. "And
I'm sure Mr. Kirschell agrees with me that it is
about time to produce that cash box—do you not,
Mr. Kirschell?"

Kirschell made no reply.

The Hawk smiled—unhappily.

"I don't think you put it back in the safe—I see
that the door is still wide open. A drawer in the

desk, then, perhaps? Ah—*would you!*" There was a sudden deadly coldness in the Hawk's voice. The Bantam had edged around the corner of the desk. "If any of you move another inch, I'll drop you as quick as I'd drop a mad dog! Now then—if the Cricket will oblige? I'll give him until I count three. One—two——"

"Damn you!—Kirschell's face was livid and contorted. He wrenched a lower drawer open, and flung the cash box on the desk.

"The Butcher, Whitie Jim, the Bantam, and the Cricket," murmured the Hawk. "It's good to see old New York faces out here, even if you do size up like bush-leaguers trying to bust into high society. You can take that towel off, if you like, Cricket, it doesn't become you particularly—and, as you've washed off the heart-rending effect of that little bag of liquid stain you smashed over your temple, I'm sure you'll look less like a comic opera star! No? Well, please yourself!" The Hawk was coolly transferring the contents of the cash box to his pockets with his left hand. "These papers," mused the Hawk deliberately aloud, "appear to be some securities you lifted on that Pullman car raid. Rather neat idea, this, establishing this office—sort of a clearing house, I take it, for the gang's drag-net—'loans, mortgages and general exchange!' I take back part of what I said—this shows a first faint glimmer of brains. Well, keep the office going, your interests are mine! You'll notice that I was considerate enough to get Calhoun out of the way before the show-down. You were very generous, magnanimous even, Cricket—I admire you! Calhoun'll swear Mr. Kirschell is the squarest man on earth— and don't forget that's another little debt of gratitude you owe the Hawk. Three thousand dollars!" The Hawk's pockets were bulging. "Must have been what you separated some one from when I wasn't looking! Glad you weren't stingy with your bait for Calhoun! I heard to-day that Mr. Kirschell kept a good deal of cash in his safe, but I had no idea that Mr. Kirschell was the Cricket—not till I came here this evening to take a look at Mr. Kirschell's safe. I must say it has been a surprise—a very pleasant surprise."

The cash box was empty. The Hawk backed away from the desk.

None of the three men spoke—they were eying him like caged and infuriated beasts.

The Hawk reached the doorway.

"You will observe," smiled the Hawk engagingly, "that this is now the only exit, and that as I walk backward across the outer office any one who steps into this doorway will be directly in the line of fire." He bowed facetiously, backed through the doorway and across the general office, and, still facing the inner room, opened the corridor door and stepped out.

And then the Hawk spoke again.

"I bid you good evening, gentlemen!" said the Hawk softly. "You will pardon me if I put you to the inconvenience of locking this door—on the outside."

VII

WANTED—THE HAWK—DEAD OR ALIVE

MACVIGHTIE had become troublesome. For two days MacVightie had very seriously annoyed the Hawk. It was for that reason that the Hawk now crept stealthily up the dark, narrow stairs, and, on the landing, listened in strained attention before the door of his own room.

Reassured finally, he opened the door inch by inch, noiselessly. The bolt, in grooves that were carefully oiled, made no sound in slipping into place, as the Hawk entered and closed the door behind him. So far, so good! He was quick, alert, but still silent, as, in the darkness, he crossed swiftly to the window, and crouched down against the wall. A minute, two, went by. The fire-escape, passing at an angle a short distance below the window sill, and at first nebulous in the blackness, gradually took on distinct and tangible shape. Still the Hawk held there motionless, searching it with his eyes—and then, abruptly, satisfied that it sheltered no lurking shadow, he straightened up, thrust his automatic back into his pocket, pulled down the shade, and, turning back into the room, switched on the light.

MacVightie, it appeared, still had lingering suspicions of this room over the somewhat disreputable saloon below, and still had lingering suspicions of its occupant. All that afternoon the Hawk was quite well aware that he had been shadowed—but the result had been rather in his favour than in MacVightie's. From the moment he had discovered that he was being followed, he had devoted his time to making applications for a job—for MacVightie's benefit—that being the reason he had given MacVightie for his presence in Selkirk. Later on, when it had grown dark, having business of his own, he had left MacVightie's satellite standing on a street corner somewhat puzzled just which way to turn! That, however, had no bearing on the watch that had been, or might be at the present moment, set upon this room.

The Hawk, in apparent abstraction, was flipping a coin up in the air and catching it. There was a slight frown on the Hawk's face. MacVightie's suspicions were still lingering for the simple reason that MacVightie, utterly at sea, was clutching at the only straw in sight, unless—the coin slipped through the Hawk's fingers and fell beside his trunk. He stooped to pick it up—yes, not only had the room been searched, but the trunk had been opened! The single strand of hair, almost indiscernible against the brass and quite innocently caught in the lock, was broken. Well, he had not finished that mental sentence. Unless—*what?*

He tucked the coin into his pocket, and, standing

up, yawned and stretched himself. With the toe of his boot he lazily pushed a chair out from the wall. The chair fell over. The Hawk picked it up, and quite casually set it down—near the door. He took off his coat, and flung it over the back of the chair.

The Hawk's face was greyer now, as it set in rigid lines, but there was no tremor in the hand that inserted the key in the lock of the trunk. He flung back the lid—and his eyes, for an instant, searched the room again sharply. The window shade was securely drawn; the coat over the back of the chair completely screened the keyhole of the door. He laughed a little then—mirthlessly. Well, the trunk had been opened! Had MacVightie found *all*—or nothing?

His fingers were working swiftly, deftly now around the inside edges of the lid. He was either caught here, cornered, at bay—or MacVightie, once for all, would be satisfied, and, as far as MacVightie was concerned, the coast would hereafter be clear. The Hawk's dark eyes narrowed, the square under jaw crept out and set doggedly. It had been a close call, perilously close, that other night when he had taken the ten thousand dollars from the paymaster's safe, and MacVightie had followed him here to this room. He had pulled the wool over MacVightie's eyes for the moment—but MacVightie had returned to the old trail again. Well, the cards were on the table now, and it was a gamble that was grim enough! Either he was quit of MacVightie, could even count on MacVightie as a sort of sponsor for his innocence; or—

"Ah!" The ingeniously fashioned false tray in the curvature of the lid had come away in the Hawk's hands. He was safe! MacVightie had missed it! In the tray, untouched, where he had left them, lay the packages of banknotes from the paymaster's safe; in the tray still glittered the magnificent diamond necklace, whose theft from the wife of His Excellency the Governor of the State had already furnished more than one of the big dailies back in the East with attractive copy for their Sunday editions; and there, undisturbed, were the contents of Isaac Kirschell's cash box, a trifling matter of some three thousand dollars; and there too, snugly tucked away in one corner, was the bundle of crisp, new, counterfeit ten-dollar bills. The Hawk grinned maliciously, as his eyes rested on the counterfeit notes. The one he had sent, inscribed with his compliments, to MacVightie, when he had returned the otherwise empty paymaster's bag to the detective, had not pleased MacVightie!

Quite at his ease now, the Hawk fitted the false top back into the lid, closed the trunk, locked it, drew a chair up to the table, and sat down. With MacVightie removed as a possible factor of interruption, there was another, and very pressing little matter to which he was now at liberty to give his attention. He produced a folded sheet of paper from his inside vest pocket, spread it out on the table before him, and inspected it with a sort of cynical curiosity. In each corner were tack holes. He had removed it less than half an hour ago—not through any misguided dislike to publicity, but simply because he had urgently required a piece of paper—from a conspicuous position on the wall of the railroad station. It was a police circular. The Hawk had not before had an opportunity to absorb more than the large type captions—he filled his pipe calmly now, as he read it in its entirety:

$5,000 REWARD—FOR EX-SING SING CONVICT

Five Thousand Dollars Reward Will Be Paid For Information Leading to the Arrest and Conviction of THE HAWK, Alias HARRY MAUL.

Here followed a description tallying with the one given by MacVightie to Lanson, the division superintendent, and which Lanson had caustically remarked would not fit more than twenty-five thousand men in Selkirk City; followed after that a résumé of the crimes recently committed on the railroad, amongst them the theft of the diamond necklace and the robbery of the paymaster's safe; and, at the end, in bold-faced type again:

$2,000 REWARD

Two Thousand Dollars Reward Will Also be Paid For Information Leading to the Arrest and Conviction of Each and Every One of THE HAWK'S Confederates.

The Hawk smiled broadly, as he held the flame of a match to his pipe bowl. The last paragraph was exquisitely ironical. Those whom MacVightie so blithely called the "Hawk's confederates" were vying with each other at that exact moment, and for the exact amount of two thousand dollars offered by the Master Spider of the gang, for the privilege of putting an even more conclusive end—in the shape of a knife thrust, a bullet, or a blackjack—to the Hawk!

"And," said the Hawk softly, as he turned the circular over, "I guess they'd make it a whole lot more if they knew that I had—*this!*"

The back of the circular was covered with line after line of what, seemingly, was but a meaningless jumble of scribbled letters—nor, in this case, were the letters any too well formed. The Hawk had laboured under difficulties when the telegraph sounder had "broke" unexpectedly with the message. He had been listening—as he was always listening when within sound of a telegraph instrument—but he had never known a message from the Wire Devils to come through at so early an hour in the evening before. He had shaken MacVightie's man off the trail and had gone down to the depot, intending to go up the line to the first small station, where, with little chance of being discovered, he could spend the night within earshot of the operator's instrument—in the hope that his vigil would not, as it sometimes did, prove futile. He had been standing under the dispatcher's open window waiting for a train, when the police circular tacked on the station wall had caught his eye. The large type was readily decipherable, but the platform lights were poor, and he had stepped closer to read the remainder—and instead, glancing quickly about him to see that he was not observed, he had snatched the circular from the wall, and, whipping a pencil from his pocket, had scrawled on the reverse side, as best he could, the message that was rattling in over the dispatcher's sounder from the room above. He had taken chances—but he had played in luck. No one had noticed him, and—well, he was here now with the message; and, since it must sooner or later have been put to the proof in any case, he was back here, too, to find that he was quit of MacVightie.

"Yes," confided the Hawk to himself, as he reached for a blank sheet of paper in the drawer of the table, "I guess I played in luck—both ways. Wonder if there's another ripe little melon here going to be shoved my way on a gold platter by the Butcher and his crowd?"

The Hawk studied the cipher for a moment.

"lqrtvy . . . key letter . . . stroke at six . . .two-three-one," he murmured.

He drew the fresh sheet of paper toward him, and began to work busily. Occasionally he paused, staring dubiously at a letter—he had taken the message under far from ideal conditions, and a mistake here and there, if not fatal, was annoying and confusing. Finally, however, the Hawk leaned back in his chair, and whistled low under his breath. The message, deciphered and arranged into words and sentences, ran:

Final orders. Number One, Three, and Six hold up Fast Mail three miles east of Burke's Siding to-night. Cut wires on approach. Express car next to engine. Uncouple and proceed. Diamond shipment in safe. Messenger drugged. No interference with remainder of train. Deliver safe five-mile crossing to Number Four and Seven. Number One, Three, and Six take engine and car further along the line. Return separately to Selkirk.

Again the Hawk whistled low under his breath— and for the second time reached into his inside vest pocket. He took out a letter that was addressed, care of general delivery, to Mr. J. P. Carrister. The Hawk puffed pleasantly at his pipe as he read it:

"Dear Friend: The folks are all well, and hope you are the same. I haven't had time to write much lately. I like my new job fine. Say, I felt like a Fifth Avenue dook for about umpty seconds to-day. One of the fellows in the office let me hold a package of diamonds in my hand just to see what it felt like. Gee! Say, you could almost shove it in your vest pocket, and it was invoiced through customs at twenty thousand plunks. They were unset stones, and came in from Amsterdam. It made me feel queer.

I wouldn't like to be the fellow that has to keep his eye on it any of the way from here to San Francisco, where it's going to-morrow by express. If you see any bright lights flashing around your burg that you can't account for about 11:15 next Wednesday night, you'll know it's the diamonds going through in the express-car safe. I'm getting to be some joker, eh? We all went down to Coney last Sunday. It's been fierce and hot here. Say, don't be a clam, write us a line. Well, I guess there ain't any more news. Yours truly, Bud."

The Hawk, instead of folding up the letter and returning it to his pocket, began meditatively to tear it into minute shreds, and with it the police circular and the sheet of paper on which he had worked out the cipher message. The Fast Mail scheduled Selkirk at 11:15—*and this was Wednesday night!*

"Twenty thousand dollars," said the Hawk gently under his breath. "Thanks, Bud, old boy! You were there with tne goods all right, but it wasn't a one-man job, and I didn't think there was going to be anything doing." The Hawk grinned at the ceiling. "And just as I was about passing up the last check, here they go and fix it for me to scoop the whole pot! Three miles east of Burke's Siding, eh?"

The Hawk relapsed into silence for a moment; then he spoke again.

"Yes," said the Hawk, "I guess that ought to

work. She won't make the three miles from the siding under five or six minutes. She's due at Burke's at ten-ten. I can make it on the local out of here at eight-thirty. Twenty thousand dollars—in *unset* stones! Just as good as cash—and a lot easier to carry!"

The Hawk looked at his watch. It was five minutes of eight. He rose leisurely from his chair, stooped for a precautionary inspection of the trunk lock, put on his coat, and, moving toward the door, switched off the light.

"If I get away with this," observed the Hawk, as he went down the stairs and let himself out through the street door, "it'll be good-night for keeps if any of the gang ever pick up my trail—and they won't quit until they do! And then there's MacVightie and the police. I guess there'll be some little side-stepping to do—what? Oh, well"—he shrugged his shoulders—"I guess I'll get a bite of supper, anyway—there's no telling when I'll have a chance to eat again!"

VIII

THREADS IN THE WEB

IT was not far to the station—down through the lane from the Palace Saloon—and close to the station, he remembered, there was a little short-order house that was generally patronised by the railroad men. Old Mother Barrett's short-order house, they called it. She was the wife of an engineer who had been killed, he had heard, and she had a boy working somewhere on the railroad. Not that he was interested in these details; in fact, as he walked along, the Hawk was not interested in old Mother Barrett in a personal sense at all—but, as he reached the short-order house and entered, his eyes, as though magnetically drawn in that direction, fixed instantly on the little old woman behind the counter.

The Hawk was suddenly very much interested in old Mother Barrett. It was not that she made a somewhat pathetic figure, that she drooped a little at the shoulders, that her face under her grey hair looked tired, or that, though scrupulously neat, her clothes were a little threadbare—it was none of these things—it was old Mother Barrett's hands that for the moment concerned the Hawk. She was in

the act of adjusting her spectacles and picking up a
very new and crisp ten-dollar bill, that a customer
from the stool in front of her had evidently tendered
in payment for his meal.   The Hawk shot a quick
glance up and down the room.   There were several
other customers at the long counter, but the stool
beside the owner of the ten-dollar bill was vacant—
and the Hawk unostentatiously straddled it.

He glanced casually at the man at his elbow; allowed his eyes to stray to the kindly, motherly old
face with its grey Irish eyes, that was puckered now
in a sort of hesitant indecision—and glanced a little
more than casually at the banknote she kept turning
over and over in her hands.   No, he had not been
mistaken.   It was one of those counterfeits which,
according to MacVightie, had flooded the East and
were now making their appearance in Selkirk, and it
was a duplicate of those in the false tray of his
trunk.   His eyes perhaps were sharper than old
Mother Barrett's—in any case, his identification was
the quicker, for his gaze had wandered to the coffee
urn, and he was drumming idly on the counter with
his finger tips before the little old woman finally
spoke.

"I—I'm afraid I can't take this," she said slowly,
handing the banknote back across the counter.

"What's the matter with it?" demanded the man
gruffly.

"Why—it's—it's counterfeit," she said a little
anxiously, as though she were fearful of giving of-
fence.

The Hawk's eyes, with mild and quite impersonal interest, were on the man's face now. The man had picked up the bill, and was pretending to examine it critically.

"Counterfeit!" echoed the man shortly. "Say, what are you giving us! It's as good as wheat! Give me my change, and let me get out—I'm in a hurry!" He pushed the bill toward her again.

She did not pick it up from the counter this time.

"I'm sorry." She seemed genuinely disturbed, and the sweet old face was full of sympathy. "I'm sure you did not know that it was not good, and ten dollars is a great deal to lose, isn't it? It's too bad. Do you remember where you got it?"

"Look here, you're dippy!" snapped the man. "I tell you it's not counterfeit. Anyway, it's all I've got. If you want your pay, take it!"

"You owe me thirty-five cents, but I can't take it out of this." She shook her head in a troubled way. "This is a counterfeit."

"You seem to be pretty well posted—on counterfeits!" sneered the man offensively. "How do you know it's a counterfeit—eh?"

"Because I've seen one like this before," she said simply. "My son showed me one the last time he was in from his run, and he warned me to be careful about taking any."

"Oh, your son—eh?" sneered the man again. "Some son! Wised you up, did he? Carries it around with him—eh? And who does *he* shove it off on?"

There was a queer little sound from the old lady—like a quick, hurt catch of her breath. The Hawk's eyes travelled swiftly to her face. She had turned a little pale, and her lips were trembling—but she was drawn up very proudly, and the thin shoulders were squared back.

"I love my boy," she said in a low voice, and tears came suddenly into her eyes, "I love him with all my heart, but I should a thousand times rather see him dead than know him for a thief. And a man who attempts to pass these things knowingly is a—*thief*. I have been very respectful to you, sir, and I do not deserve what you have said. I assumed that you had been swindled yourself, and that you were perfectly honest in offering the bill to me, but now from your——"

"What's the trouble, Mother Barrett?"—a big railroader farther up the counter had laid down his knife and fork, and swung round on his stool.

With a hurried glance in that direction, the man hastily thrust the counterfeit note into his pocket, laid down thirty-five cents on the counter—and, with a dive across the room, disappeared through the door.

The Hawk stared thoughtfully after him.

"I couldn't butt in on that, and hand him one," said the Hawk to himself almost apologetically. "Not with twenty thousand in sight! I couldn't afford to get into a row, and maybe miss the local, and spill the beans, could I?"

He looked around again to find the little old

woman wiping her spectacles, and smiling at him a little wistfully.

"I'm sorry that you had to listen to any unpleasantness," she said. "My little place isn't very pretentious, but I would not like to have you, a stranger, think that sort of thing was customary here. What can I get you, sir?"

It was no wonder that the railroaders evidently swore by old Mother Barrett, and that one of them had been quick to shift her trouble to his own shoulders!

"I guess he was a bad one, all right!" growled the Hawk.

She shook her head regretfully. There was no resentment left—it was as though, indeed, the man was a charge upon her own conscience.

"He meant to be dishonest, I am afraid," she admitted reluctantly; "but I am sure he cannot be thoroughly bad, for he wasn't very old—just a young man."

She was a very simple, trusting little old lady— as well as a sweet little old lady. Why should her illusions be dispelled? The Hawk nodded gravely.

"Perhaps," suggested the Hawk, "perhaps he hasn't had any one to keep him straight. Perhaps he hasn't got what keeps a good many chaps straight —a good mother."

The mist was quick in her eyes again. He had not meant to bring that—he had meant only to show her a genuine admiration and respect.

"Perhaps not," she answered slowly. "But if he

has, I hope she will never know." She shook her
head again; and then: "But you have not told me
yet what you would like, sir?"

The Hawk gave his order. He ate mechanically.
Back in his mind he was reviewing a rather extensive acquaintanceship with certain gentry whose mo-
rals were not wholly above reproach. Failing, however, to identify the individual with the counterfeit
note as one of this select number, he finally dismissed
the man somewhat contemptuously from his mind.

"Just a piker crook, I guess," decided the Hawk.
"I'd like to have found out though how many more
of those he's got, and who the fool was that let an
amateur skate like that loose with any of the goods!"

He finished his meal, paid his bill, smiled a good-
night to old Mother Barrett, walked out of the short-
order house, and made his way over to the station.
Five minutes later, having purchased a magazine, the
Hawk, with a ticket in his pocket for a station a number of miles beyond Burke's Siding, curled himself
up with his pipe on a seat in the smoker of the local.

The train started, and the Hawk apparently became immersed in his magazine. The Hawk, however, though he turned a page from time to time,
was concerned with matters very far removed from
the printed words before him. The game to-night
was more hazardous, more difficult, and for a vastly
greater stake than any in which he had before pitted
his wits or played his lone hand against the combined brains of the Butcher, his fellows, and their

unknown leader, who collectively were referred to by the papers as—the Wire Devils.

The Hawk tamped down the ash in the bowl of his pipe with a wary forefinger. He, the Hawk, according to MacVightie, was the leader of this ingenious criminal league! It was very complimentary of MacVightie—very! Between MacVightie and the Wire Devils themselves, he was a personage much sought after! MacVightie, however, was not without grounds for his assertion and belief—the Hawk grinned pleasantly—he, the Hawk, had certainly, and for some time back, helped himself to the leader's share of the spoils, and helped himself very generously!

The grin died away. He had beaten them so far, appropriated from under their very noses the loot they had so carefully planned to obtain, and he had mocked and taunted them contemptuously in the doing of it; but the cold fact remained that luck sometimes was known to turn, and that the pitcher that went too often to the well ran the risk of getting—smashed! If they ever caught him, his life would not be worth an instant's purchase. He knew some of them, and he knew them well for what they were, and he laboured under no delusions on that score! The Butcher, for example, who was the Number One of the message, had already nearly done for him once; and the Butcher had nothing on Number Three, who was the Bantam, or on Number Seven, who was Whitie Jim—or, it was safe to presume, on any of the others that he had not yet iden-

tified—this Number Four and Number Six, for instance, who were mentioned in the cipher message
to-night. And how many more were there? He
did not know—except that there was the Master
Spider of them all.

The Hawk had ceased now even to turn cursorily
the pages of the magazine. He was staring out of
the window.

"I wonder," muttered the Hawk grimly, "when
I'll run up against *him?* And who he is? And where
the head office is?"

He nodded his head after a moment. MacVightie
had called the turn. The Wire Devils formed as
powerful and dangerous a criminal organisation as
had probably ever existed anywhere. And not for
very long would they put all their resources at work
to pull off some coup, only to find that he, the Hawk,
had made use of their preparations to snatch the
prize away from them; they were much more likely
to put all their resources at work—with the Hawk
as their sole objective!

The Hawk's lips tightened. He might under-estimate, but he could not exaggerate, his danger! The
man in the seat behind him might be one of them for
all he knew. Somewhere, hidden away in his web,
at the end of a telegraph wire, was the Master Spider
directing the operations; and there must be very
many of them—the little spiders—spread all over
the division. Where there was a telegraph sounder
that sounder carried the messages, the plans, the
secret orders of the brain behind the organisation;

and the very audaciousness with which they made
themselves free of the railroad's telegraph system
to communicate with each other was in itself a guarantee of success. If one of their messages was in-
terferred with, they threatened to cut the wires;
and that meant, if luckily it meant no more, that
train operating was at an end until the break could
be located and repaired. Were they tapping the
wire somewhere? What chance was there to find
out where? There were hundreds of old splices on
the wires. Or, if found, what would prevent them
tapping the wire on the next occasion many miles
away? Also the sources of information that they
tapped must be far-flung. How, for instance, unless
they too had a "Bud" back there in New York, did
they know of this diamond shipment coming through
to-night?

The Hawk's lips grew still a little tighter. His
safety so far had depended on the fact that he possessed the key to their cipher messages, which not
only enabled him to reap where they had sown, but
warned him of any move they might make against
him. But it was becoming increasingly difficult to
intercept those messages. He had MacVightie to
thank for that. Where before he had only to crawl
into some little way-station where there was no night
operator, MacVightie now had every one of those
stations securely guarded. Yes, it had become exceedingly more difficult! If only he could find out
where those messages emanated from, or the system in force for receiving them!

The Hawk slid further down in his seat, tossed the magazine to one side, pulled his hat over his eyes, and appeared to sleep. All that was neither here nor there—*to-night*. He *had* the message to-night— but he had not yet got that twenty thousand dollars in unset stones! He would perhaps do well, now that he had the leisure, to give the details of that matter a little more critical attention than they had received when he had made up his mind that his best chance lay in the three miles between Burke's Siding and the point where the Butcher and his men planned to hold up the train. According to the message, the implication was that there would be nobody in the express car at that time except a drugged messenger. And now, somehow, he did not quite like the appearance of that. It seemed a little queer. What was the object of drugging the man if they did not take immediate advantage of it? He pondered the problem for a long time. No, after all, it was logical enough—since they meant to remove the safe bodily. There evidently was not a specialised cracksman amongst them who had lifted his profession to the plane of art, no "knob-twirler" such as— well, such as himself! The Hawk opened his eyes sleepily to inspect the tips of his carefully manicured fingers. Otherwise, with no one to interfere but a drugged messenger, they could have opened the safe, looted it, and, since the Fast Mail carried only through express matter, have slipped away from the car at the first stop, with no one being the wiser un-

til, somewhere up the line, the messenger returned
to life and gave the alarm.

Yes, it was very craftily worked out. The Master
Spider was far from a fool! They would have to
"soup" the safe, and blow it open. If they attempted
that while the train was en route they ran the risk
of being heard, and trapped like rats in the car; and
if they were heard, even if they managed to stop the
train and make their escape, they invited instant and
definite pursuit on the spot. The reason for drugging the express messenger became quite evident now.
If the man were already helpless when they held up
the train, they, at one and the same time, assured
their access to an otherwise guarded car without
danger to themselves, and without danger of being
balked at the last moment of their reward—which
the messenger, with a small package like that, might
easily have been able to accomplish if he were a game
man. He could have opened the safe, say, the instant the first alarm came as they tried to force the
car door, taken out the package, and secreted it somewhere. It needed only the nerve after that to defy
them, and they had evidently given him credit for it
whether he possessed it or not.

Yes, decidedly, the Master Spider was no fool in
the spinning of his web! As it was, the safe, which
would only be a small affair anyhow, would disappear
bodily; and between the point where the train was
held up and the point where they finally left the engine and express car there would be a distance of at
least ten miles, even allowing that they approached

no nearer than within two miles of Bradley, the first station west of Burke's Siding. With the wires cut and the coaches of the Fast Mail stalled three miles out of Burke's, considerable time must elapse before any one could make a move against them; and even when the pursuit finally started, MacVightie, for instance, would be confronted with that somewhat illusive stretch of ten miles in which to decide *where* the pursuit should begin. Ten miles was some little distance! MacVightie would be quite at liberty to make his guess, and there was the chance, with the trifling odds of some few odd thousand to one against it, that he might guess right—unless he guessed that the safe had been removed at the point where the engine and car were finally left, in which case MacVightie would guess wrong.

If the Hawk was asleep, he was perhaps dreaming—for the Hawk smiled. The chances were just about those few odd thousand to one that MacVightie would guess exactly that way—wrong. Yes, it was an exceedingly neat little web that the Master Spider had spun. If he, the Hawk, were permitted to make a guess, he would guess that the safe would never be found!

His mind reverted to the cipher message. The safe was to be delivered at "five-mile crossing." Where that was the Hawk did not know—except that it must necessarily be somewhere between the point where the train was held up and Bradley. However, that was a detail with which he need hardly concern himself. Long before this "five-mile crossing" was reached, his vest pocket, if he played in luck, would be very comfortably lined! He would enter the express car as the Fast Mail pulled out of Burke's Siding, trust to certain long and intimate experience to open the safe—and get off the train as it slowed down at the Butcher's very thoughtful request! For the rest, the details—circumstances must govern there. In the main, that would be his plan.

The Hawk "slept" on. Station after station was passed. His mind now dealt in little snatches of thought. There was MacVightie and the police circular; and the search of his room that day; and speculation as to how they had managed to drug the express messenger; and the man with the counterfeit ten-dollar bill in old Mother Barrett's short-order house; and the little old woman herself, with her shabby clothes and her tired, gentle face—and finally the Hawk stirred, glanced at his watch, and, as the train whistled, picked up his magazine and sauntered down the car aisle to the door.

They were approaching Burke's Siding. The Hawk opened the door, went out on the platform, and descended to the lowest step. The train slowed. A water-tank loomed up, receded—and the Hawk dropped to the ground. A minute later, as the tail-lights winked by and came to a stop at the station a short distance down the track, he had made his way back to the water-tank, crossed to the opposite side of the track, and stretched himself out on the grass in the hollow at the foot of the embankment. The Fast Mail's sole excuse for a stop at Burke's Siding

was the water-tank—which would bring the express
car to a halt directly in front of the spot where he
now lay.

The local pulled out, and racketed away into the
night. The tail-lights vanished. Silence fell. There
was only the chirping of the insects now, and the
strange, queer, indefinable medley of little night-
sounds. Burke's Siding was a lonely place. There
was a faint yellow gleam from the station windows,
and there was the twinkle of the switch lights—no
other sign of life. It was pitch black—so black that
the Hawk could just barely distinguish the outline
of the water-tank across the track.

"It's a nice night," observed the Hawk pleasantly
to himself. "A very nice night! It's strange how
some people prefer a moon!"

— IX —

THE LOOTING OF THE FAST MAIL.

THE minutes went by, ten, fifteen, twenty of them—a half hour—and then, from far down the track, hoarse through the night, came the scream of a whistle. From his pocket the Hawk took out his diminutive flashlight, thin as a pencil. It might have been the winking of a firefly, as he played it on the dial of his watch.

"On the dot!" murmured the Hawk. "Some train —the Fast Mail! I guess, though, she'll be a little late, at that, to-night—when she pulls into Selkirk!"

A roar and rumble was in the night again, increasing steadily in volume. Down the right of way, in the distance, a flash of light stabbed through the black. It grew brighter and brighter. The Hawk, wary of the spread of the powerful electric headlight, edged further away from the trackside. And now the rails gleamed like polished silver—and the water-tank stood up out of the darkness, a thing of monstrous size. There was the hiss of steam, the rasp and grind of the setting brakes, the glinting rays from the windows of a long string of coaches that trailed back to the station platform, and a big

ten-wheeler, like some human thirsty thing, was panting beside the water-tank.

The engineer, with his torch, .swung from the
gangway for an oil around. There was the creak of
the descending spout, the rush of water, and, sil-
houetted against the water-tank, the Hawk could
make out the fireman standing on the back of the
tender. And now, poking with his long-spouted oil
can, weirdly swallowed up in the darkness at intervals as he thrust the torch far in under the big machine, the engineer moved slowly along the side of
the engine, and finally disappeared around the end
of the pilot.

The Hawk stole forward closer to the track again,
his eyes on the fireman, who, now that the engineer's torch was on the other side, was more sharply
outlined than before. Came then the swish and
gush of water as it overflowed, the spout banged
back against the water-tank, and the fireman scram-
bled back over the tender into the cab. It was the
moment the Hawk had been waiting for. Swiftly,
but still crawling as a safeguard against being seen
by any of the train crew in the rear, he moved up
the embankment, and in an instant had swung himself up between the tender and the forward door of
the express car. There was no platform here, of
course, but the end beam of the car, making a sort
of wide threshold, gave him ample room on which
to stand.

The roar of escaping steam drowned out all other
sounds; the back of the tender hid him from any

chance of observation from the cab. He tried the door cautiously. It was locked, of course—there were twenty thousand dollars' worth of stones in the safe inside! The Hawk felt carefully over the lock with his fingers, classifying it in the darkness, as it were, by the sense of touch, and produced from his pocket his bunch of skeleton keys. He inserted one of the keys, worked with it for a moment, then shook his head, and selected another. This time he felt the lock-bolt slide back. The train was jerking into motion now. He exchanged his keys for his automatic, turned the knob softly, opened the door an inch, and listened. Even the Wire Devils were not infallible, and if by any chance the messenger——

The Hawk whistled low and contentedly under his breath. He had caught a glimpse of the interior of the car—and now he slipped quickly through the door, closing the door behind him.

A quarter length down the car, in the aisle made by the express packages which were piled high on either side, the messenger, a young man of perhaps twenty-two, was huddled, apparently unconscious, in his chair. In a flash the Hawk was down the car, and bending sharply over the other. The man sat in a helpless, sagging attitude; he was breathing heavily, and his head, hanging forward and a little to one side, swayed limply with the motion of the car. There was no question as to the messenger's condition—he was drugged, and well drugged. From the man, the Hawk's eyes travelled to a sort of desk,

or ledge, built out from the side of the car, and
topped by a pigeonholed rack stuffed with express
forms and official-looking manila envelopes. On the
desk was a small leather satchel containing some
lunch, and a bottle of what was evidently cold tea,
now but barely a quarter full; and, as though to supply further evidence that the man had succumbed
in the midst of his meal, a little to one side lay a
meat sandwich, half eaten.

The Hawk nodded quietly to himself, as again
his eyes shifted—this time to a small safe, about
three feet square, that stood beneath the desk. It
was quite easy to understand now. The Wire Devils had only to ascertain the fact that it was the messenger's habit to eat his lunch at a certain time,
choose the point of attack on the line to correspond
therewith, and see that a sufficient quantity of knockout drops was introduced into the cold tea—not a
very weighty undertaking for the Wire Devils!

Well, it was a bit rough on the boy—the Hawk
was kneeling now in front of the safe—but he, the
Hawk, was greatly indebted to the Wire Devils!
Twenty thousand dollars was a snug little sum—
quite a snug little sum!

The figure in the chair, with swaying head,
breathed stertorously; there was the pound, quick in
its tempo, of the trucks beating at the rail joints;
the give-and-take of the car in protesting little
creaks; and, over all, a muffled roar as the Fast Mail
tore through the night—but the Hawk heard none
of this. His ear was pressed close against the face

of the safe listening for the tumblers' fall, as his fingers twirled the dial knob.

After a little while the Hawk spoke aloud.

"Left, twenty-eight, one quarter . . . two right, fourteen . . . two left, eighteen, one-half," he said.

He straightened up, swung the handle of the safe —and a dismayed, anxious look flashed across his face. There was not much time, very little time— and he had missed it! How far along those three miles from Burke's Siding to where the Butcher was waiting had the train already come?

He tried again, coolly, methodically—and again he missed.

"I guess I'm out of practice to fall down on a tin box like this!" he muttered grimly. "But the first two are right, that's sure—it's the last turn that's wrong somewhere. Give me another minute or two"—he was twirling the dial knob with deft, quick fingers once more—"that's all I ask, and——"

A sudden jolt flung him forward against the safe. Came the scream of the whistle, the screech of the tight-set brakes, the bump, and jerk, and pound, and grind of the flying train coming to an emergency stop. The limp form of the messenger, sliding down, was almost doubled over the arm of the chair.

In an instant the Hawk had recovered his balance, and, his face set like iron, his jaws clamped hard, he snatched at the knob, and with desperate haste now made another attempt. There were a few seconds left, a few seconds before the train would come finally to a standstill and—no, they were gone **now,** those seconds—and he *had* missed again!

His automatic was in his hand as he stood up. It was no longer a question of twenty thousand dollars' worth of unset diamonds—it was a question of his life. There was a bitter smile on his lips, as he ran for the forward door. It looked as though the pitcher had at last gone once too often to the well! The train had stopped now. He reached the door, and opened it guardedly a little way. A great red flare from somewhere ahead lighted up the night. He heard and recognised the Butcher's voice, menacing, raucous, punctuated with vicious oaths:

"Get out of that cab, and get out *damned* quick! Down you come—jump now! Now, boys, run 'em back, and keep firing down the length of the train as you go; and if these guys don't run faster than you do, let 'em have it in the back! Beat it now— beat it like hell! I'll pull out the minute you're uncoupled. You two grab the rear end as she moves, there's room enough for you, and you can bust in the door, and——"

A fusilade of shots rang out. Flashes cut the black. The Butcher's two companions, evidently driving the engineer and fireman before them, were coming on the run along the trackside from the cab. The Hawk retreated back a step, and closed the car door. He heard the men rush past outside. The fusilade seemed to redouble in intensity; and now, added to it, were shouts and yells from the rear of the train itself, and—if he were not mistaken—answering shots.

His hand on the doorknob, he stood waiting tensely. With the Butcher on guard out there in front, it would have been equivalent to suicide to have opened the door again until he knew the other was back in the cab—against the background of the lighted interior he would have made a most excellent mark for the Butcher!

His eyes swept past the huddled form of the young messenger in the chair, and fixed speculatively on the safe. He nodded suddenly, grimly. Twenty thousand dollars! Well, he wasn't beaten yet—not till he threw down his own hand of his own accord—not till he lost sight of the safe for keeps!

Over the shouts and revolver shots came the sharp, vicious hiss of the air-hose, as it was uncoupled; and then, with a violent jerk, the car started forward, as the Butcher evidently whipped the throttle open. And, coincidently, there was a smash upon the rear door—and the Hawk opened the forward door and slipped out again.

A din infernal was in his ears. Like a maddened thing under the Butcher's unscientific spur, the big ten-wheeler was coughing the sparks heavenward in a volleying stream, while the huge drivers raced like pinwheels in another shower of sparks as the tires sought to bite and hold. And now the rear door of the car crashed inward; the shots came fast as a gatling, and shouts, screams and yells added their quota to the uproar.

The Hawk, crouched by the door, moved suddenly to one side, as he caught the dull, ominous *spat* of a bullet against one of the panels. The train crew and those of the passengers who were armed were, very obviously, keeping up a running fight from the stalled section of the train, and pumping their bullets through the broken rear door and up the aisle of the express car as long as they could hold the range; and, from within, he could distinguish the duller, muffled reports of the Butcher's confederates firing in return, preventing any attempt being made to rush the rear of the car.

And then the sounds began to recede and die away. The men inside the car ceased firing, and he could hear them now moving the safe out from the side of the car. It seemed as though a very long interval of time had been consumed in the hold-up; but in reality he knew it had been little more than a matter of seconds—the time it had taken the two men to run the length of the car, uncouple it, and leap on the rear end. The fight afterwards could hardly count, for once the express car began to pull away the thing was done.

They were moving fast now, and with every instant the speed was increasing. The Hawk clutched at the handrail, and lowered himself to the iron foot-rung which, on the express car, served in lieu of steps. Here, having chosen the opposite side to that of the Butcher at the throttle in the cab, he ran no risk of being observed. This "five-mile crossing," wherever it was, promised to concern him a great deal more than he had anticipated! He leaned out, and clung there, staring ahead.

The big ten-wheeler was swaying and staggering like a drunken thing; the rush of the wind whipped at his face; a deafening roar sang in his ears. The Fast Mail usually ran *fast;* but the Butcher was running like a dare-devil, and the bark of the exhaust had quickened now into a single full-toned note deep as thunder.

With a sort of grim placidity, the Hawk clung to the lurching rail. Far ahead along the right of way, a shaft of light riven through walls of blackness, played the headlight. Shadowy objects, trees that loomed up for an instant and were gone, showed on the edge of the wavering ray. They tore through a rock cut, and, in the confined space and in the fraction of a second it took to traverse it, the roar was metamorphosed into an explosion. And then suddenly, as though by magic, the headlight shot off at a tangent, and the glistening lines of steel, that were always converging but never meeting, were gone, and the ray fell full upon a densely wooded tract where leaves and foliage became a soft and wonderful shade of green under the artificial light. The Hawk braced himself—and just in time. The ten-wheeler, unchecked, swung the curve with a mighty lurch, off drivers fairly lifted from the rails. She seemed to hang there hesitantly for a breathless instant, then with a crunch, staggering, settled back and struck into her stride again.

The thunder of the exhaust ceased abruptly, and

the speed began to slacken. The Butcher had slammed the throttle shut. At the end of the headlight's ray, that was straight along the track again, a red light flashed up suddenly three times and vanished. The Hawk leaned farther out, tense now, straining his eyes ahead. It was evidently Number Four and Number Seven signalling from "five-mile crossing."

The Butcher began to check with the "air." And now, in the headlight's glare, the distance shortened, the Hawk could discern a large wagon, drawn by two horses, that appeared to be backed up close to the right-hand side of the track. Two forms seemed to be tugging at the horses, which equally seemed to be plunging restively—and then, being on the wrong side of the car, the angle of vision narrowed and he could see no more.

The Hawk turned now—his eyes on the door of the car. There was a possibility, a little more than a possibility, that the men inside, knowing that they had reached their destination, would come out this way. No—he had only to keep hidden from the men out there with the wagon until the car stopped —the men within were sliding back the side door. He swung himself still farther out on the foot-rung; then, curving back with the aid of the handrail, flattened himself against the side of the car.

They were close up to the wagon now, and he could hear voices cursing furiously at the horses, as the frightened animals stamped and pawed. And then the car bumped and jerked to a standstill, and the Butcher was bawling from the cab:

"Take the horses out, you blamed fools, and tie 'em back there on the road a bit till we're gone! We'd have a sweet time loading the wagon with them doing the tango every second! Take 'em out! We'll back the wagon up against the car."

The Hawk lowered himself silently to the ground —to find that the car had come to a stop directly over a road crossing. The men in the car had joined their voices with the Butcher's, and in the confusion now the Hawk slipped quickly along the side of the car, stole around the rear end, and from that point of vantage stood watching the Butcher and his men at work.

He could see quite plainly, thanks to the light from the car's wide-open side door that flooded the scene. The horses had been unharnessed, and were being led away along the road. One of the men in the car jumped to the ground, as the Butcher called out, and together they backed the wagon close up against the car doorway; and then, presently, the men who had accompanied the horses, one carrying a lantern, came running back. The Hawk's eyes, from a general and comprehensive survey of the scene, fixed on the man who until now had not left the car, but who had now sprung down into the wagon and was running a short plank, to be used as a skid evidently, up to the threshold of the car door, which was a little above the level of the wagon. The light shone full in the man's face.

"Number Six—Crusty Kline!" confided the Hawk softly to himself. "I'm glad to know that. The last time I chummed with Crusty was back in little old Sing Sing. Guess he got out for good behaviour—thought he was elected for five spaces yet!"

Crusty spoke now, as he jumped back into the car.

"Look here, Butcher, I'm telling you again, this guy in here's in pretty bad shape."

"Never mind about that!" replied the Butcher roughly. "Get the safe out! All hands now! We've got no time to monkey with him. He'll come around all right, I guess—anyway, it's none of our lookout!"

The men were bunched together now, three in the doorway of the car and two in the wagon, the safe between them. The Hawk was studying one of the two who stood in the wagon. One was Whitie Jim, as he already knew, but the other had had his back half turned, and the Hawk had not been able to see his face. The safe slid down the plank, and was levered and pushed forward into the middle of the wagon.

"French Pete!" said the Hawk suddenly and as softly as before, as the man he had been watching straightened up and turned around. "Say, I guess Sing Sing's gone out of business—or else somebody left the door open!"

But if the Hawk's words were indicative of a facetious mood, his actions were not. There was a

sort of dawning inspiration in the dark, narrowed
eyes; and the strong jaw, as it was outthrust, drew
his lips into a grim, hard smile. They were spreading a huge tarpaulin over the wagon and safe—and
abruptly the Hawk drew back, dropped to his hands
and knees, crawled along the trackside on the opposite side of the car again until almost opposite the
wagon, and there lay flat and motionless at the side
of the road. There was a chance yet, still a chance,
a very good chance—for that twenty thousand dollars' worth of unset stones.

"All right, now!" It was the Butcher's voice.
"Pull her away a few feet into the clear!" The
wagon creaked and rattled. "That's enough! Now
get a move on—everybody!"

Steps crunched along the trackside—the Butcher
and his two companions obviously making for the
cab—and a moment later came the cough of the engine's exhaust, and the express car began to glide
past the spot where the Hawk lay.

The Hawk raised himself cautiously on his elbows. Two dark forms and a bobbing lantern were
already speeding toward where the horses had been
left. The Hawk crawled forward, crossed the track
—and paused. The engine and express car were
fast disappearing in the distance; the lantern glim-
mered amongst the trees at the side of the road a
good hundred yards away.

There was no shadow to fall across the back of
the wagon.

"I said it was a nice night, and that it was strange

how some people preferred a moon!" observed the Hawk cheerfully—and, lifting the end of the tarpaulin, he swung noiselessly under it into the wagon, and stretched himself out beside the safe.

THE THIRD PARTY

THE Hawk felt upward with his hand over the safe. It was faced, he found, toward the rear of the wagon. This necessitated a change in his own position. He listened tensely. They were coming back with the horses now, but they were still quite a little way off. He shifted quickly around until his head and shoulders were in front of the safe.

"It was the last turn of the combination that I fell down on, though I don't see how it happened!" muttered the Hawk.

He felt above his head again, this time rubbing his fingers critically over the tarpaulin—and then the diminutive little flashlight winked, winked again as it played around him, and finally held steadily on the nickel dial. There were no inadvertent openings, and, particularly, no holes in the tarpaulin, and the texture of the tarpaulin was a guarantee that the tiny rays of light would not show through.

They were harnessing the horses into the wagon now. The Hawk, in a somewhat cramped position, due to the wagon's narrow width, his legs twisted at right angles to his body as he lay on his back, reached

143

up and began to twirl the dial knob slowly and with painstaking care.

"Left, twenty-eight, one quarter," murmured the Hawk; and, a moment later: "Two right, four——" The Hawk swore earnestly under his breath. The jolt of the wagon, coming unexpectedly as it started forward, had caused him to spin the knob too far around.

It was hot, stifling hot, under the heavy tarpaulin, that, slanting downward from the little safe, lay almost against his face. A bead of sweat had gathered on his forehead. He brushed it away, and began again to work at the dial. It was more difficult now —the wagon bumped infernally. And as he worked, he could hear the muffled clatter of the horses' hoofs, and occasionally the voices of the two men on the seat.

And then suddenly the Hawk's fingers travelled from the dial knob to the handle. Had he got it this time, or—yes! The handle swung easily— there was a low metallic thud—the bolt had slipped back to the end of its grooves. The safe was unlocked!

"Twenty thousand dollars!" said the Hawk very softly—and, without the slightest sound, he edged his body backwards to afford space for the swing of the opening door. "Twenty thousand doll——"

The word died, half uttered, on the Hawk's lips. The flashlight was illuminating the interior of the safe. On the bottom lay a single, crisp, ten-dollar counterfeit note, over the face of which was scrawled in ink—*"With the Hawk's compliments!"* Otherwise the safe was empty.

For a moment, like a man dazed, he stared at the counterfeit note. He could not seem to believe his eyes. Empty—the safe was empty! The diamonds were gone—gone! Gone—and these poor fools were driving an empty safe to the Master Spider—and another poor fool, with dropped jaw, was staring, gaping like an imbecile, into one! And then, a grip upon himself again, he laughed low, grimly, unpleasantly. "With the Hawk's compliments!" He had sent a bill like that once to MacVightie inscribed —"With the Hawk's compliments!" This was very neat, very clever of—*somebody*. Of somebody—who must have known what the Wire Devils were up to to-night! There would be no doubt in the minds of the Wire Devils, who would have heard of that little episode with MacVightie, but that the Hawk had again forestalled them, and left them a ten-dollar counterfeit bill in exchange for—twenty thousand dollars' worth of unset diamonds! Only it was this somebody, and not he, the Hawk, who was twenty thousand dollars the richer for it!

He reached in, picked up the bill to put it in his pocket—and suddenly laid it back again, and closed and locked the safe. Why deprive the Master Spider of a little joy; and, besides, it would carry a message not perhaps so erroneous after all—for, in a flash, logically, indisputably, apparently impossible though it appeared to be on the surface, he knew who that *somebody* was. The shelving of the theft to the Hawk's shoulders would have defeated its own object unless the theft were committed and discovered on this particular division of the railroad where the Hawk and, incidentally, his supposed gang of desperadoes were known to be operating. The messenger certainly had not been in a drugged condition when he went on duty, and, since it was only reasonable to assume that he would have satisfied himself everything was all right at that time, it was evident, as he had given no alarm, that the contents of the safe had been intact when he took charge—whether as a "through" man in New York, or at the eastern terminus of the road, or at the last divisional point —it did not matter which. The robbery, then, had been committed while the messenger was present in the car—and it had been committed on this division. The safe had not been forced, it showed not the slightest sign of violence—it had been opened on the combination. Some one then, an expert safeworker, in the first stages of the messenger's drugged condition, had happened into the car just ahead of him, the Hawk, and had done exactly what he, the Hawk, had intended to do?

"No," said the Hawk. "No, I guess not." He was wriggling noiselessly backward, and his feet were hanging out now over the end of the wagon. "No—coincidences like that don't happen—not very often!" The Hawk's head and shoulders were still under the tarpaulin, but his feet now could just feel the ground beneath them. "I guess," said the Hawk, as he suddenly withdrew his head, and, crouching low, ran a few steps with the wagon, then dropped full length in the road, "I guess it's—the third party."

The wagon disappeared in the darkness. The Hawk rose, and, turning, broke into a run back along the road.

He had been longer in the wagon than he had thought—it took him ten minutes to regain the railroad tracks.

Here, without pause, still running, he kept on along the right of way—but there was a hard twist to his lips, and the clenching of his fists was not wholly due to runner's "form." How far had the Butcher taken the car before deserting it? A mile? Two miles—three? He could not run three miles under half an hour, and that would be *fast* over railroad ties! How long would it be before the train crew of the stalled Mail got back to Burke's Siding and managed somehow, in spite of the cut wires, to give the alarm—or how long before the dispatcher at Selkirk, with the Fast Mail reported "out" at Burke's Siding and no "O. S." from Bradley, would smell a rat? It would take time after that, of course, before anything could be done; but, at best, the margin left for him was desperately narrow.

He ran on and on; his eyes, grown accustomed to the darkness, enabling him to pick out the ties with a fair degree of accuracy. There was not a sound save that of his own footsteps. He stopped for breath again and again; and again and again ran on at top speed. It seemed as though he had run, not three miles, but six, when finally, far ahead, he caught a glow of light. The Butcher and his confederates had evidently not taken the trouble to close the side door of the car!

Instinctively, the Hawk, in caution, slowed his pace—and the next instant, smiling pityingly at himself for the act, ran on the faster. The Butcher and the other two would long since have made their getaway! There was only the messenger—and the messenger was drugged. That was all that need concern him now—the messenger—to find some way to rouse the man so that he could talk.

The Hawk reached the car, ran along the side to the open door—and stood suddenly still. And then, with a low, startled cry, he swung himself up and through the doorway, and running forward, knelt beside a huddled form on the floor. It was the messenger, sprawled on his face now, motionless, and it was no longer a case of being drugged—*the man had been shot!* There was a dark, ugly pool on the flooring, and a thin red stream had trickled away in a zigzag course along one of the planks. The Hawk's lips were tight. The Butcher's work! But why? *Why?* Yes! Yes, he understood! The Butcher, too, in some way had discovered that the messenger was—the third party!

The boy—he was even more of a boy now in appearance, it seemed to the Hawk, with his ashen face and colourless lips—the boy moaned a little, and, as the Hawk lifted him up, opened his eyes.

The Hawk produced a flask, and forced a few drops between the other's lips.

"Listen!" he said distinctly. "Try and understand what I am saying. Did they get the diamonds from you after they shot you?"

The boy's eyes widened with a quick, sudden fear. Perhaps the drug had begun to wear off—perhaps it was the wound and the loss of blood that had cleared his brain.

"The diamonds?" he faltered.

"Yes," said the Hawk grimly. "The diamonds! You took them. Did you tell those men where they were?"

"It's—it's a lie!" The boy seemed to shiver convulsively. Then, his voice scarcely audible: "No, it's—it's true. I—I did. I—I guess I'm going out —ain't I? It's—it's true. But I—I didn't tell. There weren't any men—I——" He had fainted in the Hawk's arms.

"My God!" whispered the Hawk solemnly. "It's true—the kid's dying."

He held the flask to the other's lips again. It wasn't the Butcher, then, who had shot the boy; and, besides, he saw now that the wound was in a strangely curious place—in the back, below the shoulder blade; the boy had been sitting in his shirt sleeves, and the back of his vest was soaked with blood. And the Hawk remembered the fusillade of bullets that had swept up the interior of the car, and the *spat* upon the forward door panel as he had crouched there outside—and he understood. The boy, sitting in a stupor in his chair facing the forward door, had been directly in the line of fire, and a stray bullet had found its mark.

"I—I don't know how you knew"—the boy had roused, and was speaking again—"but—but I'm going out—and—and it's true. Two days ago, a man gave me a hundred dollars to stand for—for knockout drops on the run to-night. I—I couldn't get caught—I—I was safe—whatever happened. I'd be found drugged—and—and no blame coming to me—and——" He motioned weakly toward the flask in the Hawk's hand. "Give me—give me some more of that!"

He did not speak for a moment.

"And, instead," prompted the Hawk quietly, "you double-crossed the game."

"I—I had a counterfeit ten-dollar bill," the boy went on with an effort. "I'd heard about the Hawk —and—and MacVightie. I knew from what—the fellow said—that the Hawk—wasn't one of them. I—I got to thinking. All I had to do was empty the safe—and—and write just what the Hawk did on the bill—and—and shove it in the safe—and—and take the diamonds—and—and then drink the tea that had the drops in it. I—I would be drugged, and they—they'd think the Hawk did it while I was drugged before they—they got here—and—and that's what I did."

The boy was silent again. It was still outside, very still—only the chirpings of the insects and the night-sounds the Hawk had listened to while he had

lain below the embankment waiting for the train at
Burke's Siding. There was a set, strained look on
the Hawk's face. The kid was paying the long price
—for twenty thousand dollars' worth of unset diamonds!

"To make it look like—like the real thing"—the
boy's lips were moving again—"I—I cleaned out
everything in the safe—but—but of course there
mustn't any of that be found—and—and I tied the
stuff up—and—and weighted it, and dropped it—
into—the—river as we came over the bridge at
Moosehead. And then I had to—to hide the diamonds so they wouldn't be found on me, and yet so's
they—they'd come along with me—and—and not
be left in the car. I was afraid that when some of
the train crew found me drugged—they—they'd undress me—and—and put me to bed—and—and so
I didn't dare hide the diamonds in my clothes.
They're—they're—in——" He raised himself up
suddenly, clutched frantically at the Hawk's shoulders and his voice rang wildly through the car. "Hold
me tight—hold me tight—don't let me go out yet—
I—I got something more to say! Don't tell her!
Don't tell her! I'll tell you where the stones are,
they're in the lining of my lunch satchel—but don't—
oh, for God's sake, don't tell her—don't let her
know that—that I'm a—thief! You don't have to,
do you? Say you don't! I'm—I'm going out—I—
I've got what's coming to me, and that's—enough—
isn't it—without her knowing too? It—it would
kill her. She was a good mother—do you hear!"

He was stiffening back in the Hawk's arms. "And this ain't coming to her. She was a good mother— do you hear—everybody called her mother, but she's *my* mother—you know—old Mother Barrett— short-order house—you know—old—Mother—Bar- rett—good——"

The boy never spoke again.

The Hawk laid the still form gently back on the floor of the car, and stood up. And there was a mist in the Hawk's eyes that blotted out his immedi- ate surroundings, and in the mist he seemed to see another scene, and it was the picture of a gentle, kindly-faced old woman, who had silver hair, and who wore clothes that were a little threadbare, and whose grey Irish eyes behind the spectacles were filled with tears, and he seemed to see the thin shoul- ders square proudly back, and he seemed to hear her speak again: "I love my boy, I love him with all my heart, but I should a thousand times rather see him dead than know him for a thief."

Mechanically the Hawk moved over to the desk where the lunch satchel still lay, and emptied out the remainder of the food.

"No," said the Hawk, "I guess she'll never know; and I guess I'd have to take the stuff now, anyway, whether I wanted to or not—if she's not to know."

He was examining the inside of the satchel. It was an old and well-worn affair, and a torn piece of the lining, stuck down with paste at the edges, would ordinarily have attracted no attention. The Hawk loosened this, and felt inside. At the bottom, care-

fully packed away, were strips of cotton wadding.
He took one out. Embedded in this were a number
of diamonds, which, as he drew the wadding apart,
flashed brilliantly in the light of the oil lamps above
his head. He wrapped the stones up again, and
put them in his pocket—took out the remainder from
the satchel, put these also in his pocket, and replaced
in the satchel the portion of the lunch he had removed. It mattered little about the torn lining now!

"He kind of put it up to me," said the Hawk
slowly. "Yes, and she did too—without knowing it
—old Mother Barrett. It's kind of queer she should
have said that—kind of queer." The Hawk pulled
the drawer of the desk open, and nodded as he
found and took out the messenger's revolver.
"Thought he'd have one, and that it would most
likely be here," he muttered.

He crossed the car, and listened intently at the
open side door. There was no sound—nothing, for
instance, coming from Bradley yet. He closed the
door, and stood for an instant looking down at the
boy's form on the floor.

"I guess I can fix it for you, kid—maybe," he
said simply. "I guess I can."

In rapid succession he fired five of the seven shots
from the revolver; then, stooping, laid the weapon,
as though it had dropped at last from nerveless fingers, just beside the boy's outstretched hand. He
straightened up, stepped to the side door, and slid
it open again.

"It'll let the smoke out before anybody gets here,"

said the Hawk. "The Butcher isn't coming forward
with any testimony, and with all those shots fired at
the time of the hold-up who's to know the boy didn't
fight till he went down and out? And now I guess
I'll make my own getaway!" He dropped to the
trackside, and started forward at a brisk pace. "I'll
keep on a bit until I hear something coming," he decided. "Then I'll lay low while they're cleaning up
the line, and wait till I can hop a freight, east or
west, that will get me out of this particular locality.
After that, there's nothing to it!"

A hundred yards farther on the Hawk spoke
again, and there was a twisted smile on the Hawk's
lips.

"It'll break her heart anyway, I guess," he said;
"but it'll help some maybe to be proud of him. Yes,
I guess they'll tell her that, all right—that he died
a game kid."

— XI —

THE LEAD CAPSULE

THE Hawk yawned. He had been almost forty-eight hours without sleep. He had slept all day after he had regained his room, following the night at "Five-Mile Crossing," but after that——

He frowned in a perturbed and puzzled way. Ensconced now in a wicker lounging chair in the observation car of the Coast Limited, he was apparently engrossed in the financial page of his newspaper, and apparently quite oblivious of his fellow travellers, some four or five of whom lounged and smoked in their own respective wicker chairs around him. On a little pad of paper, which he held in his left hand, he might even, without serious tax upon the imagination, have appeared to be calculating the effect of the market's fluctuations upon personal, and perhaps narrowly held, margins—for again he scowled unhappily. The Hawk, however, at the moment, was engrossed solely with a few curiously assorted letters of the alphabet, which were scrawled across the top of the pad. They ran:

pzudlkmlqpb.

155

Beneath this his pencil had already been at work, and he had transformed the line as follows:

p̸t̸ra̸l̸k̸ ṃin̸p̸y.

He was staring at this result now in a bewildered way. Then his pencil picked out the remaining five unscored letters, and mechanically set them down as a third line:

rainy.

"Rainy"—there was one word, just one word—"rainy." What did it mean? What was the significance of the word? No message in the Wire Devils' cipher, once the message was decoded, but had been at once clear and unmistakable in its meaning before. Had they resorted now to *code* words as well, to a cipher within a cipher? Into the grimness of the Hawk's smile there crept a hint of weariness, as he slipped the pad into his pocket, allowed the newspaper to drop to his knees, and, edging his chair around, gazed out of the window.

For once his knowledge of their cipher was obviously useless to him—and useless when a foreknowledge of their plans at that moment meant scarcely less than a matter of life and death to him in a very unpleasantly real and literal sense. Not a word had come from them; not a message had gone over the wires on either of the two preceding nights; not a sign of existence had they given since three nights ago when, with an empty safe as the sole reward for their elaborately laid plans, he, the Hawk, had enriched himself with the twenty thousand dollars' worth of diamonds it had once contained. There had been something sinister, something ominous in their silence, as compared with the almost insane ravings of MacVightie, the police, and the press—yes, and the railroad men as well, who were particularly incensed over the "murder" of the young messenger found dead at his post in the express car with his revolver partially emptied on the floor beside him.

The Hawk drummed abstractedly with his finger tips upon the window pane. MacVightie, the police, and the press made no doubt but that he, the Hawk, was the leader of the desperadoes who were terrorising that particular section of the country; on the other hand, the gang itself had already had occasions enough and in plenty to be painfully aware that he, the Hawk, played always a lone hand—and won! A smile, grim and ironical, parted the firm, set lips. The police and the Wire Devils had a common interest—the Hawk. He was the storm centre.

The smile faded, the strong jaws clamped, and the dark eyes narrowed on the flying landscape. It was not the police who concerned him, it was not the impotent frothings of the press—it was the *silence* that the Wire Devils had not broken since that night until they had broken it this morning with the single word that, now that he had deciphered it, still meant nothing to him. A dozen times, stealing their cipher messages, he had turned all their carefully prepared plans to his own account, and snatched away the prize, even as they were in the act of reaching for it. But he was not a fool to close his eyes to the inevitable result. He was pitted against the cleverest brains in the criminal world; all the cunning that they knew would be ruthlessly turned against him; and, already out to "get" him, a price already guaranteed to the lucky member of the band out of the common funds, the empty safe of three nights before, with its jeering ten-dollar counterfeit bill flung in their faces, crowned, he feared, their injuries at his hands, and marked the turning point where they would leave no stone unturned to wreak their vengeance upon him.

And he did not like this silence of theirs since that night. Were they suspicious at last that he had the key to their cipher? He did not think so, and yet he did not know—it was always a possibility. But in any case, wary of any move they might make, he had, as far as it was humanly possible, remained within sound of a telegraph instrument ever since. Last night, for example, taking advantage of some repairs that were being made on the station at Elk Head, fifty miles east of Selkirk, he had lain hidden behind a mass of building material in the dismantled waiting room within earshot of the telegraph sounder—and there had been nothing. Forced to retire from there by the advent of the workmen, he had eaten a very leisurely breakfast at the lunch counter —still within earshot of the sounder. He had lingered around the station as long as he had dared

without running the risk of exciting suspicion, and
then he had taken the local east for Bald Creek—
and taken the chance, because he had no choice, that
nothing would "break" over the wires during the
three-quarters of an hour that he was on the train.
The Limited scheduled Bald Creek, and that would
give him an excuse for remaining there, an innocent
and prospective patron of the road, until the Limited's arrival some two hours later. After that, if
nothing happened, he had intended to go back on
the Limited to Selkirk—and get some sleep.

The Hawk yawned heavily again. Yes, after an
almost uninterrupted vigil of forty-eight hours one
needed sleep. Well, he was on his way back to Selkirk now—on the Limited. Only something *had*
happened. Almost at the moment that the Limited
had pulled into Bald Creek, the Wire Devils had
broken their silence, and a cipher message had flashed
over the wires. He had waited for it, fought for
it, schemed for it, gone without sleep for two days
and nights for it—and he had been rewarded. He
had intercepted the message, deciphered it, he had
got it at last—he had it now! It was the one word—
"rainy." And the word to him meant—nothing!

The Hawk's fingers ceased their drumming on the
window pane, his head inclined slightly to one side,
and he listened. His fellow travellers had evidently
scraped up acquaintanceship. The conversation had
become general—and suddenly interesting.

" . . . Yes, unquestionably! The amount I have
with me is worth quite easily a half million francs—

a hundred thousand dollars. It is not my personal property, I regret to say. Quantities sufficient to be of material service are for the most part institutionally held."

The Hawk swung around in his chair, and with frank interest surveyed the little group. He had scanned them once already, critically, comprehensively—at the moment he had first entered the car. The man who sat nearest to him was a doctor from Selkirk; and, it being the ingrained policy of the Hawk to know a reporter as he would know a plain-clothes man, he had recognised one of the others as a young reporter on the staff of the Selkirk *Evening Journal*. The others again, of whom there were three, were strangers to him. His eyes rested—with frank interest—on the man who had just spoken. There had been just a trace of accent in the other's perfect English, and it bore out the man's appearance. The man was perhaps forty-five years of age, rather swarthy in complexion, and, though slight in build, commanding in presence. The black Vandyke beard, as well as the mustache, was carefully trimmed; and his face had an air of the student about it, an air that was enhanced by the extraordinarily heavy-lensed spectacles which he wore. The excellent clothes were unmistakably of foreign cut.

"Great Scott!" ejaculated the reporter. "Is that straight?" He twisted his cigar excitedly from one corner of his mouth to the other. "I say, I don't suppose there's a chance of getting a squint at it, eh?"

"A—squint?" The foreigner's face was politely puzzled.

"I mean a chance to see it—to see what it looks like," interpreted the reporter, with a laugh.

"Oh, yes, of course—a squint. I will remember that!" The foreigner joined in the laugh. "One learns, monsieur, always, eh—if one keeps one's ears open!" He reached down and picked up a small black bag from the floor beside his chair. "No, I am afraid I cannot actually show it to you, monsieur, owing to the nature of the container; but perhaps even the manner in which it is carried may be of interest, and, if so, I shall be delighted."

The others, the Hawk among them, leaned spontaneously forward in their chairs. From the bag the man produced a lead box, some four inches square. He opened this, and, from where it was nested in wadding, took out what looked like a cylindrical-shaped piece of lead of the thickness and length of one's little finger. He held it out in the palm of his hand for their inspection.

"Inside this sealed lead covering," he explained, "is a glass tube hermetically sealed. The lead, of course, absorbs the rays, which otherwise would render the radium extremely dangerous to handle. You perhaps remember the story—if not, it may possibly be of interest. Radium, you know, was discovered in 1898 by Monsieur and Madame Curie; but the action of radium on human tissues was unknown until 1901, when Professor Becquerel of Paris, having incautiously carried a tube in his waistcoat pocket, there appeared on the skin within two weeks the severe inflammation which has become known as the famous 'Becquerel burn.' Since that time, I may add, active investigation into the action of radium has been carried on, resulting in the establishment in Paris in 1906 of the Laboratoire Biologique du Radium."

The doctor from Selkirk reached out, and, obtaining a smiling permission, picked up the lead cylinder from the other's hand. The reporter sucked noisily on the butt of his cigar.

"And d'ye mean to say *that's* worth one hundred thousand dollars?" he demanded helplessly.

"Fully!" replied the foreigner gravely. "I should consider myself very fortunate if I had the means and the opportunity of purchasing it at that price. There are only a few grains there, it is true, and yet even that is a very appreciable percentage of the world's entire output for a single year. The Austrian Government, when it bought the radium-producing pitchblende mines at Joachimsthal, you know, acquired what is practically a world's monopoly of radium. And since the annual production of ore from those mines is but about twenty-two thousand pounds, and that from those twenty-two thousand pounds only something like forty-six grains of radium are obtained, it is not difficult to understand the enormous price which it commands."

The little lead cylinder passed from hand to hand. It came last to the Hawk. He examined it with no more and no less interest than had been displayed by the others, and returned it to its owner, who replaced it in the black handbag.

"Look here," said the reporter impulsively, "I don't want to nose into personal affairs; but, if it's a fair question, what are you going to do with the stuff?"

It was the doctor from Selkirk who spoke before the foreigner had time to reply.

"I was being tempted to ask the same question myself," he said quickly. "I am a physician—Doctor Moreling is my name—and from what you have said I imagine that possibly you are a medical man yourself?"

"And you are quite right," the other answered cordially. "I am Doctor Meunier, and I come from Paris."

"What!" exclaimed the Selkirk physician excitedly. "Not Doctor Meunier, the famous cancer specialist and surgeon of the Salpêtrière Hospital!"

The other shrugged his shoulders protestingly.

"Well," he smiled, a little embarrassed, "my name is certainly Meunier, and it is true that I have the honour to be connected with the institution you have mentioned."

The reporter had a notebook in his hand.

"Gee!" he observed softly. "You don't mind, do you, Doctor Meunier? This looks like luck to me. I'm on the *Evening Journal*—Selkirk."

"Ah—a reporter!" The dark eyes seemed to twinkle humorously from behind the heavy lenses. "I have met some—when I landed in New York.

They were very nice. I liked them very much. Certainly, young man, why should you not say anything I have told you? You have my permission."

"Fine!" cried the reporter enthusiastically. "And now, Doctor Meunier, if you'll just round out the story by telling us why the celebrated Paris surgeon is travelling in America with a hundred thousand dollars' worth of radium, I'll be glad I got panned on the story I went after this morning and so had to take this train back."

"Panned?" inquired the other gravely.

"Yes." The reporter nodded. "It blew up, you know."

"Blew up! Ah!" The foreigner's face was at once concerned. "So! You were in an accident, then?"

"No, no," laughed the reporter. "There wasn't anything in the story. It didn't have any foundation."

"Again I learn," observed the foreigner, with an amused drawl. He studied the reporter for an instant quizzically. "And so I am to supply the place of the panned story that blew up—is that it? Well, very well! Why not? I see no reason against it, if it will be of service to you. Very well, then. I have been summoned to Japan to attend a case of cancer—radium treatment—and I am on my way there now." He smiled again. "I have noticed that American reporters are observant, and it may occur to you that I might have reached my destination quicker by way of Russia. As a matter of fact, however, I was in New York attending a convention when I received the summons. I cabled for the radium, and—well, young man, that pretty well completes the story."

"Yes—thanks!" said the reporter. He wrote rapidly. "Operation on a Japanese?"

"Why, yes, of course—on a Japanese."

" 'Summoned,' you said. That listens as though it might be for one of the Emperor's family," prodded the reporter shrewdly.

"I did not say so," smiled the other imperturbably. "And even if it were so——" He shrugged his shoulders significantly.

"I get you!" grinned the reporter. "Well, there's no harm in saying a 'High Personage' then, is there? That sounds good, and it would have to be some one on the top of the heap to bring a man like you all this way."

"Let us be discreet, young man, and say—well, let us say, a member of a prominent family," suggested the other, still smiling.

"All right," agreed the reporter. "I won't put anything over on you, I promise you. And now, doctor, tell us something more about radium, how it acts and all that, and how an operation is performed with it, and——"

The Hawk had apparently lost interest. He settled back in his chair, and picked up his previously discarded newspaper—yet occasionally his eyes strayed over the top of his newspaper, and rested meditatively on the little black handbag on the car floor beside the Frenchman's chair. The doctor from Selkirk, the reporter, and the French specialist talked on. The Limited reached the last stop before Selkirk. As the train pulled out again, the Hawk, as it were, summed up his thoughts.

"A hundred thousand dollars," confided the Hawk softly to himself. "Maybe it wouldn't be easy to sell, but it would make a very nice haul—a very nice haul. It would tempt—almost anybody. Yes, bad stuff to handle; the fences would be leery probably, because I guess every last grain on this little old globe is catalogued as to ownership, and they'd be afraid it would be an open-and-shut game that what they were trying to shove would be spotted as the stolen stuff—not that it couldn't be done though, at that! There's always somebody to take a chance —on a hundred thousand dollars! And what about the institution that owns it coming across big and no questions asked to get it back again? Yes, I guess it would make a nice haul—a very nice haul. I wonder——"

The conductor had entered the car, had said something that the Hawk had not caught—and now the French specialist was on his feet.

"How long did you say?" he demanded excitedly.

"I didn't say," replied the conductor; "I only guessed—twelve hours anyway, and if we're through under twenty-four it'll be because some one has performed a miracle."

"Twelve hours—twenty-four!" echoed the Frenchman wildly. "But, *mon Dieu*, I have not that to spare to catch my steamer for Japan in San Francisco!"

"But what's wrong, conductor?" asked the Selkirk doctor. "You haven't told us that."

"The Rainy River bridge is out," the conductor answered.

The *Rainy* River bridge! The Hawk reached into his pocket, withdrew his cigarette case, and made a critical choice of one of the six identical cigarettes the case contained.

"Out! How?" the doctor from Selkirk persisted.

"No details," said the conductor; "except that it was blown up a little while ago and that they think it's the work of the Hawk's gang. They just got word over the wire at the last stop."

"Jumping whiskers!" yelled the reporter. "Is that right, conductor?"

"Yes, I guess it's right, fast enough," said the conductor grimly. He turned to the Frenchman. "It's tough luck, sir, to miss transpacific connections; but I guess that's the man you've got to thank for it—the Hawk."

"The Hawk? What is that? Who is the Hawk?" The Frenchman had lost his poise; he was gesticulating violently now.

"I'll tell you," said the reporter briskly. "He's the man that's got your original reign of terror skinned a mile—believe me! He's an ex-Sing Sing convict, and he's the head, brains and front of a gang of criminals operating out here compared with whom, for pure, first-water deviltry, any one of Satan's picked cohorts would look as shy and retiring as a maiden lady of sixty who suddenly found herself in a one-piece bathing suit—in public. That's the Hawk! Yes, sir—believe me!"

Doctor Meunier waved his hands, as though to ward off a swarm of buzzing bees.

"I do not understand!" he spluttered angrily. "I do not care to understand! You do not speak English! I understand only of the delay!" He caught at the conductor's sleeve. "You, monsieur—is there not something that can be done?"

"I don't know, sir," said the conductor. "We'll be in Selkirk now in a few minutes, and the best thing you can do is to see Mr. Lanson, the superintendent."

The conductor retired.

The Frenchman sat down in his chair, mopped his face with a handkerchief, and stared from one to another of his fellow passengers.

"Messieurs, it is necessary, it is imperative, that I catch the steamer!" he cried frantically. "What am I to do?"

"Lanson's a good head; he'll fix you up some way," said the reporter soothingly. "Don't you worry. I'm mighty sorry for you, Doctor Meunier, upon my soul—but, say, this is *some* story—whale of a climax!"

The Frenchman glared for an instant; then, leaning forward, suddenly shook his fist under the other's nose.

"Young man, damn your story!" he snarled distractedly.

The Hawk retired once more behind his newspaper. The reporter was pacifying the excited Frenchman. The Hawk was not interested in that. The message, that single word which had puzzled him, was transparently clear now—and had been from the moment the conductor had spoken. The surmise of the railroad officials, even if it were no more than surmise on their part, was indubitably correct—barring the slight detail of his own participation in the affair! The Wire Devils had blown up the Rainy River bridge. This, as a detached fact, did not interest him either—they were quite capable of blowing up a bridge, or anything else. That was a detail. But they were quite incapable of doing it without a very good and sufficient reason, and one that promised returns of a very material nature to themselves. What was the game? Why the Rainy River bridge? Why this morning? Why at this time? The Rainy River bridge was but a few miles west of Selkirk, and—the Hawk's eyes strayed over his newspaper again, and rested mildly upon the Frenchman's little black handbag, that was quite slim, and not over long, that was of such a size, in fact, that it might readily be concealed under one's coat, for instance, without attracting undue attention—and with the bridge out a passenger, say on the Coast Limited this noon would experience an annoying, somewhat lengthened, but unavoidable interruption in his journey. The passenger might even be forced to spend the night in Selkirk, and very much might happen in a night—in Selkirk! It was a little elaborate, it seemed as though it might perhaps have been accomplished with a little less fuss—though lack of finesse and exceeding cunning was, in his experience, an unmerited reproach where that unknown brain that planned and plotted the Wire Devils' acts was concerned; but, however that might be, the reason that the Rainy River bridge was out now appeared quite obviously attributable—to a very excited foreigner, and a little black handbag whose contents were valued at the modest sum of one hundred thousand dollars.

"And I wonder," said the Hawk almost plaintively to himself, "I wonder which of us will cash in on that!"

The Hawk rose leisurely from his chair, as the train reached Selkirk. He permitted the Frenchman, the Selkirk physician and the reporter to descend to the platform in advance of him; but, as they hurried through the station and around to the entrance leading upstairs to the divisional offices, obviously with the superintendent's office as their objective, the Hawk, in the privileged character of an interested fellow traveller, fell into step with the reporter.

The four entered the superintendent's office, and from an unobtrusive position just inside the door the Hawk listened to the conversation. He heard Lanson, the superintendent, confirm the conductor's story, and express genuine regret at the Frenchman's

plight, as he admitted it to be a practical certainty
that the other would miss his connection in San Francisco. The Frenchman but grew the more excited.
He suggested a special train from the western side
of the bridge—they could get him across in a boat,
he said. The superintendent explained that traffic
in the mountains beyond was already demoralised.
The Frenchman raved, begged, pleaded, implored—
and suddenly the Hawk sucked in his breath softly.
The Frenchman was backing his appeal for a special
with the offer to pay any sum demanded, and had
taken a well-filled pocketbook from his pocket. The
Hawk's eyes aimlessly sought the toes of his boots.
He had caught a glimpse of a fat wad of bills, a
very fat wad, whose denominations were of a large
and extremely interesting nature. The official shook
his head. It was not a question of money; nor was
the other's ability to pay in question. Later on, he,
Lanson, would know better what the situation was;
meanwhile he suggested that Doctor Meunier should
go to the hotel and wait—that there was nothing else
to do for the moment. The Selkirk physician here
intervened, and, agreeing with the superintendent,
offered to escort the Frenchman to the Corona Hotel.

The Hawk, as one whose curiosity was satiated,
but satiated at the expense of time he could ill afford,
nodded briefly to the reporter who stood nearest to
him, and quietly left the room.

— XII —

BLINDMAN'S-BUFF

FIVE minutes later, standing in another room—his own—the Hawk rapidly changed the light-grey suit he had been wearing for one of a darker material. From the pockets of the discarded suit he transferred to the pockets of the suit he had just put on, amongst other things, his automatic and his bunch of skeleton keys. He opened his trunk, removed the false tray, and smiled with a sort of grim complacency as his glance inventoried its unhallowed contents; and particularly he smiled, as, opening a little box, he allowed a stream of gleaming stones to trickle out into the palm of his hand—the twenty thousand dollars' worth of diamonds robbed from the Fast Mail three nights ago.

"Some haul!" observed the Hawk softly. "And, with any luck, there'll be something else there worth the whole outfit put together before to-night is over." He replaced the diamonds in the box, the box in the tray, and spoke again, but now his smile was hard and twisted; not an article there but he had scooped from under the noses of the gang. "Yes, I guess I'd go out like you'd snuff a candle if

172

they ever get me, and I guess they're getting—
querulous!"

The Hawk, however, had not opened the trunk
purely for the opportunity it afforded of inspecting
these few mementos, interesting as they might be.
It was an excellent safeguard to change his clothes,
but it would avail him very little if—well, any one,
say—were still permitted to recognise—his face!
From the top of the tray, where it lay upon the
packages of banknotes that had once reposed in the
paymaster's safe, the Hawk picked up a mask and
slipped it into his pocket. He fitted the false tray
back into the lid of the trunk, closed the trunk,
locked it, put on a wide-brimmed, soft felt hat,
locked the door of his room behind him, descended
the narrow staircase, and stepped out on the street.

His destination was the Corona Hotel, but there
was no particular hurry. Undoubtedly from the
moment the Frenchman had left the train some, or
one, of the gang had fastened on the man's trail;
but the companionship of the Selkirk physician guaranteed the Frenchman's immediate safety. His own
plan, as far as it was matured, was very simple.
He meant to "spot" if he could, should that particular member, or members, of the gang be unknown
to him personally, the man, or men, selected by the
Wire Devils to shadow the Frenchman—and then
watch the *gang!* The Hawk had no intention whatever of making an attempt on the Frenchman's
property with the gang watching him—that would
have been little less than the act of a fool who was

bent on suicide! Since, therefore, he had no choice
in the matter, he was quite content to have the gang
take the initiatory risk in relieving the Frenchman
of the handbag! After that—the Hawk's old
twisted smile was back on his lips as he walked
along—after that it became his business to see that
the bag did not get very far out of his sight!

He reached and crossed the city park upon which
the Corona Hotel fronted, entered the hotel, and,
sauntering leisurely through the lobby, approached
the desk. He glanced casually over the register;
then, lighting a cigar, he selected a chair near the
front windows where he could command a general
view of the lobby, and sat down.

Doctor Meunier's room was Number 106.

Once the Hawk's eyes lazily surveyed the lobby;
thereafter they appeared to be intent on what was
passing in the street. He was in luck! The first
trick, at least, had gone to him. Lolling in a chair
near the elevator doors, and apparently drowsy
from a heavy luncheon, was—the Bantam. The
Hawk smoked on. Half an hour went by. The
Bantam appeared to awaken with a start, smiled
sheepishly about him, went over to the news stand,
bought a paper—and returned to his seat. The
Hawk finished his cigar, rose, strolled to the main
entrance, and went out. The Bantam could be
safely trusted to see that Doctor Meunier did not
vanish into thin air! He would do the like for the
Bantam! He crossed over into the park.

The Hawk chose a bench—strategically. Shel·

tered by a row of trees, he had the corner upon
which the hotel was built diagonally before him,
and could see both the side entrance on the cross
street and the front entrance on the main thoroughfare.

The Hawk's vigil, however, was not immediately
rewarded. An hour passed—and yet another—and
the greater portion of the afternoon. Five o'clock
came. A newsboy passed, crying the *Evening Journal*. The Hawk bought one. A headline in heavy
type on the front page instantly caught his eye:

ONE HUNDRED THOUSAND DOLLARS IN A LEAD CAPSULE

And beneath this, still in assertive type:

Famous French Surgeon en route to Japan with Fortune in Radium Misses Connections Through Destruction of Railroad Bridge

Offers Company Large Sum of Money for Special Train to the Coast

"Yes," observed the Hawk caustically, "and even
if I hadn't known anything about it before, I'd have
had a look-in thanks to this! Sting you, wouldn't
it! The papers hand you a come-on—and then they
wonder at crime!"

The "story" itself ran a column and a half. The

Hawk began to read—or, rather, to divide his attention between the story and the hotel entrances. The reporter had certainly set out with the intention of overlooking no detail that could be turned to account. His meeting and conversation with the Frenchman in the car were breezily set forth; the member of a "prominent family" in Japan artfully disguised, or, perhaps better, disclosed no less august a personage than the Emperor himself; the value of radium, both intrinsically and scientifically, was interestingly dealt with; and the surgeon's black handbag, with its priceless contents, was minutely described and featured.

The Hawk had reached this point, when suddenly the newspaper and the reporter's version of the story lost interest for him. Doctor Meunier, gripping his little black handbag tenaciously, had stepped out through the main entrance of the hotel, and was walking briskly down the street. A moment later, the Bantam sauntered through the doorway and started in the same direction, a hundred yards behind the Frenchman. The Hawk, with a grim smile, folded his paper, stuffed it into his pocket, rose from the bench, crossed the street, and fell into the procession—a hundred yards behind the Bantam.

It was still light, though it was beginning to grow dusk—too light for any highway thuggery, and yet —the Hawk gradually closed the gap between himself and the Bantam to half the original distance.

The chase led on for a half dozen blocks, then

turned into one of the crowded streets of the shopping district, and proceeded in a downtown direction. And then, abruptly, the Hawk dropped further behind the Bantam again, and crossed to the opposite sidewalk. It was perhaps only fancy, but intuitively he felt that he, too, in turn, was being followed. His hat brim, hiding his face, was pulled a little farther forward over his eyes, as he hurried now until he was abreast of the Frenchman. Intuition or not, it was quite possible and even likely that one of the gang might "cover" the Bantam.

The Hawk scowled. He could not be sure; and he dared not put it to more than a casual test, for he could not afford to lose sight of the Bantam. He paused, took a slip of paper from his pocket, and, as though having consulted it for an address, appeared to scan the signs and numbers on the stores in his immediate vicinity. The Frenchman had passed by; the Bantam was directly opposite to him now across the street. The Hawk's keen eyes searched the stream of pedestrians behind the Bantam. And then suddenly he shrugged his shoulders, and returned the paper to his pocket—a man, in a light suit and brown derby hat, had stepped out of the crowd, and was leisurely lighting a cigarette in a doorway just across from where he, the Hawk, stood.

The Hawk went on, but keeping in the rear of the Bantam now on the opposite side of the street. He was still not sure; but, in any case, neither could the man in the brown derby be *sure* that he, the

Hawk, was following the Bantam. So far then, granted that he *was* being followed, it was an even break!

At the next crossing the Frenchman accosted a policeman, and, as though he had received directions, at once turned down the cross street. The Hawk, as he followed, smiled grimly. The cross street automatically verified the suspicions of the man in the brown derby—if the man in the brown derby had any suspicions to verify; but, at one and the same time, it also answered the Hawk's own question.

The Hawk, in turn, made use of a doorway. He could afford to allow the Bantam, temporarily, the lead of an extra half block now, for there were fewer people on the cross street and he would still be able to keep the other in sight. A minute, two, elapsed—and then the Hawk picked up the Bantam's trail again. The man in the brown derby hat had passed by the corner and continued on along the main street.

And yet still the Hawk was not satisfied. And it was not until after he had repeated the same manœuvre some four or five times, as the Frenchman, leading, turned into different streets, that he was finally convinced that neither the man in the brown derby hat, nor any one else, was interested in his movements.

The chase, since leaving the main street, had wound its way through the less populous wholesale district—it ended at the railway station. The

Frenchman passed along the front of the building, and disappeared through the doorway leading upstairs to the divisional offices, his object being, it now appeared obvious, to obtain another interview with the superintendent; the Bantam disappeared inside the main entranceway of the station, evidently to await the Frenchman's reappearance; and the Hawk, on the far side of the street, slipped into the lane that had served him many times as a thoroughfare between the station and his room over the saloon two blocks away.

It was growing dark now. A half hour went by. Still the Hawk crouched in the shadow of the building that bordered the lane. The street lights went on. The six o'clock whistle blew from the shops over across the tracks. Either the Frenchman was a visitor not easy to get rid of, or Lanson was out and the other was awaiting the superintendent's return. But the Hawk's patience was infinite.

Another fifteen minutes dragged away; then the office door opened, the Frenchman emerged, and started back uptown. The Bantam appeared from the main entranceway, and started after him. The chase was on again. The Hawk followed.

The Frenchman, seemingly sticking to rule of thumb and following the directions he had received on the way down, took exactly the same route on the way back. But now the neighborhood presented an entirely different aspect. The wholesale houses were closed; the streets deserted, dark, and poorly lighted.

The Hawk hugged the shadows of the buildings craftily on the opposite side of the street. Was it coming now? Certainly the gang would go far before finding a more ideal opportunity, and the Bantam, if he had realised that fact, could easily have sent, or telephoned, a message from the station. He, the Hawk, had not cared to take the risk of following the Bantam inside—the Bantam *might* remember having seen him in the hotel lobby.

And then the Hawk's lips thinned. Yes—it was the old, old game! They were on the cross street, a little less than a block distant from the main street ahead. The Bantam began to close up on the Frenchman. The Hawk now, crouching low, slipped almost literally from doorway to doorway. Two men, apparently drunk and quarrelling, were coming down the block toward the Frenchman. The Bantam closed to within a few yards of his quarry. The brawl attained its height as the two men reached the Frenchman. One man struck the other. They clenched, and, smashing into the Frenchman knocked him down. His hat flew in one direction, the hand-bag in another. The brawlers curiously did not resume their quarrel, but lounged a few paces away— within call of the Bantam. The Hawk, squeezed in his doorway directly opposite the scene, kept his eyes on the Bantam. If the play had lacked originality before, it did not lack it now! The Bantam stooped, picked up the handbag, and, as he stooped again for the hat, slipped the handbag under his coat, and slipped another bag—evidently a carefully prepared duplicate—out from under his coat and into his hand. The Frenchman was rising dazedly to his feet. The Bantam stepped hurriedly forward, holding out hat and bag.

"I hope you're not hurt, sir," the Hawk heard him say—and then the two moved on together toward the corner.

The Hawk shook his shoulders in a queer, almost self-apologetic sort of way, as he followed again. And then he smiled as queerly. The Bantam had the bag now, and, if he, the Hawk, were permitted to hazard an opinion, the Wire Devils had very kindly picked the fruit again for him to eat!

At the corner, the Bantam shook hands with the Frenchman, and, stepping out into the street, signalled an approaching car. Quick, alert on the instant, the Hawk, safe in the protection of the crowded sidewalk, moved swiftly along in the direction that the car would take, his eyes searching the street on both sides for a taxicab. The street car passed him, but stopped at the next corner, and he caught up with it again. And then, over his shoulder, he saw a taxi coming up behind him. He stepped from the curb, and stopped it.

"Sorry, sir," said the chauffeur. "I'm going after a fare."

"You've got one now—and a good one," said the Hawk quietly. He had opened the door—a ten-dollar bill lay in the chauffeur's hand.

"Yes, but look here, sir," said the chauffeur, a little dubiously, "I'll get into trouble for this, and——"

The Hawk had stepped inside, and lowered the window between himself and the chauffeur.

"Follow that car," said the Hawk pleasantly. "And while we're on the crowded streets don't get so far behind it that you can't close up near enough to see who gets off every time it stops. And don't worry about your trouble—there's another ten coming on top of the regular fare. That's good enough, isn't it?"

"I guess I'm not kicking!" admitted the chauffeur. The taxi started forward. He looked back over his shoulder at the Hawk. "What's the lay? Fly-cop?"

"Maybe!" said the Hawk. "Mind yourself! It's stopping again. Keep where I can see both sides of the car."

"I get you!" said the chauffeur. "Leave it to me!"

Block after block was passed, the street car stopping frequently. The Hawk, in the body of the taxi, knelt behind the chauffeur's back, his eyes held steadily on the street car ahead. The Bantam did not alight. The street car began to run out into the suburbs. The taxicab, with lights out now, risking the city ordinance, dropped back to a more respectful distance in the rear. The district became less settled, the houses farther apart; the street lights were single incandescents now, and these few

and far between.   There was one passenger left in
the car—the Bantam.

The chauffeur spoke abruptly.

"We're pretty near the end of the line," he said.

"All right," the Hawk answered.   "Stop when
the car stops—keep about this distance, we're not
likely to be noticed."   A moment later he stepped
from the taxi.   "Wait for me here!" he directed.

The Bantam, leaving the street car, had started
off at a sharp pace past the end of the car line.   It
was little more than a country road now; only a
house here and there.   The Bantam, just discern-
ible in the darkness, had a lead of perhaps a hundred yards, and the Hawk, moving stealthily, began
to creep nearer, and still nearer, until the hundred
yards were fifty—and then suddenly, with a low
muttered exclamation, he threw himself flat on the
ground.   The Bantam, abreast of a house from
which there showed a light in the side window, had
turned in abruptly from the road.   A glow of light
spread out as the front door opened.   The Hawk
lay motionless.   Then the Bantam entered, and the
door was closed again.   A little later, a form appeared at the side window, a hand reached up, and
the shade was drawn.

"Nice respectable neighborhood, too!" observed
the Hawk tersely.   "Wonder if it's *the* lair, and if
the Master Spider's in there now?"

He was creeping forward now across a small
lawn.   He neared the side window; it was open,
and the shade lacked a tiny, though inviting, space

of reaching to the sill. A murmur of voices came from within. There was not a sound from the Hawk. And then, from beneath the window, which was low and not more than four feet from the ground, he raised himself up cautiously, and suddenly his dark eyes narrowed. It was not the Master Spider—it was the Butcher, whose treachery had nearly done for him that night in the paymaster's office, the man whom he had promised should one day *remember!*

He could hear now, and he could see. It was a sitting room such as one might find anywhere in a house whose occupants were in comfortable circumstances. It was cosily and tastefully furnished. It bore no sign of criminal affiliation; it was, as it were, a sort of alibi in itself. A telephone stood on the table beside a pile of magazines, the latter flanked by an ornamental reading lamp; deep leather lounging chairs added to the inviting and homelike appearance of the room—the incongruity was in the Butcher's thin, hatchet-like face, and in the coarse, vicious features of the short, stocky Bantam, as they faced each other across the table.

"Where's the others, d'ye say?" demanded the Bantam.

"Out," said the Butcher. "The chief called 'em an hour ago. I don't know what's up. I guess you and I keep house here to-night; he said you were to stay. Mouser and Jack were to report to Kirschell, weren't they?"

"Yes, that's what they said."

"Well, all right!" The Butcher shrugged his shoulders. "That's none of our hunt. I suppose you got it, didn't you—or you wouldn't be here?"

"Sure, I got it!" answered the Bantam. "What d'ye think?"

"Let's have a look," said the Butcher eagerly. "The chief says we can cash in on it for fifty thousand."

"Fifty thousand!" The Bantam growled, as he unbuttoned his coat, and, taking out the bag, laid it on the table. "I thought it was worth a hundred thousand!"

"So it is." The Butcher was opening the bag. "But it's no cinch to turn it into money without a big split—savvy?"

The Butcher opened the lead box, took out the lead cylinder, and balanced it speculatively in the palm of his hand.

The Bantam regarded it distrustfully.

"It don't look like fifty cents to me!" he commented finally.

"I know," said the Butcher facetiously; "but your eyesight's bum, Bantam! Have any trouble?"

The Bantam grinned.

"Not what you'd notice! After the Mouser and Jack smashed into him, the poor old boob didn't know what had happened till I was handing him his hat and the other bag. I guess he bumped his bean kind of hard on the sidewalk."

The Butcher nodded approvingly. He was still

twisting the lead cylinder around and around in his hand.

"Say," suggested the Bantam impatiently, after a moment, "when you've done chucking it under the chin, put it to bed somewhere, and if there's any grub in the house lead me to it. I'm hungry!"

"All right!" agreed the Butcher. He replaced the lead cylinder in its box, and the box in the bag, crossed the room, opened a little cupboard in the wall opposite the window, laid the bag inside, and closed the cupboard door again. "Come on!" he said.

— XIII —

THE MAN WITH THE SCAR

THE two men left the room. The Hawk did not move. He was fingering in a curiously absent-minded sort of way the edges of the newspaper that still protruded from his pocket. It was very simple, very easy. The window was open, the cupboard was not locked, the room was empty, there were only the Bantam and the Butcher to look out for, and they were in another part of the house; he had only to lift aside the window shade, step in, steal across the room, and steal out again—with a hundred-thousand-dollar prize. It was very inviting. It seemed suddenly as though it were a pressing invitation to enter that room—*and never leave it alive!*

Flashing quick through the Hawk's brain now was a résumé of the afternoon, of each separate and individual occurrence since he had left the train. Had he, after all, been followed? If so—how? Had the Bantam been warned? He shook his head, as though impatient with himself. Even apart from that, what he had begun to suspect now would be thoroughly logical on the part of the gang. The newspaper supplied the key. He would un-

questionably have seen the newspaper that afternoon, and he would, apart from being spared several aimless hours in the park, have done exactly as
he had done, and just as unquestionably be where
he was now at this precise moment even if he had
not been with the Frenchman on the train. The
newspaper placed him in possession of the same
facts that the Wire Devils possessed. They must
know that. They were therefore justified in as-
suming that he, quite as rabidly as themselves, would
make an attempt to steal the bag. They knew, in
that case, that he would have discovered that they
were already at work; and they knew that, on a
dozen occasions before, that had not prevented him
from snatching the prize they had already counted
within their grasp. Were they on their guard now
—or a little more than on their guard! Were they
offering him, on the chance or with the knowledge
that he was here now, the opportunity to snatch
another prize—and seeing to it that it was for the
last time!

The Hawk edged back from the window; and,
silent as a shadow now, began to circuit the house.
And then suddenly his suspicion became a certainty.
It was only a little thing—a slip—but it was
enough. The Butcher had made a misplay! There
was no light in any other window—and a man did
not usually eat in the dark! It was fairly, even
painfully, evident now that the Bantam and the
Butcher were in, say, the adjoining room, waiting

for him to enter through that window into their trap.

But there was still the little black bag—and one hundred thousand dollars! The Hawk's smile was more ominous than pleasant. There were other ways apart from a window—and even two men, especially if they were caught napping, had been known to be quite amenable to the influence of the muzzle of an automatic!

The Hawk found the back door entrance, found it locked—and used a skeleton key. He was perhaps five minutes in opening the door; but in those five minutes there was no click of lock as the handle turned by infinitesimal fractions of an inch, no creak of hinge as the door little by little swung back and was closed again.

The silence was almost uncanny. It was utter blackness. By feeling out with his hand he discovered he was in a passageway. He moved along, guiding himself by the sense of touch against the wall, his weight balanced and full upon one foot before he lifted the other for the next step.

It seemed a passage of interminable length, that led on and on through blackness and silence. In reality he had come possibly thirty feet, and had passed one door. And then he began to catch the sound of voices whispering. The whisperings grew more distinct and became low, guarded tones, as he moved forward—and now he could distinguish words. He flattened back against the side of the passage. Opposite to him was an open door; and within the room, instead of blackness now, was a sort of murky gloom which was created by a ray of light that seeped in through a partially open door at the far side of the room. The Hawk's fingers slipped into his pocket—and slipped his mask over his face. He had his bearings now. The room from which the light came was the baited trap; the room immediately in front of him was the room from which the trap was to be sprung! His hand went to his pocket again, and came out with his automatic. It was their move now. If, when they finally grew impatient, they went back into the lighted room, or turned on the light in the room where they were now waiting, they sprang the trap upon themselves.

Came the Bantam's low growl—and the twitching of the Hawk's jaw muscles.

"I don't like it, I tell you! Where is he? What's he waiting for? I know he followed me. You saw him yourself from the front room creeping across the lawn out there. 'Twouldn't take him all this time to get in through that window."

"Aw, shut up!" snarled the Butcher. "You'd give any one the creeps!"

"That's all right," whispered the Bantam hoarsely; "but I said from the start it was a fool game not to cover him close on the way back, and——"

"Yes—and scare him off!" sneered the Butcher. "There ain't but one guy that'd pick up that trail —and that's the Hawk. He's butted in enough, but he's butted in for the last time to-night! The two of us are aplenty, aren't we? Sure—cover him close on the way back—and scare him off! D'ye think he's a fool!"

"No, I don't, curse him!" retorted the Bantam. "And if I'd had my way, I'd have croaked him in broad daylight with a bullet through his bean, and finished him for keeps the minute Jack spotted him following me! Instead of that, Jack never even gets a look at his mug."

"You're some bright guy!" grunted the Butcher. "We'd have had a hot chance making a dead man tell us where he'd planted those diamonds off the Fast Mail, not to speak of a few other little trifles the swine did us out of!"

"And you think——"

"You bet, I do!" the Butcher cut in viciously. "He'll talk to-night to save his life—and then I'll toss you, Bantam, if you like, to see who bumps him off!"

The Hawk's fingers played in a curious, caressing motion over the stock of the automatic in his hand; the twist on his lips grew a little harder, a little more merciless.

There was movement in the room now. One of the two, the Bantam undoubtedly, in growing uneasiness, was moving softly, erratically, up and down the room. It proved to be the Bantam.

"Well then, where the blazes is he!" he burst out nervously.

"Aw, shut up!" snarled the Butcher savagely for the second time.

The Bantam's shadow, as the man paced up and down, passed the doorway, repassed, and passed again.

"I tell you, I don't like it!" he flung out suddenly. "Something's wrong! If he's outside the house, he can't see, anyway. I'm going to take a chance, and——"

There was a click, the light in the passageway went on—then a yell from the Bantam in the doorway—a lightning spring from the Hawk, as the other jerked a weapon upward—and the Bantam went down in a heap, as the Hawk's clubbed weapon caught him on the head. It was quick, like the winking of an eye. From back in the room, the Butcher sprang forward for the doorway—and fired—and missed—and the Hawk's left hand, as they came upon each other, darting out, closed with the strength of a steel vise on the Butcher's right wrist, and with a terrific wrench twisted the other's arm halfway around. It was lighter now in the room—light enough to see. The two forms swayed strangely—a little apart—the Butcher's body bent over, as though queerly deformed. Slowly, remorselessly, the Hawk turned the other's arm in its socket. Sweat sprang to the Butcher's forehead, his face writhed with pain—and, with a scream of agony, his revolver clattered to the floor.

"You're breaking it——for God's sake, let go!" he moaned.

The Hawk kicked the revolver to the other side of the room.

"Take the Bantam by the shoulders and drag him into that lighted room!" The Hawk's tones were flat, unpleasant. "I don't think I hit him hard enough to take the chance of leaving him there alone!"

The Butcher obeyed—with the muzzle of the Hawk's automatic pressed persuasively against the small of his back. He left the Bantam in the middle of the sitting room floor, and himself accepted a chair—at the Hawk's invitation.

"You again—eh, Butcher?" The Hawk's voice had become a drawl. With his automatic covering the Butcher, he had backed to the cupboard, opened it, and was feeling inside with his left hand. "My grateful thanks, and you'll convey my compliments —the Hawk's, you know—to our friend—the chief." He had slipped the little black bag under his arm, and now his hand was back in the cupboard again; he had felt a ball of heavy cord there. "Sorry I haven't a phony ten-spot with me—my card, you know—unpardonable breach of etiquette —really!" He smiled suddenly. The ball of cord was in his hand, as he advanced toward the Butcher's chair. He set the little black bag down on the table.

The Butcher seemed to have lost all his characteristic ferocity; the sharp little ferret eyes rested anywhere but on the Hawk, and on his face was a sickly grin.

"Stand up!" commanded the Hawk curtly—he was knotting the end of the cord into a noose. "Now—your hands behind your back—and together! Thank you!" He slipped the noose over the Butcher's hands, and began to wind the cord around the other's wrists.

The Butcher winced.

"I'm sorry," said the Hawk apologetically; "but it's all I have. The cord *is* rather thin, and I'm afraid it may cut into you—not strong enough to allow you any play, you know. And, by the way, Butcher, I heard the Bantam say that I was spotted on the way down—I presume he meant on the way down to the station. I'll be honest and admit I'm disappointed in myself. Would you mind explaining, Butcher—I was quite convinced there was no one behind me."

"There wasn't!" The Butcher risked a sneer. "Mabbe the French guy was heard telephoning to the station, and the Bantam passed on the word. Nobody had to follow behind. All there was to do, knowing where the Frenchy was going, was to dodge around the blocks ahead, and keep hidden down the different intersecting streets, and see if the same guy kept going by the corners after the Bantam."

"Thank you, Butcher," murmured the Hawk gratefully. "That lets me out a little, doesn't it?" He wound the cord again and again around the Butcher's wrists, knotted it, shoved the other unceremoniously back into the chair, and tied the Butcher's legs.

The Hawk then gave his attention to the Bantam. The Bantam was just beginning to regain consciousness. The Hawk knelt down, rolled the man over on his side, and secured him in the same manner as he had the Butcher. But with the Bantam he went a little farther. He transferred the Bantam's handkerchief from the Bantam's pocket to the Bantam's mouth—and tied it there.

He turned once more to the Butcher.

"I must apologise again," he said softly. "I hate to do this"—he felt for, and obtained, the Butcher's handkerchief—"but the house is unfortunately close to the road, and you might inadvertently make yourself heard before I got decently away."

The Butcher's reply was a shrug of the shoulders.

The Hawk, about to cram the handkerchief into the other's mouth, paused.

"Butcher," said the Hawk, almost plaintively, "if you'll permit me to deal in mixed metaphors, you appear to have shed your spots—you're too awfully docile!"

"You got the goods," muttered the Butcher sullenly. "What more do you——"

He stopped suddenly. His eyes met the Hawk's. The telephone on the table was ringing.

The Hawk hesitated. Into the Butcher's eyes, narrowed now, there seemed to have come a mocking gleam. The telephone rang again. And then the Hawk reached out abruptly, and took the receiver from the hook.

"Hello!" he said gruffly.

"Four X. Who's that?" responded a voice.

There was something familiar about the voice, but he could not on the instant place it. The Hawk's mind, even as he answered, was swiftly cataloguing every member of the gang known to him in an effort to identify it.

"The Bantam," he said.

"All right," replied the voice. "Give me the Butcher."

"Hold the line," answered the Hawk.

He placed his hand over the transmitter. The voice was still eluding him. He turned, and eyed the Butcher.

"Four X wants you, Butcher." All the drawl, all the insouciance was gone now; his voice was hard with menace, cold as death. "And you're going to speak to him—but you're going to say what I tell you to say. But before you begin, I want you to remember the little account between us that's been hanging over since that night in the paymaster's office. If you make a break, if you try to frame me—*I'll settle that account here to-night,* while you sit in that chair. If you hesitate on a word, I'll fire—and not through my pocket, you yellow cur! Understand? Don't kid yourself on this, Butcher! If I nod my head, say 'yes'—and no more. Now!"

The Butcher had sunk back in his chair. There

was fear in his face; it was white, and he circled his lips with his tongue.

Beneath the mask, the Hawk's lips were a straight line. He laid down his automatic on the table, placed the receiver to his own ear, and held the transmitter to the Butcher's lips.

"Go ahead!" ordered the Hawk. "Ask him what he wants." His fingers, cupped and pressed over the transmitter, lifted.

"Hello!" said the Butcher. "What is it?"

"That you, Butcher? Everything all right?" inquired the voice.

The Hawk nodded.

"Yes," said the Butcher.

"Well, open up a bit!" complained the voice. "Did you get him, and——"

The voice was speaking on. The Hawk's lips had set a little tighter. He had recognised the voice now. His fingers were pressed over the transmitter again.

"Tell him you laid me out cold," instructed the Hawk; "and that I haven't regained consciousness yet. Now!" The voice had ceased speaking; the Hawk's fingers lifted again.

"We beaned him," said the Butcher morosely. "He's still asleep."

"Good!" chuckled the voice. "I'll be up there by and by, and——"

"Tell him to stay where he is, that it will be—— *safer*." The Hawk clipped off his words.

The Butcher delivered the message, the snarl in his voice entirely to the Hawk's liking.

"What?" questioned the voice. "I didn't get you."

"Repeat!" whispered the Hawk.

The Butcher repeated.

"O. K.," came back the answer. "Yes, I guess you're right. So long, Butcher."

"Say 'good-night,' " prompted the Hawk.

" 'Night!" growled the Butcher.

The Hawk replaced the receiver on the hook, and the instrument on the table.

The Butcher's lips were livid.

The Hawk picked up his automatic and leaned forward, his eyes on a level with the Butcher's.

"What's that fellow's moniker, Butcher?"

The Butcher hesitated.

The automatic crept forward an inch.

"Parson Joe." The Butcher's voice choked with mingled rage and fear.

"Parson Joe, eh?" repeated the Hawk ruminatingly. "Was he the chap who pulled that con game on the Riverdale Bank back in New York State about six years ago, and afterwards got cornered by the police in Ike Morrissey's gambling hell, and was caught because he nearly bled to death, with his wrist half off, trying to get through a broken window pane? He got four spaces. That him?"

"If you say so, it must have been!" There was a leer in the Butcher's voice.

"Was it?" The automatic touched the Butcher's breast.

"Yes," said the Butcher.

"Thank you!" smiled the Hawk. "Now——!" He gagged the Butcher with the handkerchief, tied it securely into place, stood up, picked up the little black bag, switched off the electric reading lamp, moved to the window, and drew aside the shade. "We'll let that account stand open for a little while longer, Butcher," he said softly. "Just a little while longer—good-night!"

He swung out of the window, dropped to the ground, ran across the lawn, and gained the road. His mask and automatic were back in his pockets. His fingers felt and patted the little black bag under his coat.

"Always play your luck," whispered the Hawk confidentially to himself. "It seems to me I saw a little loose change in Doctor Meunier's pocket-book, and I don't think he's opened the duplicate bag yet and stirred up a fuss. It isn't much compared with a hundred thousand, or even fifty, to quote the Butcher, but 'every little bit added to what you've got——' " He fell to whistling the tune pleasantly under his breath, as he hurried along the road.

A minute later he had regained the taxicab.

"Drop me a block this side of the Corona—and give her all she's got!" he directed crisply.

"D'ye get him?" demanded the chauffeur eagerly.

"My friend," replied the Hawk gently, as he stepped into the taxi, "if you'll think it over, you'll

come to the conclusion that you really don't **want**
to know. Take it from me that the less you're **wise**
about to-night the wiser you will be to-morrow. Now,
cut her loose!"

It had taken a good thirty minutes on the trip
up; it took less than half of that, by a more direct
route, for the return journey. At the corner, a block
from the hotel, the Hawk crumpled two generous
bank-notes into the chauffeur's hand, and bade the
man good-night. He traversed the block, entered
the hotel lobby, and, ignoring the elevators, leisurely
and nonchalantly ascended the staircase to the first
floor. From the landing he noted the room numbers opposite to him, and with these as a guide passed
on along the corridor to where it turned at right
angles at the corner of the building, and halted
before room No. 106. A light showing above the
transom indicated that the Frenchman was within.
He had passed one or two people. No one had paid
any attention to him. Why should they! He
glanced up and down. The corridor, for the moment, was empty. He tried the door gently—it was
locked. His right hand, in his side pocket, closed
over his automatic. He pressed close to the door,
knocked gently with his left hand—and with his left
hand reached quickly into his pocket for his mask.

"Who's there?" the Frenchman called out.

"Message for you, sir," the Hawk answered.

Footsteps crossed the room, the key turned in **the**
lock—and, in a flash, the Hawk, slipping on **his**
mask, had pushed the door open, closed **it behind**

him, and the Frenchman was staring into the muzzle of the automatic.

"*Mon Dieu!*" gasped the Frenchman faintly.

"That's right!" said the Hawk coolly. "Don't speak any louder than that, or——" He shrugged his shoulders significantly, as he locked the door.

The Frenchman, white-faced, was evidently fighting for his nerve.

"What—what is it?" he stammered. "What is it that you want?"

It was almost a reassuring smile that flickered on the Hawk's lips, and his voice did not belie it—it was purely conversational in its tones.

"I was reading in the paper this afternoon about the famous Doctor Meunier. I'm a bit of a scientist myself, in an amateur way, and I'm particularly interested in radium when there's enough of it to——"

"Ah! My radium! That is what you want!" cried out the Frenchman wildly. The duplicate bag lay on the bed. He ran for it, and snatched it up. "No! That you shall not have! You come to steal my radium, you——"

"You jump at conclusions, doctor," said the Hawk patiently. "Since it is already stolen, I——"

"Stolen!" The Frenchman stared—and then with feverish fingers opened the bag. He looked inside. The bag dropped to the floor, his hands went up in the air. "It is empty—empty!" he cried distractedly. "It is gone—gone! *Mon Dieu,* my radium is gone! What shall I do!" His hands were rumpling through his hair like one demented. "What shall I do—it is gone!"

"Well," suggested the Hawk suavely, "I thought perhaps you might like to buy it back again."

"Buy it back! Are you crazy? Am I crazy?" The man appeared to be beside himself; he flung out his arms in mad gesticulation. "With what would I buy it back? It is worth a hundred thousands dollars—a half million francs!"

"You are excited, Doctor Meunier," said the Hawk calmly. From where it bulged under his coat he drew out the black bag. "I said nothing about a hundred thousand dollars."

The Frenchman reached out a shaking hand, pointing at the bag.

"It is you then, after all, who stole it—eh? The bags—they are identical! *Mon Dieu,* what does this mean? I am mad! I do not understand!"

There was a chair on each side of the small table near the bed.

"Sit down!" invited the Hawk, indicating one with the muzzle of his automatic. The Frenchman sat down with a helpless and abandoned gesture of despair. The Hawk took the other chair. He opened the bag, opened the lead box, and laid the lead capsule on the table. "Do you identify this?" he inquired pleasantly.

The Frenchman reached for it eagerly.

The Hawk drew it back.

"One moment, please, Doctor Meunier!" he murmured. "You recognise it? You are satisfied that it is your tube of radium?"

"Yes, yes—*mon Dieu!* But, yes!"

"And it is worth, you say, a hundred thousand dollars?"

"But, yes, I tell you!" cried the Frenchman. "A hundred thousand—certainly, it is worth that!"

"Quite so!" said the Hawk placidly. "Therefore, Doctor Meunier, a comparatively small sum—eh?—you would be willing to pay that—a sum, I might add, that would be quite within your means."

"Quite within my means?" repeated the Frenchman a little dazedly.

"Yes," said the Hawk sweetly. "And to be specific, let us say—whatever is in your pocketbook."

The Frenchman drew back in his chair. His face blanched.

"You—you mean to rob me!" he exclaimed hoarsely.

"I do not see it quite in that light." The Hawk's voice was pained. "But we will not discuss the ethics involved—we probably should not agree. I did not steal your precious capsule from you, and I am returning it, not, I might say, without having incurred considerable personal risk in so doing. Perhaps we might better agree if we called it—a reward."

"No!" said the Frenchman desperately.

The Hawk's automatic tapped the table top with a hint of petulance.

"And—and what guarantee have I," the Frenchman burst out, "that you will give me the tube after you have taken my money?"

"My word," said the Hawk evenly. "And—I am waiting, Doctor Meunier!"

The Frenchman hesitated, then, with an oath, flung his pocketbook upon the table. The Hawk opened it, extracted the wad of bills that he had seen exhibited in the superintendent's office, smiled as he fingered them, and put them in his pocket. He pushed the lead capsule across the table—and suddenly, as the other reached for it, the Hawk was on his feet, his automatic flung forward, his left hand grasping the other's sleeve.

They held that way for an instant, eying each other—the Hawk's left hand slowly pushing back the other's right-hand sleeve. And then the Hawk's eyes shifted—to a long, jagged, white scar on the bare forearm just above the wrist.

"Shall I introduce myself—Parson Joe?" purred the Hawk.

The other's face was a mottled red—it deepened to purple.

"No, blast you!" he said between his teeth. "I know you—but I didn't think you knew me. So you called the turn when the Bantam followed me—eh?"

The Hawk shook his head.

"I never saw you in my life before to-day," he said grimly; "and, if it will do you any good to know it, I fell for that radium plant—until you telephoned the Butcher half an hour ago."

"And how did you know me, then?" The other
flung the question fiercely.

Again the Hawk shook his head. He had no desire that Parson Joe should know he had been on
the Limited that morning—Parson Joe might possess an inconveniently retentive memory for faces,
and he, the Hawk, did not always wear a mask.

"Maybe I guessed it, Parson!" he said insolently.
"I must have—it was the only thing that wasn't in
the paper! What encyclopedia did you get that
'Becquerel burn' dope out of? And was the reporter
lying, or how did you work it to get him on the
train?"

Parson Joe was leaning forward over the table,
fingering the lead capsule. He suddenly crushed it
with a blow of his fist, twisted it in two, and hurled
the pieces across the floor.

"We got him up the line on a fake that didn't
come off!" he snarled.

There was an instant's silence, then the Hawk
spoke.

"Nice, amiable crowd, you are, Parson!" The
Hawk's voice was silken. "I'm just beginning to
appreciate you. Let's see! You had to pull a story
that any newspaper would jump at and *feature,*
didn't you? And you had to have a big enough bait
to make sure I'd rise to it. And you had to account
for the celebrated Doctor Meunier's layover in Selkirk; and, not expecting I'd pick up the trail quite
so quickly, say, not until after the paper had been
out a little longer and you had made another baiting

trip or two to Lanson's office, you had to account
for the famous gentleman's enforced stay through
the night if necessary; and it gave a big swing to the
story, and let you work your stunt for the special
train that you knew you couldn't get; and you figured
I'd be even more sure to see it in the paper if it was
connected with some pleasant little episode of yours
—and so, on several counts, you blew up the bridge."

The man's teeth were clamped together.

"Yes!" he choked. "And we'd blow a dozen more
to get you!"

"You flatter me!" said the Hawk dryly. "I'm
afraid I've put you to quite a little trouble—for
nothing!"

Sullen, red, furious, Parson Joe's face twitched.

"You win to-night"—the heavy-lensed spectacles
were off, and the black eyes, the pupils gone, burned
on the Hawk—"but you're going out! As sure as
God gave you breath, we'll get you yet, and——"

"The Butcher told me that, and so did the Cricket
—some time ago," said the Hawk wearily. "I'm—
keep your hands above the table—I'm sure you
mean well!" He was backing toward the door. "I
won't bother to relieve you of your revolver; and I
don't think you'll telephone down to the office. It
might be awkward explaining to the police how Doctor Meunier lost his pocketbook—and got his medical degree! I shall, however, lock the door on the
outside, as I shall require a minute or two to reach
the street, and I cannot very well go through the ho-

tel corridor with—this"—he jerked his hand toward his mask.

The other's hands were above the table, obediently in plain view—but they were clenching and unclenching now, the knuckles white.

The Hawk reached behind him, took the key from the lock, listened, opened the door slightly, and, still facing into the room, still covering the other with his automatic, reached around the door and fitted the key into the outside of the lock.

"When you get out," said the Hawk, as though it were an afterthought, "I'm sure the Butcher will be glad to see you—I am afraid he is not as comfortable as he might be!"

The black eyes, with a devil's fury in them, had never left the Hawk's. And now the other lifted one of his clenched hands above his head.

"I'd give five years—*five years* of my life—for a look at your face!" he whispered hoarsely.

The Hawk was backing through the door.

"It's not enough, Parson," he said softly. "Make it another—pocketbook."

— XIV —

THE CLUE

TWO days had passed—two days, and a night. The Hawk's fingers drummed abstractedly without sound on the table top; his eyes, in a curiously introspective stare, were fixed on the closely drawn window shade across the room. From the ill-favoured saloon below his unpretentious lodgings, there came, muffled, a chorus of voices in inebriated and discordant song—an over-early evening celebration, for it was barely seven o'clock.

The finger tips drummed on. At times, the strong, square chin was doggedly outthrust; at times, a frown gathered in heavy furrows on the Hawk's forehead. The net at last was beginning to tighten ominously—every sign pointed to it. He would be a blind fool indeed who could not read the warning, and a fool of fools who would not heed it!

His eyes strayed from the window, and rested upon the trunk that stood between the table and the foot of the bed; and his fingers abruptly ceased their restless movements. Within that trunk, concealed in its false lid, was the loot, totalling many thousands of dollars, obtained through his knowledge of the

Wire Devils' secret code, which had enabled him to
turn their elaborately prepared plans on more occasions than one to his own account. But it was no
longer a question of outwitting them in order to add
to that purloined store; it was a question of outwitting them in order that—in very plain English—
he, the Hawk, might *live!*

Nor was it the Wire Devils alone who threatened
disaster. There were other factors; and, even if
these factors were less imminent, as it were, less in
a measure to be feared, they were by no means to be
ignored. The police were showing increasing ac-
tivity. The police circular, which he had once torn
down from the station wall, was now replaced by
another, only with this difference that, where the reward for the Hawk's capture had then stood at five
thousand dollars, it now stood at ten. Also, last
night—quite inadvertently!—while crouched under
the window of the turner's "cubbyhole" at the rear
of the roundhouse, the chosen spot for Lanson's and
MacVightie's confidential conferences, he had overheard a conversation between the division superintendent and the head of the railroad's detective force
that was certainly not intended for his ears. According to MacVightie, a man by the name of Birks, the
sharpest man in the United States Secret Service,
had been detailed by the Washington authorities to
the case. MacVightie had even taken a generous
share of the credit for this move to himself. Thefts
there might be until the country rang with them,
murders might add their quota to the reign of terror,

yet all this was outside the province of the Secret Service. It was, so MacVightie had said, through MacVightie's insistence that the systematised thefts and murders were inseparable with the counterfeit notes then flooding the country that had induced Washington to act. The Hawk and his gang, according to MacVightie again, were at the bottom of both one and the other—and counterfeiting *was,* very pertinently, within the province of the Secret Service!

The Hawk permitted a twisted smile to flicker across his lips. MacVightie, the police in general, and Birks of the Secret Service in particular, might be classed as complications, even decidedly *awkward* complications, but his immediate peril lay, not in that direction, but from those whose leadership MacVightie so blandly credited to—the Hawk!

The smile twisted deeper—into one of grim irony. While MacVightie placarded the country with circulars offering rewards for the capture of the Hawk and his gang, the "gang" was moving heaven and earth to capture the Hawk for its own exclusive purposes—which purposes, in a word, were an intense desire to recover the proceeds of the robberies that he, the Hawk, had filched from under the gang's nose, and thereafter, with such finality as might be afforded by a blackjack, a knife thrust, or a revolver bullet, to expedite the Hawk's departure from this vale of tears!

The Hawk's hand curled suddenly into a clenched fist, and his face grew set. He was facetious—and he had little enough warrant for facetiousness! They had already shown their teeth. They had shown the grim, ugly *deadliness* of their challenge in the thrust with which they had opened their attack upon him. He had parried the thrust, it was true—but there would be another—and another. There was something of remorseless promise, that would stop at nothing, in the extravagantly laid plans with which they had just attempted to lure him into the open and trap him. They had failed, it was true, and he had even scored against them again—but their cunning, their power, their resources, their malignity remained unimpaired. They would try again. It was like two adversaries in a dark room, each conscious of the other's presence, each striving to *place* the other, each conscious that the death of one was life for the other. That was the pith of the situation.

The Hawk's teeth clamped together. It was quite certain that they would run him to earth—unless he were first at the same game! An organisation as widespread as the one against which he had elected to pit his wits and play a lone hand, an organisation clever enough to have seized and put to its own use the entire divisional telegraph system of a railroad, an organisation callous enough to have counted a score of murders but incidents in its schemes, and, above all, an organisation guided by an unknown brain that was a master of cunning and unhampered by scruples, was an antagonist as sinister as it was powerful. For days now, in the great majority of cases, he, the Hawk, had turned their plans to his own account, skimmed, as it were, the cream from their milk—and there could be but one answer. And they *had* answered—and in the opening attack they had just launched against him it was obvious enough that every resource at their command was to be thrown into the balance to settle scores with him. They might, and did, laugh at the police, but to have their prizes pocketed and carried off by a competitor admitted of but one solution—the annihilation of the competitor!

The Hawk rose abruptly from his seat, stepped over to the trunk, opened it, and in an instant had removed the secret tray from the curvature of the lid. He laid the tray down upon the table; and his fingers, brushing aside a certain magnificent diamond necklace whose thousand facets glittered in the light, delved swiftly in amongst pile after pile of banknotes, and secured a package of papers.

He pushed the tray to one side, sat down again at the table, removed the elastic band from the package, and began to examine the papers. It was not the first time he had done this—he did it again now in a sort of desperation, and simply because it presented the one possibility at which he might grasp in the hope of obtaining a clue. There were many papers here, loose sheets, documents in envelopes, and, careful as he had been before, there *was* a chance that he had missed the one thing—in a sentence, in perhaps only a word, or a pencilled note on the back of an envelope—that would save him from disaster now.

It was the night before last that Parson Joe, with his fake tube of radium, had headed the gang in the attempt upon his, the Hawk's, life. The twisted smile returned to the Hawk's lips, as he turned first one paper and then another over in his hands. He had been fool enough to imagine that, besides failure, they had left a well-marked and clearly defined trail behind them—in the shape of that very comfortably, very cosily furnished house just on the outskirts of the city, where the Butcher had proposed to play the rôle of spider to his, the Hawk's, rôle of fly! It had even seemed a childishly simple matter to pick up such a thread and follow it. A house was neither rented nor furnished out of thin air. But the next morning the house was closed and deserted. It had been sublet—furnished. The subtenant, whose name was of no consequence, since it was of course assumed, had vanished—that was all. As far as the gang was concerned the house had lost its usefulness, and, having lost its usefulness, had simply been evacuated, and, together with the furniture, left to its own resources!

And it had been the same, on a previous occasion, with Isaac Kirschell's office. The morning after he, the Hawk, had appropriated the contents of Kirschell's cash box and had recognised Kirschell as one of the gang, the suite of rooms in the office building had been vacant.

The Hawk withdrew the last paper in the pile from its envelope, and read it with a sort of miserable realisation that its perusal, like the others, was foredoomed to futility. It was an alleged mortgage, spurious, of course, for these were Kirschell's papers that had been in the cash box, and, in the very nature of things, Kirschell's business had been only a blind to cover a sort of branch headquarters for the gang. He read it through, however, doggedly—and for his pains the printed words in their precise legal phraseology seemed to mock at him and chuckle with devilishly perverted humour.

He tossed the document upon the table, and, his face strained, pushed back his chair, got up, and began to pace the length of the room with a tread that, in its quick, nervous litheness and its silence, was like the pacing of a panther in its cage.

Nothing! And yet there must be something— somewhere! It was his move now, and there was little time to spare. It had become simply a question of which of the two, he or the gang, would win this game of blindman's-buff. It no longer sufficed that he should intercept those secret code messages in the former haphazard way, for, consistently as he had haunted the telegraph sounders, he was well enough aware that he must of necessity have missed many of the messages. He could afford to miss *none* of them now. Formerly, a message missed meant but a lost opportunity to thwart their plans, to add a little more to the contents of the trunk's false lid; now, since they had shown that they would stop at nothing to trap him, his life was dependent on having, with certainty, foreknowledge of their every plan. His defense lay in attack. He must trace those messages to their source, and trace them quickly before the Wire Devils should strike again, or leave the field to the Wire Devils—in other words, quit and run for it!

"Quit!" It was the first sound the Hawk had made, and it was only a whisper—but the whisper was gritted out through set teeth. Quit! He laughed a little, low, with menace, without mirth. It was not an alternative—it was the sting of a curling whip-lash to spur him on.

Well? What was he to do then? It was his move—and there was no time to spare. He approached the table again, and began to rearrange the papers into a pile, preparatory to replacing them in the tray. It was veritably a game of blindman's-buff! They knew him through personal contact, but only as a man who had always been masked; he knew many of them, and knew them personally—but only in the play-off of their schemes, when he had, as it were, snatched the plunder from their hands as he made his own escape, had he ever seen any of them. Well—the question came again, more insistent, more imperative, more vital—well, his life was in the balance, what was he to do? Go out again to-night and haunt a telegraph sounder, trust to——

He turned suddenly, the spurious mortgage, and the long envelope that had contained it, in his hand. The document, for some reason or other, refused to fit into the envelope as neatly or as readily as it had previously done. He held the envelope up to the light—and the next instant, flinging the document down on the table, he had ripped the envelope apart, and from under the inner flap, where it had undoubtedly been forced by the document itself and afterwards, as he had handled the envelope, had obviously worked its way partially out again, he extracted a small, thin slip of yellow paper.

And then for a moment the Hawk stood motionless, but into the dark eyes there leaped a triumphant flash. In his hand was the return portion of a railroad ticket that read:

Conmore to Selkirk City.

He whipped the ticket over to scrutinise the date stamp on the back—it was that of the day prior to his visit to Kirschell's office. And he laughed a little again, but there was no bitterness in the laugh now. The clue that he had sought, the clue that Lanson's men had in vain patrolled and scoured the division's right of way to obtain, was in his possession.

"It fits—like a glove!" muttered the Hawk, with grim complacence. "Kirschell had the envelope in his pocket, of course, and in putting his return ticket in his pocket it slipped into the envelope without his knowing it, got crowded under the flap, and he thought he had lost it!" The Hawk turned sharply to the table. "Conmore—eh?" He was working with feverish haste now, replacing the papers in the tray, and fitting the tray back into the curvature of the trunk lid. "Number Thirty-Eight, if she's on time, is due at seven-thirty." He pulled out his watch. "Seven-twenty! Conmore—eh?" The light

was out, the door locked behind him. "That's twenty
miles east of here, and *between* here and Bald
Creek." He was out of the house now, and running
along the lane that gave on the station street. "Yes,"
said the Hawk again, and there was suppressed ela-
tion in his voice, "it fits! It fits—like a glove!"

The Hawk reached the station, and purchased a
ticket; but, as usual, the ticket did not indicate his
destination—it read, not to Conmore, but to several
stations farther along the line. The local pulled in
on time. As it pulled out again, the Hawk, having
appropriated the rear seat of the smoker, lighted,
though he inclined little toward that particular form
of tobacco, a cigar.

His slouch hat was jerked a little forward over his
eyes. He settled back in his seat. Like links in a
chain, the keen, alert brain was welding the events
of the days gone by into a concrete whole. The
headquarters of the gang, the heart of the web from
which the Wire Devils operated was, logically, as
he had known, as MacVightie had known, *outside*
the city, where the telegraph line could be tapped
without observation and at will. MacVightie's initial and only attempt to "ground out" the "tap" had
indicated that the wire was being tampered with
between Selkirk and Bald Creek. Conmore was between Selkirk and Bald Creek. And what interest
could Kirschell, a New York crook, have in a place
like Conmore, that was little more than a hamlet?
What, then, had prompted Kirschell's trip to Conmore and return? The Hawk smiled whimsically.

It was not proof absolute, but in his own mind it was proof quite sufficient. Kirschell's visit to Conmore had been a visit to the headquarters of the gang. Also, material proof apart, he sensed intuitively that he had struck the right trail. Those messages, keeping the unknown brain that schemed and plotted each move in instant touch with every unit of the widespread organisation, making it possible for them to strike at a moment's warning at any point over a hundred miles of country, emanated—from Conmore.

The train stopped at a station, and went on again. The Hawk nursed his cigar sedulously, and stared out of the window. Twenty minutes went by. And then the train stopped again—at Conmore.

The Hawk did not move, save that his eyes rested casually on a passenger who was making a hurried and belated dash for the door. It was quite possible that the man was not one of the gang, and equally possible that the man was—he, the Hawk, did not recognise the other. But he would do the Wire Devils less than justice to credit them with lack of interest in passengers for Conmore—or in any occupant of any car who might have left his seat and found the platform attractive, say, just *before* Conmore was reached! If the man was a spy, then—well—the Hawk smiled at his now burned-to-the-butt cigar—the man would have little to report!

The train jerked forward into motion again. The station was on the same side as the Hawk's seat— the Hawk did not look out of the window, but he

was far from being oblivious to the fact that *no*
platform lights had shown through the car windows on the opposite side of the aisle. The speed
increased a little, but still the Hawk did not stir.
The train rattled over the east-end siding switch of
the Conmore yard. And then the Hawk rose lan-
guidly, tossed his cigar butt into the cuspidor,
brushed a very noticeable quantity of cigar ash from
his vest, paused for a drink at the water-cooler, and,
as though, his smoke finished, he was seeking the
clearer atmosphere of a rear car, opened the door,
and stepped out on the platform.

The Hawk dropped to the right of way from the
side of the train opposite to that of the station,
landed as sure-footed as a cat, flung himself instantly flat down at the edge of the embankment,
and lay still. The local racketed its way past—the
red tail-lights winked, and vanished—and there fell
a silence, a drowsy night silence, broken only by
the chirp of insects and the far-distant mutter of the
receding train. The Hawk raised his head, and
looked about him. A few hundred yards away glint-
ed the station semaphore and window lights; the siding switch light, nearer, showed green like a huge
glowing emerald in the black; there was nothing else.
There was no sign of habitation—nothing—the little hamlet lay hidden in a hollow a mile away on the
station side of the track.

— XV —

THE LADYBIRD

THE Hawk rose, and began to move forward. Conmore was certainly an idealistic spot—from the Wire Devils' standpoint! He frowned a little. There was no doubt in his mind but that in a general way he had solved the problem, that somewhere in this vicinity the right of way held the wire tappers' secret; but, as he was well aware, his difficulties were far from at an end, and that particular spot might be anywhere within several miles of Conmore, and it might, with equal reason, be east or west of the station. And then the Hawk shrugged his shoulders. The night was early yet, early enough to enable him to cover several miles of track on both sides of the station, if necessary, before daylight came. If he had luck with him, he was on the right side now; if not, then, by midnight, he would start in on the other. It required the exercise of a little philosophical patience, nothing more.

It was black along the track—a black night, no moon, no stars. And it was silent. A half hour passed. Like a shadow, and as silent as one, the Hawk moved forward—from telegraph pole to telegraph pole. A pin point of light showed far down the right of way, grew larger, brighter, more luminous—and the Hawk sought refuge, crouched beneath a culvert, as a big ten-wheeler and its string of coaches, trucks beating at the fishplates, quick like the tattoo of a snare drum, roared by over his head.

Still another half hour passed. It was slow work. He was perhaps, at most, a mile and a half from the Conmore station. And then, suddenly, the Hawk dropped to his hands and knees and crawled down the embankment, and lay flat and motionless in the grass—faint, almost inaudible, a footstep had crunched on the gravel of the roadbed ahead of him. The Hawk's only movement now was the tightening of his fingers around the stock of his automatic, as, out of the blackness, a blacker shape loomed up, and a man sauntered by along the track.

The Hawk's lips compressed into a grim smile. His caution had not been exaggerated! The Wire Devils' guard! Luck, at least initial luck, was with him, then! The "tap" was here *east* of the station, and at the next pole probably. But it was more than likely that there was another guard patrolling on the other side. They would certainly take no chances, either of surprise, or of being unable to dismantle their apparatus instantly at the first alarm—and it would almost necessarily require more than one man for that. He crept forward again, and again lay still. The man on the track returned—passed by— and, close to the telegraph pole now, two blurred shapes showed; and then, low, there came voices, and a laugh.

But now the Hawk was wriggling swiftly *away* from the track. There was no longer any need to examine the telegraph poles—the sense of touch guiding him, he was following an insulated wire, two wires, that lay along the ground, and, following these wires, he reached the barbed-wire fence that enclosed the right of way, worked his way through, and here paused. The wires had apparently disappeared abruptly into the ground.

For perhaps a minute the Hawk lay still, save that his fingers worked and dug at loose earth; and then, his coat extended on either side of him, he raised himself an inch or two from the ground, and, beneath his body, his tiny flashlight glowed for a brief instant, and was restored to his pocket.

The Hawk began to crawl forward again. He was on the edge of a ploughed field—a piece of farm land. It was all very simple, and it was very clear now. In the loose earth there was embedded a small, rough, wooden box. In this receptacle was a junction box, and from the junction box, through holes bored in the outer wooden casing, the wires continued on into a small, flexible conduit. The Hawk smiled grimly. Lanson, and Lanson's section men might search a thousand years and never solve the problem. The Wire Devils were not limited to any one single or particular telegraph pole. They were limited only in the radius of their operations by the length of the "tap" wires they used. They had only

to tap the line, run their "tap" back, brush the loose
earth away from the top of the wooden casing, open
the latter, connect with the junction box, and their
"tap" became an integral part of the railroad's telegraph system. It was very simple! When they were
not operating—they reversed the process. They dis-
connected from the main line, coiled their "tap"
wires up, hid them in the wooden casing, restored the
loose earth over the latter's surface, and, save for
one of those thousands of splices on the main line
incident to years of service and differing in no way
from any of its fellows, no sign or vestige of their
work remained. It required, of course, a lineman's
outfit and the necessary appliances for work at the
top of the telegraph pole—but that the Wire Devils
were adequately equipped in this respect was so
obvious as to make any consideration of that detail
absurd. For the rest, the little conduit laid in a
ploughed furrow with the earth spread back over it
completed in perfection and simplicity the unholy
little scheme!

On the Hawk crawled across the field. All this
premised a house, a farm house probably, in the immediate vicinity. The ploughed field must, of course,
never be disturbed, therefore the tenancy of the
land axiomatically was for the moment vested in the
Wire Devils, and——ah! The Hawk, far enough
from the railroad now to be secure from observation,
had risen from his hands and knees, and, in a
crouched position, was moving forward more rapidly. A small, wooded tract of land was showing

a little way in front of him; the house undoubtedly was there.

He gained the trees, made his way through what appeared to be an open grove of pines, and, on the other side, at the edge of the clearing, halted, and listened intently. He could just make out a little group of buildings—the house itself, a barn, and one or two smaller structures, probably wagon and implement sheds. No light showed from anywhere, nor was there any sound. Cautiously, silently, the Hawk crossed the clearing, and began to circuit the house. It was a little strange! The place seemed absolutely deserted. Had he made a mistake? Naturally, he could not follow the direction of the buried conduit! Was there another house in the neighbourhood? He shook his head. There might be another house, many of them for that matter, but the ploughed field, from its location, surely belonged to this one. And yet—he halted once more, and, listening again intently, looked sharply about him.

He was around on the other side of the house now, and now his eyes were fixed on one of the lower windows. It was not the window of a lighted room, yet still a faint glow seemed to emanate most curiously from it. He crept toward it, crouched beneath it, listened again, then partially straightening up—the window sill was but breast high—peered in. Of the room itself he could see nothing—only the dull glow of light, extremely faint, that came, he now discovered, from an open door across the room. He tried the window; and then, finding the catch unfastened, with a deft pressure of his fingers upon the sash, he began to raise it slowly, silently.

And now into the Hawk's dark eyes there leaped for the second time that night a triumphant flash. Yes, beyond doubt, beyond question, beyond cavil, here was the heart of the spider's web at last! Muffled, low, indistinct, barely audible, but equally unmistakable, there came the clicking of a telegraph instrument.

The Hawk drew his mask from his pocket, slipped it over his face, swung noiselessly over the window sill, and began to creep across the room toward the opened door and the glow of light. And, as the clicking of the sounder grew more distinct and there mingled with it now a murmur of voices, the Hawk's lips compressed into a thin, straight line. If he were caught, if a single inadvertent sound betrayed his presence, it needed no effort of the imagination to picture what would follow. Death, if it were sudden, would be a very merciful ending—but it would not be death, if the Wire Devils could prevent it, until they had exhausted every means, torture ingenious and devilish, for instance, to extort from him the whereabouts of the plunder taken from them, and which they knew to be in his possession. He knew much now, he knew their lair at last, and for a moment, as these thoughts flashed across his mind, he was prompted to retreat again while he had the chance. An inner voice called him a fool to persist; another bade him go on. But the latter voice was right. He knew much—but he did not know enough.

If his life was in peril in the one sense, it was equally in peril in the other. He did not know *enough.* Who, for instance, was the master brain behind the organisation? Where and how, for instance, was the next trap they would set for him to be laid?

Brief snatches of conversation now began to reach the Hawk, as he drew nearer to the door:

". . . Twenty-five thousand dollars . . . Traders' National Bank . . . superintendent's car . . . dummy package . . . counterfeit seals . . . that's all right, but MacVightie says the Secret Service is sending a man by the name of Birks out here. . . ."

And then a voice at which the Hawk involuntarily held his breath, and to which, at the door now, he listened in a sort of stunned incredulity, as though he were indeed the sport of his own ears. It was a very quiet voice, very soft, a velvet voice, a voice whose tones were cultured tones—and whose language was the language of a pirate of the Spanish Main.

"Time enough to attend to this Birks personage— what I want is the Hawk!" came in limpid tones. "And if I were not tied down here in this damned and double-damned wheel chair, I would have twisted his throat for him long ago. I furnish brains— and I am cursed with a miserable, crawling mob of gnats upon whom they are wasted! That's it— gnats! Gnats—insects—moths—anything that, if shown the light, knows nothing but to singe its own wings!" The voice was not raised; it was like a mother's, like a woman's voice, talking plaintively to a spoiled child—but there was something absolutely deadly in its inflection.

"The Ladybird!" The Hawk's lips framed the words without sound, and in a sort of numbed hesitant way. "I—I thought he was dead."

The telegraph sounder kept on spluttering at intervals, but it was only stray stuff, routine railroad business, going over the wires. The Hawk, flat on the floor and at one side of the jamb now, stared through the doorway. It was the doorway leading to the cellar. The stairs, halfway down, turned abruptly at right angles. The Hawk was rewarded with a view of the stone foundation wall of the house, nothing more. But for the moment the Hawk was lost to his immediate surroundings. The Hawk's criminal acquaintanceship was wide, varied and intimate, and his mind was still not entirely recovered from the startled amazement which the recognition of that voice had brought him. He was quite fully conversant with the Ladybird's record—only he had thought the Ladybird dead!

The Ladybird was not an ordinary criminal; instead of having spent twenty years in Sing Sing, as was very justly his due, the police had spent those twenty years in trying to put him there—and the Ladybird was still to know the restrictions of a cage! Clever, fearless, cunning, Napoleonic in the scope and breadth of his operations, the biggest scoops on the blotters of the New York police, and, higher up, on the Federal records, were laid to the Ladybird's door; but always, somewhere, the thread

of evidence broke—sometimes not till the door itself was reached—but always it broke; the thread
had never crossed the threshold. The man himself
was highly educated, a man now well on toward fifty.
In the underworld there were a thousand different
stories of his early life—that he had been a professor of science in a great university; that he came
of a rich family high up in the social scale; that he
had been, in fact, everything that the spice of imagination could supply to enhance the glamour that surrounded him in the sordid empire of Crimeland,
where so many were his followers and worshippers.
But here, too, the thread was broken. None knew
who he had been; none knew where he had come
from. They knew him only as one who was invul-
nerable against the attacks and efforts of the police,
as a peer of their own unholy realm, as one whose
name was a name to conjure with—for in the name,
the "moniker" they themselves had given the Ladybird on account of his effeminate voice and manner,
derision was neither intended nor implied. There
were limits and bounds to even the underworld's
temerity, and none knew better than the underworld
the sinister incongruity of those effeminate charac-
teristics. Where another might bellow and roar his
rage, and threaten, the Ladybird lisped his words—
and *struck*.

But he, the Hawk, had thought the Ladybird
dead! The man had been badly hurt a year ago in
a railroad accident somewhere in the East, and the
report had spread, and had been credited even in

the inner circles of the underworld, that he was dead. The Hawk's lips twisted grimly. The Ladybird had seen to it evidently that the report was not denied! And so, instead, the man was a cripple now, weaving his plots, and scheming with that black, cunning brain of his from a wheel chair! Well, he——

The Hawk reached quickly into his pocket for pencil and paper—there would be just light enough to enable him to see. The sounder was rattling a brisk, tattoo, but it was no longer stray stuff. The message, in quick, sure "sending," was coming in the Wire Devils' secret code. Letter by letter the Hawk jotted it down:

"plkxtfbmezbyqetbqfslkgqmbokufecsrfijojeremb sthfgsbkbnfebvwqjduuvsfpqxwfsnlipbouflmnfsbg jeborrettjupujohllsppn."

The sounder ceased abruptly. There was silence. The Hawk replaced pencil and paper in his pocket. The minutes passed—the message was evidently being decoded. Then the Ladybird's voice:

"Very well! Code a message to Number One, and tell him Number Seven has completed his work. Tell him again to take no chances by hurrying things; that he is to wait until they are asleep. And warn him again that under no circumstances is our hand to show in this to-night."

A slight confusion followed from below—the scuffling of feet, the murmer of voices mingling with curious, indefinable metallic sounds. And then suddenly the Ladybird's voice again:

"No—never mind that message! Damn my cursed, useless legs!" A flow of unbridled oaths followed—the sacrilege the more horrible, the menace the more ghastly for the languid, conversational tones in which the blasphemy rolled so smoothly from the man's lips. "I'll trust to no message tonight! Curse my legs! If I could only get there myself! Failure! Failure! Failure! Gnats! But I will not have my plans ruined to-night by any fool! Here, you, Dixer! Where's Dixer?"

"I'm here," a voice answered.

"Listen, then!" murmured the Ladybird. "You haven't got any more brains than any of the rest of them, but you're so cautious you wouldn't take a chance on swapping a Mexican dollar for a gold eagle unless you had a bottle of acid in your pocket —for fear the eagle was bad! I want caution to-night, and I want orders obeyed to the letter, and that's all I want. You take the runabout and go down there. You've lots of time. Tell Number One you're in charge. I'll wire him to that effect. And now pay attention to me so you won't have ignorance for an excuse! It's time the police and the rags they call newspapers around here had a little something to divert their attention—from us. They're getting to be pests, and I want a lull in which to devote a little more attention to—the Hawk. It's about time they understood we are modest enough not to hog all the lime-light!" He laughed

a little, a low, modulated, dulcet laugh, that rippled
like a woman's—but in the ripple there was something that was akin to a shudder. "Twice in the
last month, the Traders' National has made remittances to its banking correspondent at Elkhead for
the mine country pay rolls and on account of general business. They did it very neatly, they fooled
us completely—because the remittances were only
piker amounts, and because it was only a question
of letting them get fed up enough with their own
cleverness to pull a good one! They're pulling a
good one to-night!" The Ladybird's laugh rippled
out again. "To outwit us, and paying us the com-
pliment of not daring to trust to ordinary means of
shipment, they've had a little arrangement in force
with Lanson, the division superintendent. It was
very simple. Lanson, in his car, making a trip over
the division, could never interest us—certainly not!
Why should it? Only they did not count on Number
Eleven *inside* the bank. Very well! They wrapped
their banknotes up in small packages, sealed them
with the bank's seal, wrapped these small packages
up again into an innocent looking parcel *without* a
seal, and handed it over to a trusted young employé
by the name of Meridan—Paul Meridan. On both
the former occasions, Meridan left the bank at the
usual closing hour, took the parcel with him, and
went home; but, later on, in the evening, he slipped
down to the railroad yard, boarded Lanson's private
car, locked the parcel up in a small cupboard at the
bottom of the bookcase with which the main com-

partment of the car is equipped, smoked a cigar with
Lanson, turned in, the car was coupled to the night
express, and in the morning Meridan delivered his
package in Elkhead.

"That was the way it was done before, Dixer"—
the Ladybird's voice, if anything, grew softer—"and
that's the way it is being done this time—only there
are *more* little sealed packages in the parcel to-night.
And to-night Meridan will sneak out of his home
again, and go down to the private car with the money
as usual. *Your* way, yours and the Butcher's, and
that of the rest of you, would be to lay a blackjack
over Meridan's head on the way to the railroad
yard, and snatch the parcel. It's not *my* way. It's
too hot, as it is, around here now, and there's got
to be a big enough noise made to attract attention to
the other side of the fence and give us a breathing
spell. *Paul Meridan stands for this to-night.*
There's nothing new about one of those ubiquitous
'trusted employés' going wrong, but everybody
sucks in their breaths just the same every time it happens, and the splash is always just as big. Understand? Number One has got a dummy package
identical in appearance with Meridan's—each of the
small packages is sealed with the bank's seal in dark-
green wax, and the whole is wrapped up with the
bank's special wrapping paper and tied precisely as
is the one Meridan has in his possession. Number
Eleven did his work well. There was, of course, no
opportunity to effect the exchange in the bank itself,
and the dummy parcel had to be made up outside,

but there was no difficulty in carrying away enough wrapping paper and wax for the purpose—and, as far as the seal was concerned, it was you, Dixer, who engraved it a week ago, wasn't it?"

"Yes," said Dixer. "You took me off the new twenty-spot plate for that."

"Exactly!" lisped the Ladybird. "Well, though this exchange could not be effected in the bank, there was no great ingenuity required to get Meridan to handle, perhaps only to lift, say, a pile of the bank's wrapping paper from one position on a table or desk to another. If the under sheet happened to be slightly smeared, and so left a not too evident, but still well-defined finger print, it was, I am afraid, our friend Meridan's great misfortune! That was one of the sheets Number Eleven took away with him. Very good! Meridan delivers his package to his bank's correspondent in Elkhead to-morrow morning. When the seals are broken, the little packages are found to contain—piles of blotting paper, neatly and carefully cut to the size of banknotes! There could be no reason for suspecting Meridan, the trusted employé—no one would think of such a thing. He had simply been the victim of a clever substitution. He was entirely blameless. Naturally! That would be the way Meridan would reason, and that would be the way they would figure *he had reasoned* when they read the letter from 'a friend' that we are sending to-night, and which they will receive in the morning. Meridan *did* have an ample opportunity to effect the substitution himself. The letter simply suggests a close inspection of the wrappers for finger prints, and directs attention to Apartment B, on the ground floor of The Linden—a rather fashionable abode for a young and newly married bank clerk—where there might possibly be found certain articles such as, say, a counterfeit of the bank's seal, a quantity of the bank's special dark-green wax, and some *superfluous* sheets of the bank's particular wrapping paper!"

There was utter silence from the cellar below for an instant, then there came a callous guffaw.

"*Some* plant, all right!" applauded a voice hoarsely. "And it was twenty-five thousand dollars, you said, wasn't it, chief?"

Again that rippling laugh, soft, low and silvery.

"Twenty-five thousand dollars is correct," corroborated the Ladybird. "And now, Dixer, if you fail, you'll talk to me—you've seen all the cards. Number One has a duplicate key to the private car, and a duplicate key to the bookcase cupboard. Don't enter the car until you are sure Meridan, Lanson and the porter are asleep. I want *caution*—and I will settle with the man until he will wish he had never been born who lets our hand show in this tonight. The car won't be moved from the siding until the Eastern Express is made up at midnight, but don't touch the car while it is on the siding at all if it means taking any chances; in that case you and Number One can get berths in the Pullman, and, with the private car right behind you, you can then make the exchange sometime during the night.

You'll find Number One and the rest of them in the old freight shed near the roundhouse, and——"

The Hawk was wriggling silently back across the floor. There was no scheme on foot to-night that was aimed at him; there was, instead, twenty-five thousand dollars—*in cash*. He gained the window, and swung to the sill. Footsteps, hurried, sounded from the direction of the cellar stairs. The Hawk dropped to the ground, stole noiselessly around the rear of the house, and reached the shelter of the grove of trees. Here, he paused, slipped his mask into his pocket, and, for a moment, a look of puzzled hesitation was in his face; then, running again, but making a wide detour to avoid the guarded section of the track, he headed for a point that would intercept the right of way quite close to the Conmore station. And, as he ran, he jerked his watch and flashlight from his pockets. It was a quarter past nine. It was early yet, very early, and they certainly would not make any attempt on the car much before midnight, but, for all that, the Hawk, who was intimately conversant with the train schedules, shook his head impatiently, as he sped along—there were twenty miles between himself and Selkirk, and the quickest, as indeed the only way to get there, since, unlike Dixer, he was not possessed of a runabout, was slow at best. There were no westbound passenger trains scheduling Conmore for two hours or more, and he would scarcely have dared to risk boarding one at the station if there had been—there remained, then, not by choice, but by necessity, the way freight. The way freight "made" Conmore at about ten o'clock, and Selkirk at about eleven-thirty. It would serve admirably, of course, if—— He shook his head again, and then laughed shortly. There were no "ifs"—he would be a passenger on the way freight.

AN EVEN BREAK

IT took the Hawk some twenty-five minutes to reach the spot he had selected as his objective, a spot some fifty yards east of the Conmore siding switch, and here he lay down in the grass under the shelter of the embankment. It was very quiet, very still, very dark; there was nothing in sight save the winking station lights in the distance, and the siding switch light nearer at hand.

"Twenty-five thousand dollars!" said the Hawk very softly to himself. He rolled the words like some sweet morsel on his tongue. "Twenty-five thousand dollars—*in cash!*"

The Hawk spread out one side of his coat, and under its protection, in a diminutive but steady little glow of light, the tiny flashlight played its ray upon the sheet of paper across which he had scrawled the Wire Devils' code message.

"Key letter—x. One-two-three—stroke at four," muttered the Hawk—and in parallel columns set down the letters of the alphabet, one column transposed.

It took the Hawk much longer to decode the message than it had taken those in the house to perform the same task. The Hawk was working under difficulties. A stone, none too flat, served to rest his paper upon, and he had only two hands with which to manipulate pencil, flashlight and coat. At the expiration of perhaps half an hour the result of his work looked like this:

```
(plkx) tfbm (e) zbyq (et) bqfs (lkg) qmbo
          seal      waxp      aper       plan
(k) ufec (sr) fijo (jer) embs (t) hfgs (bk)
       tedb      ehin      dlar      gefr
bnfe (bvw) qjdu (u) vsfp (qn) wfsn (ljp) bouf
amed       pict      ureo      verm      ante
(l) mnfs (bg) jebo (rre) ttju (p) ujoh (ll)
     lmer      idan      ssit      ting
sppn
room
```

And then the Hawk looked up—the throb and mutter of a distant train was in the air. Pencil, paper and flashlight were restored to his pockets, and he drew further back from the right of way. Far down the track the way freight's headlight flashed into view. A minute passed, another, and still another. And now, where the Hawk had lain, the ground was ablaze with light—then black again; there was the roar of steam, a grind and clash and shatter ricochetting down the string of cars, the scream and shriek of brake-shoes, and then, a panting thing, as though the big mogul were drawing in deep breaths after great exertion, the way freight

came to a standstill a few yards from the siding
switch.

The Hawk crept forward, his eyes sweeping down
the length of the train in a keen, tense gaze.   There
was a flat car—it showed in a curious open space, like
a break in the black thread stretched along the
track—but it was too far away, and too perilously
close to the caboose.   His eyes travelled back; and,
being nearer to the train now he discerned a boxcar, empty, its door open, almost in front of him.
He crawled forward until he was abreast of it, and
until he lay close up against the rails, looked cautiously up and down the length of the train, sprang
to his feet, and in an instant lay stretched out far
back in the interior of the car.

The train moved forward, stopped again at the
station, and again moved forward.   The Hawk reverted to his pencil, paper and flashlight.   The code
message now read:

> seal waxp aper plan tedb ehin dlar gefr amed
> pict ureo verm ante lmer .idan ssit ting room

It was now simply a matter of grouping the letters properly, and the Hawk wrote out the message
at the bottom of the sheet:

> Seal, wax (and) paper planted behind large
> framed picture over mantel Meridan(')s sitting
> room.

The Hawk stared at it grimly.

"Yes," said the Hawk, "I guess that's right!   I

guess the job is wished on the young fellow to a finish; he wouldn't have a hope, and MacVightie would never look any further." The Hawk was silent for a moment. "Twenty-five thousand dollars—in cash!" murmured the Hawk again.

The way freight ran slowly, very slowly—and it had already been from ten to fifteen minutes late in reaching Conmore. At the next station the train crew seemed possessed of a perversity infernal for shifting, shunting and lifting cars. The Hawk, fuming with impatience, consulted his watch, as they finally pulled out into the clear again. It was twenty-five minutes of eleven.

The train rattled, bumped and jerked its way along—and at the remaining intermediate stations there was more delay. And when, approaching Selkirk at last, the Hawk consulted his watch again as the train whistled, he was conscious that his impatience was tempered with a sort of sullen, philosophical expectation of defeat. His luck had been too abundant during the early part of the evening! It was now ten minutes of twelve. He leaned out of the doorway, peering ahead. They were just rolling into the Selkirk yard.

The Hawk swung himself out from the car, dropped to the ground, darted quickly to one side over several spur tracks, and stood still. The way freight, like a snail, dragged past him, opening, as it were, a panorama of the scene in the yard: the low switch lights, red, green, purple and white, like myriad and variegated fireflies hovering everywhere over the ground; the bobbing lantern of a yardman here and there; the dancing gleam of a headlight, as the little yard engine shot fussily away from a string of lighted coaches—the Eastern Express—which it had evidently just made up and backed down on the main line beside the station; while to his right, up the yard, on one of the spurs, perhaps a hundred yards away, its platform showing in the glow of the dome light, stood the superintendent's car; and to his left, not quite so far up the yard, and therefore nearer to him than the private car, the Hawk could make out the black, irregular outline of the old freight shed.

The yard engine wheezed its way importantly up past the station, stopped, a switch light winked, changed colour, and the shunter began to puff its way back. The Hawk shrugged his shoulders resignedly. The game was up and he was too late, unless Dixer had been forced to defer his attempt until some time during the run that night, which was hardly likely. The yard engine was backing down now to take the superintendent's car up to the main line, preparatory to running it back and coupling it to the string of coaches beside the station platform. The Hawk smiled in the darkness without mirth, as he lost sight of the little switcher on the other side of the private car. Well, at least, he could gamble on the one chance that was left! There was only one thing to do—go over to the station and get a Pullman berth. If Dixer and the Butcher—the Butcher was "Number One"—were on the Pullman, the money was still in the private car, and——

The Hawk's eyes narrowed suddenly. A man, crouched and running swiftly, circled the end of the private car, and headed in the direction of the freight shed—and like a flash the Hawk whirled and leaped forward, running silently toward the same goal. The Hawk's brain, stimulated, keen, alert, worked with lightning speed, and suddenly a strange low laugh was on his lips. Their courses were convergent, his and that black running shape's, and the other had not noticed him, and there appeared to be something, a package, under the other's arm. The Hawk, as he ran, slipped his mask over his face. Was it the dummy package—or the twenty-five thousand in cash? Had the man succeeded, or had the yard engine, backing down to couple on, disturbed him in his attempt just at the psychological instant? Again that strange low laugh, in a panting breath, was on the Hawk's lips. It did not matter! There was a way now. He was not too late. If he got *both* of the packages he could not lose—and there was a way to accomplish that, a wild, dare-devil way, but a *sure* way!

It was black, pitch black, in near the shed, and the Hawk, with the shorter distance to cover, reached the edge of the freight shed platform, and crouched down on the track. Came the faint crash and bump of the yard engine coupling to the private car; then the short, quick gasps of a runner out of breath, and a flying form bounded across the tracks, sprang to the platform, and dashed for the freight shed door—and the Hawk, his muscles, rigid, taut as steel, released suddenly, as a coiled spring is released, leaped and hurled himself upon the other.

There was a yell of dismay, of surprise and fury, that seemed to echo from one end of the yard to the other. The man went down in a heap from the impact. The package, from under his arm, rolled off along the platform—and the Hawk in a swoop was upon it. He snatched it up, and running like a deer now, headed for the yard engine and the private car.

Came another yell from behind him. He heard the freight shed door flung violently open; and then, in grim emphasis of a sudden chorus of wild, infuriated shouts from Dixer's waiting companions, the vicious tongue flame of a revolver split the black, and the roar of the report reverberated through the yard like a cannon shot.

And now from the yard itself, the roundhouse and the station came answering shouts. On the Hawk ran—he was alongside the private car now, which was already in motion—and now he was opposite the cab of the yard engine. The fireman, at the sudden pandemonium, head thrust out, was hanging in the gangway. The Hawk's automatic swung to a line with the other's head.

"Get out!" gritted the Hawk coldly. "Both of you—you and your mate! Get out—*on the other side!*"

The man, with a dazed oath, retreated, and the Hawk sprang through the gangway. The engineer, jumping from his seat, hesitated, and in the yellow

light of the cab lamp looked for the fraction of a
second into the muzzle of the Hawk's automatic, and
into the hard, uncompromising black eyes behind the
mask—and followed the fireman in a hasty exit
through the opposite gangway.

The Hawk snatched at the throttle, pulled it
wider—and, like a beast stung to sudden madness
under the spur, the yard engine quivered, and in a
storm of exhausts, coughing the red sparks skyward
from the stack, the drivers racing, spitting fire as
they sought to bite and hold the steel, plunged forward. Ahead the way was clear to the main line,
but behind—— The Hawk dropped his package on
the floor of the cab, leaned suddenly far out through
the gangway, and as suddenly fired, his automatic
cutting a lane of flame through the darkness. He
had fired at the ground, but his shot had been ef-
fective. The engineer or the fireman, he could not
distinguish which, leaping to board the private car
by the rear platform, leaped back instead, and with
a series of wild gesticulations, in which arms and
fists waved furiously, vanished in the darkness.

The yard engine, as though playing snap-the-whip
with the private car behind it, took the main line
switch with a stagger and a lurch, and straightened
away into the clear. There was speed now, and the
speed was increasing with every second. The
shouts, the yells, the cries, the pandemonium from
the yard was blotted out in the pound of the drivers
and the belch of the exhaust; and the station and
switch lights were lost to sight as engine and car

flew on, heading west into the foothills. The Hawk chuckled to himself. There would be wild confusion in the dispatcher's office, and wild confusion all along the line west of Selkirk, as regulars, extras and traffic of all sorts scurried for safety to the sidings—but there would be no interference with *him!* Where they would otherwise have ditched him, given him an open switch at the first station and sent him to destruction without compunction, he possessed, as it was, a most satisfactory hostage in the person of the division superintendent, whom they would hesitate about sending to eternity at the same time!

Possibly a minute and a half, two at the outside, had passed since he had jumped through the gangway. He eased the throttle a little now, reducing the speed to a rate more nearly commensurate with safety; and, placing the package on the driver's seat, ripped off the outside wrapper. There was a queer, hard smile on the Hawk's lips, as his fingers tore at the covering of one of the small sealed packets within. Was it the dummy parcel—or the twenty-five thousand in cash? Had Dixer succeeded—or was the money still behind him there in the private car?

The cab lamp above the dancing gauge needles seemed to throw its meagre yellow glow with strained inquisitiveness over the Hawk's shoulder—and then the Hawk laughed softly, and laughed again. In his hands were banknotes. He riffled the stack through his fingers. It was here, in his possession—*twenty-five thousand dollars in cash!*

And he laughed again, and glanced around him—

through the cab glass at the white ribbons of steel glistening under the headlight's glare, around the murky cab that in its sway and jolt seemed to endow a legion of shadows with movement, vitality and life, at the platform of the private car, which he could see by looking along the edge of the tender, and which, like its fellow at the rear, was bathed in the soft radiance of a dome light. Well, he might have known from the fact that the occupants of the car had not made any move as yet, at least from the forward end, that they had been in bed and asleep when the disturbance began; and he might, on that count, if he had stopped to think, have known that Dixer had succeeded even before he, the Hawk, had put it to the proof by opening the parcel.

A lurch of the cab sent him against the seat, and scattered the sealed packages. He gathered them together again hurriedly. He had only to slow down the engine a little more, jump to the ground, let the engine and car go on, make his own way back through the fields, and he would be safe unless —that strange, queer smile, half grim, half whimsical, was flickering across his lips—unless he cared to risk his life for that dummy package back there in the car behind, that contained nothing more valuable than neatly trimmed pieces of blotting paper!

The smile lost its whimsicality, and the grimness gathered until his lips drooped in sharp, hard lines at the corners of his mouth—and, abruptly, lifting up the seat, he swept the packages of banknotes into the engineer's box, leaped across the cab, and began to claw his way up over the coal, making for the back of the tender.

"Twenty-five thousand in cash for me, and twenty years in the 'pen' for the kid, doesn't look like an even break," muttered the Hawk, as he clawed his way up. "Maybe I'm a fool—I guess maybe I am—but it doesn't look like an even break. You see," said the Hawk, continuing to commune with himself, "they'll know, of course, that some one who wasn't Meridan tried to get the package, but with the package still there they'll think that the 'some one' made a bull of it, and to-morrow morning when they open the package and spot the finger prints, and get that bank seal in Meridan's home, they'll hold him for it cold, because what's happened around here to-night'll only look like somebody making a try for the goods without knowing they were already gone. The kid wouldn't have a hope—the Ladybird wasn't dealing any aces except to himself—the kid would go up for having *previously* stolen the goods on his own account. Yes, I guess he would—wax, seal and paper in his house to make dummy packages with—yes, I guess the kid would stand a hot chance!"

The Hawk rose to his feet at the rear of the tender, preparing to negotiate a leap down over the ornamental brass platform railing of the private car—and instantly flung himself back flat on his face on the coal. The car door was flung open, and Lanson, the superintendent, in pajamas, a revolver in his hand, stepped out on the platform. He was closely followed by a young man—Meridan, the bank clerk, obviously—also in pajamas, but apparently unarmed; and, behind Meridan again, came the negro porter.

Lanson's voice, raised excitedly, carried to the Hawk:

"Damn it, there's no one in the cab! What the devil sort of a game is this!"

The Hawk edged up to the top of the coal again —and the next instant, with catlike agility, he launched himself forward. Lanson, clambering over the platform railing, with the very evident intention of making his way via the tender to the throttle, gasped audibly over the racket of the beating trucks, and in a sort of stunned surprise and irresolution remained poised inertly on the railing, as the Hawk, clinging now with one hand to the rear handrail of the switcher, his feet planted on the buffer beam, thrust the muzzle of his automatic into Lanson's face.

"Drop that gun!" invited the Hawk in a monotone.

The weapon, from Lanson's hand, clattered down, struck the coupling, and dropped to the track.

The Hawk spoke again—with unpleasant curtness:

"You—Sambo! Move back, and stand in the doorway! Yes—there! Now, you, young man, you stand in front of Sambo—your back to him!" And then, as Meridan too obeyed, though more slowly than the porter and with a sort of defiant reluctance, the Hawk addressed the superintendent: "Now, you—your name's Lanson, isn't it?" he snapped. "You, Lanson, back up against the young fellow. Yes—that's it! Sambo, put your hands on the young fellow's shoulders—and you, young fellow, do the same on Lanson's!" The Hawk swung over to the car platform—and then the Hawk smiled uninvitingly. "It's the lock-step backwards," he explained insolently. "You get the idea, don't you? If either of you two behind lift your hands, Lanson in front here pays for it. Now—back with you!"

They shuffled backward into the observation compartment of the car, through this, and through a narrow side corridor, and emerged into the main compartment of the car. The Hawk, guiding their movements by the simple expedient of prodding the muzzle of his automatic none too gently into Lanson's body, here ranged the three along the side of the car; and, backing over to the opposite side himself, halted in front of the bookcase, and stood surveying his captives with his former insolent stare. The porter was patently reduced to a state of nervous terror; Meridan, young, clean-cut, was white to the lips, and his lips quivered, but his eyes, a hard, bitter light in them, never left the Hawk's face; Lanson, too, was white, but there was a stern composure in his face that was absent from the younger man's.

It was Lanson who spoke.

"I presume," he said evenly, "that you are the

abandoned scoundrel, known as the Hawk, whom one of these days we are going—*to hang."*

The Hawk shrugged his shoulders.

"I haven't a calling card with me, but we'll let it go at that," he answered flippantly.

The car swayed and lurched suddenly; the trucks beat a louder tattoo as they clattered over a switch; lights, a row of them from without, scintillated through the car windows—and were gone. They were not running perilously fast, but fast enough to prohibit the possibility of any one, even an acrobatic brakeman from a stalled train, swinging aboard. The Hawk laughed low. Also, he had been quite right—they had just passed a station, and, thanks to the superintendent's presence, no attempt had been made to interfere with the train.

From one of the Hawk's pockets—with his left hand—the Hawk produced a small steel jimmy. He knelt down, and, still covering the three men, inserted the jimmy in between the cupboard doors. There was a creak, the rip and split and tear of rending wood and lock, and the doors flew apart. The Hawk reached in, laughed again, as, with the dummy package under his arm, he stood up and began to back away toward the corridor leading to the forward end of the car—and the laugh died on his lips. In the winking of an eye Meridan had swung his hands from Lanson's shoulders, and was springing forward.

"You'll never get it!" The boy's voice was a hoarse whisper. "Not while I——"

"Keep away, you fool!" snarled the Hawk, and fired—at the floor. His brain seemed instantly in a riot of ironical mockery. He could not fire at the boy—it was the boy who had brought him here— and now the other was upon him—like a wild cat— snatching at the automatic.

It was only another step backward to the opening of the corridor, and the Hawk gained it; but still the boy clung on, fighting furiously. He saw Lanson and the porter leap forward, but for the moment that mattered little—no more than one at a time could get at him in the confined and narrow space here. To hold the package rendered his left arm useless. He dropped the package to the floor, and kicked it deftly back behind him, as the boy, with both hands, wrenched and battled madly for posses- sion of the automatic.

They were swaying now, the two of them, bump- ing their shoulders and their arms and elbows against first one side of the corridor and then the other. There was the crash of splintering glass as they lunged into a window—another crash, louder, more ominous, and with it a tongue of flame, as the auto- matic went off in their hands—and something like a red-hot iron seared the Hawk's side, and a blur came before his eyes.

He reeled, recovered himself, and, massing all his strength for the effort, as, with a cry of triumph, Meridan closed again, he tore himself free from the other's grasp. There was one way—he was still in possession of the automatic—only one way now.

With a lightning swing he whipped the butt of the weapon to the other's head, backed rapidly away as the boy slid a limp thing to the floor, and, picking up the package as he moved backward, holding the narrow corridor with his automatic, though Lanson was kneeling now at Meridan's side, he reached the observation compartment, whirled, ran for the door, opened it, and stepped out on the platform.

He stood panting here, a little dizzy, a sort of nauseating weakness upon him, as he fumbled in his pocket. He was not as quick as usual in his work, not as expert now in the use of his skeleton keys, but, swiftly for all that, he locked the car door.

The car and the engine seemed to sway and lurch and pitch and toss as they had never done before. Was the speed greater? What was it? He stumbled and nearly fell as he climbed to the tender. He fell, unable to maintain his footing in the shifting coal, as he reached the cab. There was something hot and wet that seemed to be working its way down his leg; his side was giving him intolerable pain.

He looked at the package in his hands, looked at it queerly for a moment, and then his drawn lips parted in the old whimsical smile, as he lurched forward and opened the fire-box door. The red glow filled the cab and spread upward, tinging the sky with a rosy light—and the Hawk thrust the package into the fire, and, swaying unsteadily, watched it burst into flame.

He glanced at the gauge now. The steam was

dropping rapidly. He swept his hand across his eyes. He had two things to do, and it seemed as though his brain clogged in its decision as to which he should do first—he had to get more coal on the fire, or else the engine would run down, and he did not want it to run down, for it must keep on going a long way, a very long way if possible, after he left it; and he must stop the flow of blood from his wound somehow, or else——

He put coal into the fire-box. It was painful, dizzy work, and he spilled a great deal of it, and the lumps rolled over the floor of the cab, and he stumbled over the lumps.

The Hawk's teeth were biting into his bloodless lips, as he finally shut the fire-box door, and, staggering to the side of the cab, lifted up the engineer's seat again. Here, under the packages of banknotes, he found a bunch of waste and some cord; and then, reeling with the lurch of the cab, reeling with his own weakness that only an iron nerve held back from mastering him, he examined his wound, found it, though painful and bleeding profusely, to be only a bad flesh wound, and, making a thick pad of the waste, he laid it against his side, and bound it there by passing the cord tightly several times around his body. It was a crude bandage, but it should, at least, check the flow of blood—afterwards, if he had luck, there would be opportunity for a better one!

His mind reverted, seemingly without volition of his, to the fight in the car, and he spoke aloud.

"I guess," said the Hawk, "I didn't hit him as hard as twenty years in the 'pen' would have hit him—I guess I didn't hit him that hard."

He rested for a moment, sitting on the floor of the cab; then from the engineer's box he removed the sealed packages, the torn outside wrapper, and likewise an evening newspaper which he found there. He wrapped up the banknotes in the newspaper, tied the bundle securely with the remainder of his cord, replaced the seat, and, crouched low enough on the floor to be protected by the tender from, say, a shot fired through the observation window of the private car, kept his eyes fastened on the right of way ahead.

The next station must be close at hand, and there was but one way in which he could get back to Selkirk—and he *must* get back. There was that letter —the Ladybird's letter—that would be received in Elkhead in the morning! His brain was clearer now. He must be on Extra No. 92, the eastbound fast freight's, running time, and she must be somewhere very near here, must have taken to the siding at the next station probably to avoid him, and to give clearance to what was, undoubtedly now, coming behind him—a detective's special, with MacVightie, naturally, in command.

He straightened up painfully. Ahead, he had caught the glint of switch and station lights. The siding was on the left-hand side. He moved to the left-hand side of the cab, and lay on the cab floor by the gangway. That letter! It seemed to obsess him now. If, when the letter was read, the bank seal, the wax, and the wrapping paper were *found* hidden in the boy's home, the fact that some one—he, the Hawk—had stolen the package from the car in no way changed anything. The boy's apparent prior guilt was as glaring as ever. On the other hand, with the package gone, and if the seal and those other things were *not* found, the letter became simply the expression of some practical joker's perverted sense of humour, or the irresponsible work of some fool or crank. He frowned in a sort of dazed irritation. He had known that all along, hadn't he? He had known when he started after that dummy package in the first place that he would have to go *all* the way—so why was his mind dwelling now on useless repetitions!

The Hawk raised his head slightly—a deafening racket was in his ears. The freight was here—on the siding. He was roaring past it now. He could not hope for an open boxcar on the fast freight. His eyes were searching eagerly for a flat car—a flat car loaded with anything that would afford him shelter. Yes—there was one—two of them—loaded with steel girders.

The roar subsided; he was past the station and into the clear again—and now the Hawk was at the throttle, easing the speed craftily. He did not dare to "shut off" entirely, for, behind there at the station, they would know, if the sound of the exhaust ceased, that he had stopped. He checked a little with the "air" now. And now, calculating the speed reduced enough to risk a jump, he opened the throttle to its former notch, took up his newspaper package, lowered himself to the bottom gangway step, and swung off.

He rolled down the embankment. The switcher and private car went by, and, gradually gaining speed again, racketed on up the right of way. With a groan, the Hawk readjusted his displaced and makeshift bandage, and began to make his way back toward the station. If he had slowed enough to allow of a safe landing for himself, he had, of course, given Lanson the same opportunity—but he had no fear of that. Lanson might have jumped, but Meridan, whom he had left unconscious, *couldn't,* and Lanson would stick to Meridan. As for the porter —the Hawk shrugged his shoulders, as he looked about him—the porter had *not* jumped.

He stumbled on. If he were right, if they had started a posse on a special in pursuit, he had plenty of time. The fast freight could not pull out until the special had gone by. It seemed a long way, an interminable way, an immeasurably greater distance than he had covered coming up on the switcher. And then, at last, the tail-lights of the stalled freight came into sight around a bend, and grew brighter. And then, too, there came from the eastward the rumble of an approaching train. He grew cautious now, and, creeping far out from the side of the track, passed the caboose, crept in again toward the line of cars, located the position of the flat cars, climbed aboard one of them, and crawled in under the shored-up girders.

The Hawk lay very quiet. He was weak again, and his head swam, and he was dizzy. An engine and car—MacVightie and his posse presumably—passed by on the main line; and then, presently, the freight, with a clatter and bang echoing from one to another down the length of cars, drew out of the station.

When the Hawk moved again, it was as the train whistled and slowed for the Selkirk yard. Perhaps twenty minutes had passed—the fast freight, with no stops and already late, had made time. He put his mask in his pocket, wormed his way out from under the girders, and peered ahead and behind. They were just crawling into the upper end of the yard. He slid to the ground, found himself a little more steady on his feet, slipped across the spur tracks, dodged in between two buildings that flanked the side of the yard, and came out on the street.

Under a street lamp the Hawk looked at his watch. It was one o'clock. He swayed a little again, but his lips set hard. There was not very much time. Somewhere up the line the switcher and the private car would come to a stop, and they would bring Meridan home—and once that happened, with its consequent stir in Meridan's apartment, it would be impossible to get in there, and the game, as far as the boy was concerned, would be up.

"Yes," said the Hawk, as he forced himself along

the street, "I guess maybe that's right—I guess maybe I'm a fool—but it wasn't an even break."

A street car at the next corner took him across
town; and fifteen minutes more found him standing
in the unlighted vestibule of the Linden Apart-
ments. The tiny flashlight swept the ground floor
apartment doors—and an instant later the door of
Apartment B yielded noiselessly to the deft manipu-
lation of a skeleton key.

The Hawk closed the door, and stole forward.
It was a rather fashionable apartment, as the Ladybird had said, but it was also a very small one, small
enough to warrant the presumption that the young
couple did not keep a servant, and that there would
probably be no one there except Meridan's wife.
A door at his right, as he felt out in the darkness,
he found to be open. He listened—for the sound
of breathing. There was nothing. The flashlight
winked—and the Hawk stepped forward into the
room. It was the sitting room. The flashlight was
sweeping about now in an inquisitive little ray. A
door, closed, leading to an inner room, was on his
right; facing him was a heavily portièred window,
the portières drawn; and a little to the left of the
window was the mantel.

The flashlight's ray wavered suddenly, unsteadily
—and the Hawk caught at the nearest thing to him,
the table in the centre of the room, for support, a
sense of disaster upon him, a realisation that, lashed
on as it might be by force of will, there was a limit
to physical endurance, and that the limit had well-

nigh been reached. His hand brushed across his eyes, and brushed across them again to clear his sight, as he tried to follow the flashlight's ray to where it played jerkily on a massively framed picture over the mantel. He bit his lips now, bit them until they bled—and moved forward—and laid his parcel of banknotes on the floor that he might have the use of both hands—and climbed upon a chair, and felt in behind the picture. Yes—it was there! His fingers closed on a roll of paper, twitched and shook a little as they pulled it out—and a small package from inside the roll fell with a slight thud to the mantel, and from the mantel bounded off to the floor.

The Hawk caught his breath, as he listened, and descended from the chair.

"Clumsy fool!" he gritted fiercely, as he knelt on the floor. "I—I guess I'm pretty near the count to do a thing like that."

The flashlight came into play again, and disclosed a metal seal and several pieces of dark-green wax peeping through the paper wrapper that had been split apart in the fall. He picked them up, and put them in his pocket; then, loosening his vest, he tucked the roll of wrapping paper inside his shirt. Well, it was done now; he had only to get back to his room, and there was surely strength enough left for that. Again his hand swept across his eyes, and pressed hard against his temples—and then, stooping swiftly, he clutched at his package of banknotes on the floor beside him, and stood up, rigid and tense.

Out of the darkness, almost at his elbow, with a startling clamour that clashed and shattered through the silence, and seemed to set a thousand echoes reverberating through the room, came the ringing of the telephone.

Some one in the inner room stirred. The Hawk drew back hurriedly into the window recess behind the portières. The telephone rang again. There came a step now, and now the room was flooded with light, and a woman, a dressing gown flung hastily over her shoulders, crossed from the inner doorway to the table, and picked up the instrument.

"Yes? . . . Hello! . . . What is it?" she asked, a little sleepily. "Yes, this is Mrs. Meridan . . . *What!* . . . My husband!" Her voice rang out in sudden terror. "What did you say?" she cried frantically. "Yes, yes—the Hawk—my husband—unconscious . . . You are not telling me all the truth—you are trying to keep the worst from me—for God's sake tell me the truth! . . . Not dangerous? . . . You are sure—you are *sure?* . . . Yes, yes, I understand! . . . At the station in half an hour . . . I will be there."

Mechanically she hung the receiver on the hook, and clung for a moment to the table's edge, her face grey and bloodless; and then her lips moved, and one hand clenched until the tight-drawn skin across the knuckles was an ivory white.

"I pray God they get this Hawk!" she whispered. "I pray God they do! And I pray God they *kill* him! The coward! The miserable, pitiful coward!"

The Hawk's fingers were digging at the window sill, because somehow his knees were refusing to support his weight. What was she saying? He did not quite understand. Well, it did not matter, she was gone now into that other room—only she had left the light on. It was very strange the way his hand on the window sill seemed to keep pulling his body around in circles!

Time had lost concrete significance to the Hawk. She appeared again, fully dressed now, and, switching off the light, went out into the hall, and the front door closed behind her.

The Hawk parted the portières, and staggered across the room—and, a moment later, a dark form, a newspaper parcel clutched under its arm, emerged stealthily from the vestibule, and, reeling like a drunken man, disappeared in the darkness down the street.

— XVII —

A HOLE IN THE WALL

THE wound was healed—partially, at least. If the Hawk had unduly shortened his period of convalescence, he was perhaps justified, and not wholly without excuse! He stood now in the black shadows, hugged close to the wall of the roundhouse. And now he moved stealthily forward, until, from a crouched position, he straightened up against the wall at the side of one of the few windows which were lighted. Lanson had strolled aimlessly across the tracks from the station some ten minutes before, and, five minutes later, MacVightie had followed Lanson—to their chosen spot for secret conferences, this little "cubbyhole" of a turner's office in the roundhouse, as the Hawk, from more than one experience in the past, had very good reason to know. They were in there now, and, as the Hawk was likewise exceedingly well aware, the events of the next few hours, and incidentally his own particular movements, depended very pertinently upon the movements of MacVightie and Lanson.

Lanson's voice in quietly modulated tones reached the Hawk:

"Yes, both trains are on time to the minute; I've taken care of that. And so far there doesn't seem to be a hitch anywhere, and with your men boarding the trains west of here at different stations along the line, and mixing quietly with the passengers, I don't see how any one could be the wiser on that score. Yes, it looks as though everything were all right— eh, MacVightie?"

"I don't know; I hope so," MacVightie's deep growl came in reply. "Anyhow, we've carried out instructions from Washington, and it's up to the Secret Service crowd as to how it pans out."

"No, it isn't!" declared Lanson, still quietly. "It isn't up to a soul on earth except those of us who have got the responsibility of this division on our shoulders! I believe the plan is a good one, but because it came from Washington doesn't let us out—not for a minute! What about Birks; has he shown up yet?"

"Not yet," MacVightie answered—and swore suddenly under his breath. "And I don't mind admitting that the crowd down there in Washington make me tired! It's over two weeks ago that I put it up to them. They said they would take the matter under consideration, and in any case would send one of their men, this Birks, out here to make an investigation. But nothing doing! Then, as you know, I wrote them again a week ago, when we knew this Alaskan gold shipment was coming through, and you know their reply; they outlined a plan for us, and stated definitely that Birks would be on deck to-night. Maybe he will—in time to tell us what we *should* have done!"

"The Secret Service isn't a police force," said Lanson tersely. "The only excuse they would have for acting at all would be if your pet theory were correct—that the Hawk and his gang, apart from their systematised murders and robberies, were also the ones who have been flooding the country with those counterfeit ten-dollar notes. You had no actual proof to offer, and Washington evidently hasn't felt quite so sure about it as you have. However, there's no use discussing that to-night. If Birks shows up, all right; if he doesn't—well, I don't see that he could make any difference one way or the other now."

There was silence for a moment, then Lanson spoke again.

"What worries me as much as anything," he said slowly, "is the express company making a shipment of money at the same time—forty thousand dollars in the car's safe. Of course, it's logical enough with a half million to guard anyway, but it's an added incentive to those devils, that's all. A half million in raw gold isn't any easy thing to pick up and walk off with, and there's more than an even chance that the Wire Devils might pass it up on that account; but with banknotes alone in so large an amount——"

"If they know about it!" interrupted MacVightie brusquely. "And it's not likely they do! You can't send a heavily guarded express car on from the coast and keep it mum that gold is going through, especially when the papers print pictures of the cases being swung out of the steamer's hold on arrival from Alaska—but the other's different.   I'm not banking on them passing up the gold on any account, though they may, at that; but in any case they'll be welcome to open the safe now, won't they?"

Again there was an instant's silence; and the Hawk now, as though fearful of losing a word that might be spoken, strained forward closer still to the side of the window.

"Yes, that's right!" Lanson laughed now in a grimly humorous way.   "It's in the biggest case of all!   Yes, I guess it's all right, MacVightie; anyway, another hour or two will tell the story.   The shift should have been made at Mornleigh without any trouble, and the Limited will come through here without a thing in the express car except the guards! If they hold her up anywhere on the division, that's all they'll find—the guards, and one of your posses. Yes, it ought to work."   Lanson's voice took on a curiously monotonous drone, as though he were checking over the details in his own mind, and unconsciously doing so audibly.   "The Limited takes water at Mornleigh, and No. 18 always takes the siding there to let the Limited pass, so there's nothing in that to arouse suspicion.   In the darkness, with the door of the Limited's express car only a foot or so away from the door of No. 18's baggage car, and a picked crew to transfer the gold, I don't see how there could be any 'leak.'   The Limited pulls in here with its guarded express car—everything looks

just as those Wire Devils would expect it to look—
and they know the gold left the coast on that train,
and in that car. Yes, I think we win to-night. If
they hold up the Limited they'll catch a Tartar, and
without any risk on our part as far as the gold is
concerned. How many men in the posse scattered
through the cars on that train?"

"Twenty," said MacVightie tersely.

"Good!" said Lanson approvingly. "That ought
to be enough to round them up—if they nibble at
the bait at all. And if they don't, if they let the
Limited go through unmolested, it will be pretty
nearly safe to assume, as I said before, that they
figure gold in the bulk is too awkward a thing to
handle, and too hard to get away with. But even
there we are not taking any chances; they *might*
have discovered that it had been transferred. How
many men in the posse on No. 18?"

"The same number," replied MacVightie—and
then MacVightie's fist crashed down into the palm
of his hand. "I hope they start something!" he exclaimed savagely. "I'd give a year's salary to get to
grips with them, and if I ever do I'll clean 'em out!
And I'll see that some of them, and particularly
that damned Hawk, swing for it! I haven't forgotten the murder of old Mother Barrett's boy in the
express car that night, or a dozen others, or——"

"That's your end of it, MacVightie," said Lanson grimly. "Mine's to see five hundred thousand
dollars' worth of bullion and forty thousand in cash

over this division and safely on its way East. If the plan——"

The Hawk, slipping silently out of the shadows, began to cross the railroad yard, heading for the station.

"Forty thousand dollars," said the Hawk softly to himself—and chuckled suddenly. "Forty thousand dollars in a big packing case! The *biggest* case of the lot, he said, wasn't it?" The chuckle died away, and the Hawk's face grew hard. "I don't know!" muttered the Hawk. "It's no cinch! I guess there'll be something doing to-night!"

A glance at the illuminated dial of the clock on the station tower showed it to be half past eight, as the Hawk stepped to the platform. He hesitated an instant in indecision, then went on into the general waiting room. There was ample time. The Limited was not due for another hour; and No. 18 —in which alone he had now any concern—did not schedule Selkirk until forty minutes after the Limited. Nearly two hours!

The Hawk, standing in the doorway of the waiting room, ostentatiously consulted a time-table which he drew from his pocket, frowned, glanced about him, and, finally, approaching the news-counter, which appeared for the moment to be minus an attendant, helped himself to a newspaper, tossed a copper on top of the pile, and appropriated the nearest seat. The Hawk opened his paper in front of him—and over the top of the paper inspected with some interest the view afforded by the open doorway

of the news-counter, which was directly facing him
and but a few feet away. The news-counter was
a long, narrow affair, glass enclosed, with big sliding windows, making one corner of the waiting room,
and at its further end boasted a little office of its own.
The door of this private domain was closed, but it,
too, was glass panelled, and the apparent absence of
any attendant was explained. The Hawk permitted
a curious smile to flicker across his lips behind his
newspaper. Inside the little office a man, sprawled
forward in a chair, his head resting on his arms,
which were outflung across the desk in front of him,
appeared to be sound asleep and magnificently oblivious to anything so grossly material as business.

The Hawk shifted his glance, this time for a more
critical survey of the waiting room. He found himself, strangely enough, quite sheltered from observation. True, it was "between trains," and there were
very few people in the room—he had noted several women and an elderly man with a little boy, as
he had come in—but these were now screened from
his view by the large, boxed-in posts, or pillars, that,
in the remodelling and enlargement of the station
some years before, had sought to combine, evidently,
ornamentation with stability.

The Hawk's eyes, under cover of his newspaper,
reverted to the man at the desk. The minutes
passed—five, ten of them. The man's hours were
long undoubtedly, and usually there were two in
charge of the news-counter, which might perhaps account for the man's weariness, and the profound

slumber that was possible even in such an uncomfortable position! The Hawk turned to the editorial page of his newspaper. There were almost two hours before No. 18 was due, and, though he had a little business of a purely personal and intimate nature to transact before then, there was time in abundance and to spare, and it might possibly be utilised as profitably here as anywhere else. In any case, there was usually an editorial diatribe, interesting principally for the virulent language in which it was couched, anent the Hawk and the Wire Devils, with whose leadership he, the Hawk, was universally credited. The Hawk smiled thinly. If leadership was vested in the lion's portion of the spoils, then MacVightie, and Lanson, and the newspapers, and the public generally were unquestionably right—but, since those spoils had been snatched from under the noses of the Wire Devils, thanks to his possession of their secret code, the Wire Devils and the Ladybird in particular, that peer of the underworld who, as he had discovered a few nights ago, was the moving spirit of the gang, held a very different and even more decided opinion on the subject!

He folded the paper over, and sprawled himself out lazily on his seat—but if the editorial in question was on the sheet before him, he did not see it. The man at the desk raised his head, yawned, stretched himself, and, as though wearily resuming his work, reached into a small drawer that stood open in the upper section of the roll-top desk, took out a pad of paper, and began to write.

Still another five minutes passed; and then the man tossed his pencil away from him, and reached out for the telephone at his elbow. But now he seemed to hesitate, then evidently changed his mind. He pushed back his chair, stood up, tore the sheet of paper on which he had been writing from the pad, replaced the pad in the drawer, closed the drawer, and, turning quickly, opened the office door. He came down the narrow space behind the news-counter itself, stepped out into the waiting room, glanced hurriedly about him, and, breaking suddenly into a run, disappeared through the waiting room door in the direction of the platform.

The Hawk's lassitude seemed suddenly to have vanished. In a flash he had covered the few feet of space that separated his seat from the doorway of the news-counter, and now, crouched low, hidden by the counter itself, he darted silently for the little office, gained it, wrenched open the drawer of the desk—and over the Hawk's set, tense features there flickered again that curious smile. Faint, muffled, but none the less distinctly, there came from the interior of the drawer, which, as he reached in his hand, he found was open through to the wall, the clicking of a telegraph sounder. But, while he listened, the Hawk was working with breathless haste. His fingers closed on the pad of paper, and tore off the topmost sheet. Without folding or crushing the paper, he laid it carefully inside his vest, buttoned his vest over it again, closed the drawer of the desk noiselessly—and in another instant was lolling again in his seat in the waiting room, apparently immersed once more in his newspaper.

It had taken the Hawk a matter of less than a minute to go and come, but for all that his margin of safety had been small. The man returned almost instantly, and again entered the office. The Hawk, finding that for once the editorial which might have afforded him a genuine, if passing, interest, was absent, turned another page of the paper, spent a few minutes in the somewhat unprofitable perusal of what proved to be massed columns of "Help Wanted" and "Situations Vacant" advertisements, and, finally, throwing the paper down on the seat beside him, got up leisurely, and strolled out through the main entrance of the station to the street.

The Hawk crossed the road, and slipped into the lane that was almost opposite the station. This being accustomed ground to the Hawk, he made his way quickly along in the blackness, reached the first intersecting street, dove through the doorway of the dirty and squalid three-story building, the ground floor of which was occupied by a saloon, and, mounting the narrow staircase, entered the room that was directly over the saloon on the first landing. The Hawk locked the door behind him. If his temporary abode in Selkirk City could be so designated, the Hawk was at home.

He switched on the electric light, drew a chair up to the cheap and somewhat dilapidated table that stood against the wall opposite the door, and from under his vest took out the sheet of paper he had purloined a few minutes before. He spread it out eagerly before him on the table, scanned it closely, and into his dark eyes there came a half mocking, half triumphant gleam.

"I thought so!" murmured the Hawk. "He didn't dare telephone it. I thought the messages must be coming in pretty hot to-night—the other fellow must have gone up to the East End to shoot some mighty important reply back, or else he'd never have left his pal short-handed. It's no wonder I never tumbled to that lay until the Ladybird opened the bag! I didn't recognise those news-counter fellows, did I? Why should I? They're new ones just breaking into the game, or they'd never have pulled a fool stunt like this!"

The Hawk bent over the paper. In places the impression left by the pencil was faint and, indeed, illegible, and had not come through from the upper sheet at all; but the Hawk patiently and painstakingly settled himself to his task. The first few lines were but a confused and, to all outward appearances, meaningless jumble of letters run together—one of the Wire Devils' code messages. And here, if this had been all, the Hawk would have been hopelessly astray; but lower down on the sheet the man had decoded the cipher, and here, where letters and words were too faintly impressed on the paper or were missing altogether, the Hawk was able to supply them by following the general sense of the message. He began by tracing over the impressions carefully with a sharp lead pencil, and at the expiration of a few minutes was staring, a grim smile on his lips, at the following:

"Gold transferred to No. 18 at Mornleigh. Keep away from Limited. Probably big posse on No. 18. Every man will join Number One on Train 18 to-night. Those boarding No. 18 at Selkirk must on no account excite suspicion. All other details to stand."

The Hawk's remark, as he reached into his inside coat pocket and brought out several small slips of paper, which he laid on the table in front of him, was seemingly quite irrelevant.

"Yes," said the Hawk. "I've been curious ever since yesterday to get a look at that desk—yes, I guess the Ladybird's no fool!"

The Hawk arranged the slips of paper in what appeared to be a sort of chronological order, and studied them for a moment. Prefacing the message he had just obtained, these others, messages that he had intercepted at intervals during the preceding few days, made a complete and decidedly enlightening record. The first one, decoded, read:

"Reported movement of half million in gold to be made from coast. Number Three will proceed to coast, verify, and secure details."

The Hawk nodded shortly. Number Three was the Bantam. He passed on to the next message:

"Gold coming through on Limited on Thursday night. Express car well guarded. Numbers One, Seven, Eight, Six and Four will board Limited at different stopping points west of Mornleigh; all others to hold themselves in readiness at Selkirk."

Again the Hawk nodded. This was Thursday night! Mornleigh was the Limited's last stop west of Selkirk. Number One was the Butcher, and the others were—he shrugged his shoulders. As he had once facetiously remarked, somebody must have left the door of Sing Sing open!

There was still another message:

"Hold up train three miles East of Echo Rock. Detach express car, and run to Willow Creek bridge. Load gold on wagon, and disperse."

The Hawk consulted his watch. It was a quarter past nine. He took out his pipe, lighted it, put his feet up on the table, and gathering together the various slips of paper abstractedly began to tear them into shreds.

Pieced together, the whole affair was quite simple. In a word, every move that had been made by Lanson and MacVightie at the instigation of the Secret Service men, and, presumably, in particular by one Birks, was known to the Ladybird and the Wire Devils. Lanson and MacVightie had waited until the last moment before making the transfer at Mornleigh, the final stop before Selkirk, but the Bantam was already accompanying the gold east on the Limited, and, added to the Bantam by that time, there would have been those others who were detailed to board the Limited at the various points still further west of Mornleigh.

It was very simple. The Bantam had not been asleep at Mornleigh, and it was not the contents of the express car alone that had been transferred there—the Bantam and his companions had likewise transferred themselves to No. 18! Also, either because the Bantam had spotted some of MacVightie's men, or because logical deductions in the Ladybird's very shrewd brain had led to that conclusion, it was known that No. 18 harboured a posse. It was evident, however, that this in no way dismayed the Ladybird; and it was equally evident that both Lanson and MacVightie were very far astray, in their estimate of the nerve and resourcefulness of the brain behind the Wire Devils' organisation, to have even considered it as a possibility that the physical difficulty in the way of handling a half million in raw gold would have caused the Ladybird to hesitate an instant in an effort to get his hands upon it. A half million—was a half million! That was the answer! The only change the Ladybird had seen fit to make was to mobilise, as it were, the entire strength of the Wire Devils to offset MacVightie's posse. Apart from that, according to the final message, the prearranged plan was to stand.

It was not a plan that was markedly original, paralleling very closely, as it did, the Wire Devils' removal of the safe from the express car of the Fast Mail on a certain night not very long since, but this could hardly be held up against the Ladybird—there were limitations to originality, and originality was a secondary consideration as compared with feasibility and success. Echo Rock station was two stations east of Conmore, the Wire Devils' headquarters—just far enough distant to preclude the immediate search from spreading to the neighbourhood of Conmore, and yet not too far away to make the transport of the gold to the isolated old farmhouse impractical before daylight. The details of the hold-up itself required little elucidation. In whatever manner they might elect to bring the train to a stop, all that was necessary, once that was accomplished, was to keep MacVightie's men from No. 18's baggage car while the car itself, into which the Wire Devils would naturally retreat, moved off down the line to the Willow Creek bridge some two or three miles further on.

The Hawk took his pipe from his lips, polished the bowl by rubbing it along the side of his nose, and inspected the result critically. And then the Hawk smiled pleasantly to himself. In none of the messages had the Wire Devils given the slightest evidence of any knowledge of a fact that was very near to his, the Hawk's, heart. It was quite possible, even probable, that on one point, at least, Lanson and MacVightie were right—that the Wire

Devils were ignorant of the presence of that forty thousand dollars in bills—but even supposing that they *did* know, they would scarcely give him, the Hawk, credit for being in possession of the knowledge as well. Therefore, bitter as was the feud between them, the Ladybird would be almost certain to ignore his, the Hawk's existence in so far as this night's work was concerned. The Hawk's smile broadened. It was quite true, single-handed he would have no excuse on earth for attempting the impossible feat of carrying away a half million in gold—but forty thousand dollars in banknotes was not as prohibitory in its weight! His problem, therefore, simplified itself into an intimate investigation of No. 18's baggage car before Echo Rock was reached, and before either MacVightie's posse, or the Butcher and his ungentle crowd in the cars behind, should have started anything on their own account.

"Yes," said the Hawk confidentially to the toe of his boot, "yes, I guess I'll sit in for a hand in the game myself; yes, I guess it looks pretty good—if the luck holds."

The Hawk relapsed into silence, still studying the toe of his boot. His last remark seemed suddenly to have obsessed him, and he frowned. If the luck still held! It wasn't altogether luck—indeed, it was far from luck. The Ladybird, and, for that matter, a half dozen others of the Wire Devils whom he could name, were not to be lightly reckoned with. He had no delusions on that score! Since the day

he had begun to trespass on the Wire Devils preserves, listening when and where he could, he had
intercepted enough of their cipher messages as they
came over the wires to enable him to pull from the
fire and pocket for himself the chestnuts they had
been so carefully roasting for themselves, to turn in
fact the entire labour and effort of their organisation to his own account—and in their turn they had
sought by every means within their power to trap
him. And they had nearly caught him, very nearly
caught him once, and he had realised that the haphazard method in which, not knowing their source,
he had been able to obtain the cipher messages would
no longer do. It was through those messages alone
that he could hope to get a hint of, and thereby fore-
stall, the *next* trap they might set for him. And then
the way had seemed to clear a little when he had
at last discovered that source in the old farmhouse
near Conmore, and had discovered that the Ladybird, thought dead and mourned by the underworld
as one of its greatest, from a wheel chair now, a
maimed thing in all save brain, moved and guided
what MacVightie had been pleased to call the most
powerful and dangerous criminal organisation that
had ever known existence. Only on the night that
he, the Hawk, had made those discoveries he had
been wounded! That was a week ago. For three
days, not daring to let it be known that a *wounded*
man was in the house, he had remained here in his
room, nursing his hurt as best he could. It had only
been a flesh wound, and those three days were all

he had allowed himself to remain inactive; for in those three days, temporarily blindfolded as to any move against him that the Ladybird might make, he had lived like a hunted man, wary of every passing moment, of every sound without his door, his automatic never for an instant out of reach. After that, during the past four nights, he had resumed his vigil at the farmhouse again.

The Hawk smiled grimly. No, he laboured under no delusions as to the craft, the cunning, and the power of those against whom he had elected to play a lone hand! The four nights just past had resulted in something more than the mere accumulation of those code messages he had just read, in something besides a more intimate acquaintanceship with the farmhouse and its surroundings, even including the underground passage, for instance, that led from the wagon shed to a trapdoor in the cellar—it had resulted, last night, in a still further insight into the ingenuity and the sort of remorseless mastery of detail through which the organisation attained its ends. The method by which they tapped the wires, commandeering the telegraph system of the railroad, the primary purpose of which was undoubtedly to supply them with the vital information that must of necessity pass over the wires and on which they based their own plans, this gold shipment to-night, for example, or the shipment of diamonds from New York of a few weeks back, was ingenious enough; but still more ingenious, when using their secret code and putting the wires to another purpose, that of enabling the Ladybird to direct his operations and send his orders as he had done to-night, was the method by which those messages were received. Every sounder on the line carried them, of course, and when, in isolated cases, the gang was working at smaller places along the line, they could readily enough, if expecting a message, as he, the Hawk, had often done, keep within sound of an instrument by the simple expedient of occupying a waiting room, or of lounging on the platform outside the operator's window; but the vast majority of the messages were for those of the gang who maintained a sort of branch headquarters in Selkirk, and such a method was neither practical nor possible, since the first essential in making the scheme of value was that, without the chance of a single message being missed, the messages should reach their destination at any hour of the day and night.

Again the Hawk smiled grimly. It had puzzled him a good many times—but it puzzled him no longer! Last night the Ladybird, quite unconscious of a rapt audience, had, by a chance remark, disclosed the secret; and to-night he, the Hawk, had seen the plan in operation! The news-counter! It was simple enough; but it held a deadly significance in its proof of the fact that there were no obstacles too great, no details too minute to stand in the way between the Ladybird and the end he sought. The news-counter was directly beneath the operator's room upstairs. In the old days, before the station had been enlarged and modernised, it had been a somewhat diminutive affair, and where the news-counter now stood had been the superintendent's office. This had connected with the room above by means of an old-fashioned speaking tube. When the alterations had been made, the mouthpieces, both above and below, had been removed, the room above had been papered over, and the waiting room had been plastered; but, as the wall had been left intact, the speaking tube had remained embedded—in the wall. Yes, it was very simple! Say, a dint in the wall in the operator's room above, and a slight tear in the paper that, if it attracted any attention at all in surroundings where the call boys backed their chairs against the wall and kept their hair on end with nickel thrillers, would at least never excite suspicion! And below, with the desk in the little office of the news-counter backed up against it, who was to know that a hole had been punched in the wall, or, for that matter, in the back of the desk itself behind the convenient little drawer, so that one could sit there and listen to the sounder upstairs! Also, it was quite obvious now why, several months ago, the old lessee of the news-counter had been bought out by some newcomers!

The Hawk's lips tightened. The game to its full extent was wide open now. The news-counter ran day and night, operated by four of the gang in pairs, one always on duty at the desk; while, should there, by any chance or at any time, be an unwelcome intruder in the office, the drawer had only to be shut and the sound was thereby eliminated. When a message "broke" over the wires above, the man on duty had only to decipher it and telephone it to what the Ladybird had referred to as the "boarding house"—the disguise, it appeared now, under which the gang maintained its headquarters in the city. That was all there was to it! To-night, it was true, the operation had been a little different; but the reason for that, as the Hawk had already decided in his own mind, was obvious enough. With MacVightie, Lanson, and the authorities generally, on the alert, due to the gold shipment coming through, the man had not dared to take the risk of telephoning any such message as he had received, but had taken it outside to where one of the gang, undoubtedly, in view of the importance of the night's work, was on additional duty and in readiness to receive and transmit it on the instant, say, to the local headquarters. As for the absence of the second man at the news-counter, who ordinarily preserved the pretence of catering to the public, it was quite possible, and indeed likely, that he had gone on a similar errand with a previous message; or, if one of the rare occasions when it was necessary to telegraph a cipher message *from* Selkirk had arisen, he might have gone—according to the Ladybird again—to the little suburban station at the East End of the city, which was closed at night, but to which an entry and the subsequent use of the wire would present little difficulty, since MacVightie had finally given up as impossible the task of guarding all the numerous stations of that description on the division.

"Yes," said the Hawk suddenly, under his breath, "I guess they'd go a long way to get their hands on what I've got off their bat; and I guess, after that, I'd go out—like a pricked bubble!" He sucked meditatively at his brier for a moment; then a mirthless smile parted his lips, and he spoke again. "Forty thousand dollars," whispered the Hawk. "Yes, I guess that's the play—and the last one! If I win out to-night, and I guess I will, this is where the curtain drops, and the Hawk makes his fade-away for parts unknown!"

— XVIII —

THE HAWK PACKS HIS VALISE

THE Hawk looked at his watch again, removed his feet from the table, knocked the ashes from the bowl of his pipe, stood up, and crossed leisurely to the window. The window gave on the fire escape. He lifted aside the shade, and stood there for a moment staring out into the darkness, then drew the shade very carefully back into place again. From the window he crossed to the door, reassured himself that it was locked, and, as an extra precaution, draped his handkerchief on the door handle, completely screening the keyhole.

He returned now to the other side of the room, and from under the bed pulled out a large, black valise. He laid this on the bed, and opened it. It was quite empty.

Between the bed and the table stood his trunk. He unlocked the trunk, and threw back the lid.

"It's quite possible," muttered the Hawk, as his fingers worked deftly and swiftly around the edges of the lid, "that I may not return. I've forgotten just how I stand on my rent, though I fancy I've paid up for a week in advance! In any case, there's the trunk for old Seidelberger downstairs, and like-wise its contents, with the exception, scarcely worth mentioning—of this!"   There was a grim chuckle on the Hawk's lips, as the false tray came away in his hands.   "Yes," said the Hawk, as he laid the tray on the bed beside the valise, "I hardly think that I'll be back!   I guess they're pretty peeved as it is, and after to-night I've a notion their sentiments aren't going to improve any!"

He stood looking down at the tray, that bulged to repletion with the proceeds of a dozen robberies that were almost country-wide in fame, and which, more pertinent still as far as the Hawk was con-cerned, represented the loot that the Wire Devils had already counted their own—when he, the Hawk, instead, had helped himself to the prize at their expense!

The Hawk began to transfer the contents of the tray to the valise.

"I don't know how big the lot would size up, but it looks like a garden villa at Palm Beach—which is going some!" observed the Hawk softly.   "Yes, just one more little play to-night, and I guess I retire!"

He held the magnificent diamond necklace up to the light, causing its thousand facets to leap and gleam and scintillate in fiery flashes, then laid it in a curiously caressing sort of way in the bottom of the valise.   The Hawk seemed peculiarly entranced with diamonds, as though in their touch and in their re-sponsive life and fire he found a pure and unalloyed delight. From their little box he allowed the score or two of unset stones to trickle into the palm of his hand, and again he brought the light to flash and play upon them. And for a moment he held them there—then a sudden hardness set his jaws and lips, and impulsively he thrust the stones back into the box, and tossed the box into the valise.

"Damn it!" said the Hawk through compressed lips. "They make me think of the kid—and old Mother Barrett."

He laughed harshly, and shrugged his shoulders as though literally to throw off the weight of an unpleasant memory—and reached again into the tray. He worked more quickly now. Into the valise he packed away in rapid succession a very large collection of valuables, amongst them the ten thousand dollars in banknotes that he had taken from the paymaster's safe, the contents of the cash box, amounting to some three thousand dollars, of which he had once relieved one Isaac Kirschell, and, still in its newspaper wrapper, the Trader's National Bank's twenty-five thousand dollars, likewise in banknotes, which had been his last venture, and which he had appropriated on the night he had been wounded.

The tray was empty now, save for a black mask, a steel jimmy, and a neat little package of crisp, new, ten-dollar counterfeit notes. The two former articles the Hawk laid aside on the table; and the latter, after an instant's hesitation, was added to the horde in the valise. He closed and locked the valise. There remained now but the empty tray. He stared at this ruefully.

"I hate to lose that trunk, upon my soul, I do!" he muttered. "But I can't afford to take any chances of spilling the beans by trying to get it out of here!"

He took out his knife, and slashed away the canvas bottom of the tray, then broke the framework into a dozen pieces. The lid of the trunk itself was innocent of fastenings, or of any evidence that it had ever concealed a tray; and the tray itself, when the Hawk was through with it, was an unrecognisable debris of splintered wood and ribbons of torn canvas. He made a bundle of this, tying it together with a strip of the canvas.

The Hawk now emptied his pockets, and proceeded to change his clothes. If he were destined to sacrifice the greater part of his wardrobe, he at least need not linger long in indecision over the choice of what should be preserved! There was an exceedingly useful and ingeniously devised pocket concealed in the back lining of a certain one of his coats. The suit, of which this coat was an integral part, was a trifle worn and threadbare, not in quite as good repair as any of the rest of his clothing, and for that reason he had not worn it of late; but one could not at all times afford to be fastidious! What he left behind would be minutely searched and examined. The secret of that pocket, a little invention of his own, was worth preserving from the vulgar eye, even at the expense of sacrificing a better suit of clothes for the sake of it! He resurrected the suit in question from the bottom of the trunk, and put it on. And into the concealed pocket he tucked away his mask and his bunch of skeleton keys. A side coat pocket, more instantly accessible, served for his automatic—the other pockets for his various other belongings, including the steel jimmy.

The Hawk made a final and comprehensive survey of the room, then closed and locked the trunk, and again consulted his watch. It was five minutes after ten, and No. 18 scheduled Selkirk at ten-twenty. The Hawk nodded. It was time to go—just time. He took from his pocket his automatic, tested and examined its mechanism critically, and restored it to his pocket. He crossed the room, turned out the light, unlocked the door without opening it, and took his handkerchief from the keyhole. Without a sound now the Hawk moved back to the bed, picked up the valise, tucked the bundle of what had once been the tray under his arm, returned to the door, opened it silently, and stood peering out into the dark hallway—and the next instant, the Hawk, stealing like a shadow down the stairs, gained the street, and in another had swung around the corner into the lane.

It was only the length of a block to the station, but here in the lane the Hawk found means of disposing of the irksome bundle under his arm by the simple expedient of dropping pieces of the wreckage in the various refuse barrels as he went along. Nor had the Hawk, evidently, any intention either of hampering his movements with the care of the valise, or of risking the valise's contents in the night's work that lay ahead of him. The Hawk was, perhaps, possessed of a certain ironical sense of humour. Since his possession of the loot which the valise contained was due in a more or less intimate degree to the railroad, it seemed eminently fitting that it should be restored to the railroad for safe-keeping temporarily. The Hawk, as he entered the station, nonchalantly exchanged his valise for a parcel-room check, paid down the dime for the service to be rendered, and passed on into the general waiting room.

He glanced at the news-counter on his way through to the platform. Its full complement of two attendants were present now; but, contrary to all precedent, it being an all-night stand, obvious preparations for closing it for the night were in progress—the two men were engaged in removing the magazines, newspapers, and various small wares from the outside ledge of the counter, and in pulling down the large sliding windows that enclosed the place. The Hawk's dark eyes flashed a gleam of grim appreciation. It was then literally a mobilisation of the Wire Devils to the last man to-night! A half million in gold—was a half million in gold!

The Hawk bought a mileage book in lieu of a ticket to any specific destination, both because his immediate destination was peculiarly his own private concern, and because in the very near future he expected to put a considerable quantity of mileage to excellent use. He strolled out to the platform, and along to the east end of the station.

Here, quite unobtrusively, he awaited the arrival

of No. 18. The platform was fairly well crowded —but not unusually so, or rather, perhaps, not noticeably so. A half dozen, or even a dozen, extra men circulating amongst the ordinary press of traffic would hardly be expected to make any appreciable difference. The Hawk, back under the shadows of the building, surveyed the lighted stretch of platform narrowly. They were there, the Wire Devils' reserve, he knew; but he recognised none of them. He smiled a little whimsically. His acquaintanceship with the gang so far had been with its more prominent members, as it were, and these, as likewise MacVightie's posse, had already boarded the train far west of Selkirk—that each might not excite the other's suspicion! Nor was MacVightie himself in evidence. Not that this surprised the Hawk! He was interested, that was all. It was simply a question of whether MacVightie had elected to stay with the gold, or had gone on with the first posse on the Limited on the assumption that the Limited was the more likely to be attacked. It made little difference, of course, as far as he, the Hawk, was concerned, whether it was MacVightie or some one else who was in command of the posse—his own plans would in no way be affected on that account.

There was a stir along the platform. Up the yard, past the twinkling switch lights on the spurs, the glare of a headlight flashed into sight around the bend. Came the roar and rumble of a heavy train, and a moment later No. 18, its big mogul panting like a thing of life from a breathless run, its long string of coaches behind it, rolled into the station.

The Hawk did not stir. By coincidence, perhaps, the baggage car had come to a stop directly opposite the position he had chosen. The rearmost sliding door of the car was slammed back, and the baggageman, a powerfully built, muscular fellow of perhaps thirty, appeared in the doorway. The Hawk, from his place of vantage, eyed the other appraisingly, and then his glance travelled on into the interior of the car—what he could see of it. What he saw was a mass of trunks, some of which the man now unloaded on the waiting trucks, and in turn piled others, as they were heaved up to him from the platform, into the formers' places. The Hawk nodded his head shortly. True, the forward door of the car had not been opened, but MacVightie had done his work well. There was no hint of concealment, the baggage car of No. 18 was as frankly innocent in appearance on its run tonight as it had ever been.

The train was starting into motion again when the Hawk finally moved. He crossed the platform, and swung himself on the forward steps of the smoker, that was immediately behind the baggage car. His slouch hat pulled a little over his eyes, he opened the door, stepped into the car, sauntered down the aisle, and out of the rear door to the vestibuled platform of the first-class day coach behind. But here, the Hawk paused a moment, and his face, impassive before, was stamped now with a twisted smile. His reconnaissance of the train so far had proved fruitful. The four men in the forward double seat of the smoker, a lap board across their knees, and apparently engrossed in their card game, were the Butcher, Whitie Jim, the Cricket and the Bantam! And further down the aisle, unwittingly rubbing shoulders quite probably with some of Mac-Vightie's men, Parson Joe occupied a seat, and the keen, pale, thin face of Kirschell peered out from another.

"Yes, they're all here," decided the Hawk, his voice drowned in the rattle of the train. "Counting those who got on at Selkirk, they're all here to the last man—except the Ladybird and his wheel chair!"

The Hawk moved forward, reached out for the handle of the day coach door—and sucked in his breath, as he drew sharply back again. Through the glass panel he had caught sight of two men he had not expected to see. Sitting together on the right-hand side about a quarter of the way down the aisle were MacVightie and Lanson. The Hawk frowned. He had waited until the train was in motion, and he had not seen them get on; and *they,* as witness that little conference in the roundhouse of a while back, had not been amongst those who had boarded the train west of Selkirk. And then the frown gave place to a sort of self-commiserating expression. Where were his wits to-night! It was simple enough! They had boarded the car from the yard side of the train, and not from the platform, of course!

Well, that put an end to any further reconnaissance through the train! In one sense it was not
altogether true that it made no difference whether
MacVightie was aboard or not. He and MacVightie were not altogether strangers. They had met
once in his, the Hawk's, room, and on that occasion,
the night, to be precise, he had cleaned out the paymaster's safe of that ten thousand dollars, Mac-
Vightie had been in a decidedly suspicious frame
of mind. MacVightie, it was quite certain, had not
forgotten that night; nor, it was quite equally safe
to assume, had MacVightie forgotten his, the
Hawk's face—and at that exact moment the Hawk
had no desire that MacVightie should recognise him
again!

The Hawk turned, re-entered the smoker, found
the always unpopular crosswise seat behind the door
vacant, and appropriated it. His eyes straying forward over the car located two more acquaintances in
the person of Crusty Kline and French Pete, and
came back to fix musingly on the worn nickel faucet
of the water-cooler. No. 18's first stop was at
Barne's Junction, fifteen miles out from Selkirk, and
some five miles this side of Conmore; the next stop
was Lorraine, and Lorraine was on the *other* side—
in fact a good many miles on the other side—of
Echo Rock and the Willow Creek bridge. The de-
duction was obvious; and the Hawk's destination, in
so far as his occupancy of a seat in the smoker was
concerned, was therefore quite plainly—the Junction.

"Three miles east of Echo Rock," repeated the

Hawk to himself. "No, I don't think so! This is where the Ladybird has another guess! Maybe I couldn't get away with a half million—but maybe I'm not the only one! There's one or two guys in this car that haven't got the high-sign to my lodge! It seems to me I promised the Butcher something the night he tried to shoot me through his pocket, and it seems as though I promised Parson Joe something too—yes, it seems to me I did!"

— XIX —

BIRDS OF A FEATHER

IT took twenty minutes for the run to the Junction. And at the Junction, as far as the Hawk could tell, since, yielding to what had become a sort of habit with him, he descended to the ground on the opposite side from the station, he was the only passenger for that stop. It was dark here; strangely silent, and strangely lonely. Barne's Junction owed its existence neither to a town site, nor to commercial importance—it existed simply as a junction, and for purely railroad operating purposes only. It was, in fact, the other extreme as compared to Selkirk with its lighted and busy platform, its extensive yard, and its ubiquitous and, perhaps, too inquisitive yardmen!

The Hawk dropped on all fours and began to creep along the side of the smoker toward the forward end of the train, his eyes strained warily through the darkness against the possibility of one or other of the engine crew descending from the cab. He passed the smoker and kept on along the length of the baggage car, still crawling, moving without a sound. When he rose from his knees finally, he was crouched down in between the tender and the forward end of the bagage car; and a moment later, as the train jerked forward into motion, he was crouched again—this time on the end beam of the baggage car which, in lieu of platform, served as a sort of wide threshold for the door.

The train was beginning to gain momentum now, and against the jolt and swing of the increasing speed the Hawk steadied himself by clinging with one hand to the iron handrail at the side of the door —with the other hand he tried the door cautiously, and found it locked.

From the pocket in the back lining of his coat he produced his mask, fingered it speculatively for an instant, then slipped it over his face. True, this was to be his last venture in the Wire Devils' preserves, but he had always worn a mask, and—there came a twisted grin—they perhaps would not recognise him *without* it. And it was quite necessary that they should recognise the Hawk—if he was to keep that promise to the Butcher! It might be a farewell, as far as he was concerned, but he intended that it should be a memorable one, and that no doubt should be permitted to linger in their minds as to the identity of the parting guest they had so lavishly, if ungraciously, entertained!

From the same pocket came his skeleton keys. The Hawk now felt tentatively with his finger over the keyhole, nodded his head briskly, and from the bunch of keys, still by the sense of touch, selected one without hesitation. The Hawk, however, for the moment, made no effort to open the door. The rush of the wind was in his face now; like some black, monstrous, uncanny wall confronting him, the tender clashed and clattered, and swayed in dizzy lurches before his eyes; while heavenward the sky was tinged with a deep red glow, and the cab was ablaze with light from the wide-flung fire-box door, and the top of the baggage car door, and the individual particles of coal on the top of the tender's heap stood out in sharp relief against the background of the night.

And then the darkness fell again.

The Hawk's hand shot forward to the keyhole, lingered there an instant, as he crouched again swaying with the lurch of the train, then the skeleton keys were returned to the pocket in the back lining of his coat—and the Hawk was in action. In a flash he had opened and closed the door behind him, and, with his back against it, his automatic flung significantly forward in his hand, he stood staring down the length of the car.

There was a hoarse, startled yell, that was lost in the roar of the flying train, and the baggageman, from his chair at one side of the car and in front of a shelf-like desk topped with a rack of pigeon-holes, leaped to his feet.

"Sit down!" invited the Hawk coldly.

The man hesitated, but the next instant dropped back into his chair, as the Hawk moved suddenly forward to his side.

"What do you want?" he demanded sullenly.

"This—to begin with!" The Hawk's voice was

an insolent drawl now, as his deft fingers, like a streak of lightning, were into the other's pocket and out again with the man's revolver. "How long since they've been arming the baggagemen on this road? You needn't answer—I'm only talking to myself. Those are the cases up there by the forward door, aren't they? And the big one's got the green boys— eh?" He was backing away from the man now. "Don't move, my bucko—understand? That chair you're sitting in is the only health resort in this car!"

The man's hands clenched, as his eyes narrowed on the Hawk.

"You damned thief!" he rasped out. "I—I'd like to——"

"Quite so!" said the Hawk softly. "I know how you feel about it, and if it helps any to get it off your chest, go to it! Nobody'll hear you but me, and I'll try and make the best of it!"

Piled along the side of the car from the doorway were a number of solidly made, heavy-looking cases that obviously contained the gold shipment. In front of these, between them and where the baggageman sat, and acting too perhaps as a screen when the rear sliding door was open, as, for instance, it had been at Selkirk, was a large, innocent-appearing, flimsily-constructed packing case. The Hawk, beside this now, moved it slightly. It was very light, so light as to warrant the presumption that it might even be empty.

The baggageman had relapsed into a scowling silence, his eyes still on the Hawk. The Hawk took his steel jimmy from his pocket, shifted his automatic to his left hand, and inserted the jimmy under the cover of the case. There was a rip and tear of rending wood; the operation was twice repeated—and the Hawk threw the shattered cover on the floor. He glanced inside. At the bottom of the case lay a large paper package, strongly tied, and heavily sealed with red wax.

Under his mask, the Hawk's lips parted in a smile, as, his eyes on the baggageman again, he noted that the other was watching his every movement now with a sort of intense expectancy. The Hawk, however, made no effort to reach down into the four-foot depth of the packing case; he canted the box over, and picked up the package from the floor of the car. With the point of his jimmy he tore a rent in the paper wrapper—and his smile broadened.

"I apologise," said the Hawk, with an engaging nod to the sullen figure in the chair. "They're not green boys—they're yellow backs!"

"You damned thief!" said the man, in a choked voice.

The roar and sway of the train seemed suddenly to increase, as the wheel trucks, jolting and beating at a siding switch, set up a sort of infernal tattoo. They were passing the first station after the Junction—Conmore.

The smile left the Hawk's face. A little further along, and *they* would stop the train. There came a sort of dare-devil set to the Hawk's clamped jaws.

He was taking chances, but he had already weighed those chances well. The Wire Devils, the Butcher and his crowd, would be on the alert; but equally so would be MacVightie—and the posse that must far outnumber the gang. And there was that promise to the Butcher! With their plans awry, and taken by surprise, instead of profiting by surprise themselves, their chances, rather than of securing a half million in gold, were most excellent of securing quite as generous a reward, though of another nature—at the hands of MacVightie!

"I'm going to get off here," said the Hawk coolly to the figure in the chair. "And the only way to get off without cracking my bean is to let that guy there in the engine know that he's infringing the speed laws! You remember what I told you—the only healthy place in this car for you is where you're sitting now. Something may crack loose around here—keep out of the wet!"

The Hawk reached above his head for the bell cord, and pulled it sharply. The engine crew, too, were evidently on the alert! The shrill blast of the whistle answered the signal instantly. There was a sudden jerk that almost threw the Hawk from his feet, the pound and slam of buffer plates, and the vicious shriek of the "air." The Hawk recovered himself, and, cool and quick in every movement now, thrust his jimmy into his pocket to free his hands, flung the package of banknotes up the aisle made by trunks and boxes behind him, and began to retreat toward the forward door, pulling the empty case along as a shield between himself and the other end of the car.

The rear door of the car smashed inward. The Hawk caught a blurred glimpse of faces and forms surging through the doorway, and streaming across the platform from the smoker behind—and, in the lead, the Butcher's crafty face, with its little black, restless, ferret eyes fixed down the trunk-made aisle of the car on *him!"*

"The Hawk!"—it came in a scream of abandoned fury from the Butcher—then a headlong rush—a flash, the roar of the report, as the Butcher fired—another, as the Hawk's automatic answered—and the *spat* of a bullet splitting the panel of the forward door.

The Hawk, stooped low behind the packing case now, still edged backward toward the door, still dragging the case after him. A smile that was deadly grim and far removed from mirth curved his lips downward in hard, merciless lines. He had, at least, attained his object! There was no doubt concerning their recognition of him as the Hawk! Well, he had weighed the chances. They would be on him now, but only one at a time; there was not room for more, with the packing case blocking the way—and it would be the Butcher first. After that—well, after that, he counted on MacVightie creating a diversion from the rear, and——

The Butcher had flung himself against the packing case. It toppled to one side, and the Hawk, like a crouched tiger, sprang and closed, making of the Butcher's body, as a substitute for the packing case now, a shield from the onrush behind. There was a furious oath from the Butcher; a lurch, a stagger, as the train jerked and jerked again—and both men, gripped and locked together, went to the floor.

For an instant they rolled over and over, the Butcher snarling like a mad beast, wrenching and twisting for an opening at the Hawk's throat—and then suddenly the car was in an inferno. A voice, MacVightie's, rang out sternly from the rear door. It was echoed by a yell from one of the Hawk's companions, then a shot, another, a fusillade of them—and then a voice above the uproar:

"It's MacVightie, an' de bulls!"

There was a scurrying of feet, a stampede for cover behind trunks and boxes by the Butcher's men—and the Butcher's grip was tense upon the Hawk.

"Cut it out!" he whispered hoarsely. "My God, we're trapped—the lot of us! Make a break for the door—get me? Crawl—that's the only chance!"

Blue eddies of smoke hung in queer, wavering, hesitant suspension up and down the length of the car; the air was full of the acrid smell of powder. The firing broke out again. The Hawk released his hold.

"All right!" he panted. "I'm with you!"

The Butcher was right, it was the only chance— and a chance that was theirs alone, for, as they lay on the floor, the packing case hid them, and it was barely two yards to the door. The train was almost at a standstill now. MacVightie's men had gained an entrance and a position for themselves behind the trunks at the lower end, firing as they crept forward, while back on the smoker's platform, through the baggage car's open door, others commanded the sweep down the center of the car.

The Hawk snatched at the package of banknotes, snuggled it under his coat, and, with the Butcher beside him, began to wriggle toward the door.

MacVightie's voice rang out again from the rear of the car:

"Marston, take ten men, and surround the car! And——" His voice rose suddenly in a bull-like roar. "The forward door, there—two of them! Watch which way they jump—not a man of them gets away to-night! *Quick!*"

The Hawk had wrenched the door open, and, with the Butcher behind him, flung himself out, and leaped to the ground. With the Hawk leading, running like hares, the two men dashed down the embankment, and hurled themselves over the barbed-wire fence that enclosed the right of way. Shouts, the crackle of shots, echoed from behind them—the short, vicious tongue-flames of the revolvers, a myriad of them, it seemed, stabbed yellow through the blackness.

The Hawk glanced back over his shoulder. He could just make out perhaps a half dozen dark forms in pursuit—and perhaps fifty yards away. The dark-ness and the distance made the shooting at best uncertain. It was only a chance shot that would get either the Butcher or himself, and ahead, unless he was mistaken, for the train must have come to a stop at just about that distance from Conmore, must be the wooded tract of land that surrounded the old farmhouse. Yes—there it was! The old dare-devil set clamped his jaws again. Yes, and so was the Ladybird—there! Well, it was obvious enough that there was no other cover! He glanced at the Butcher's face that he could just discern in the darkness. The Butcher might decide against it, but the Butcher evidently had not recognised his surroundings. The man's lips were working, and he was cursing in abandon as he ran.

The Hawk spoke in short, gasping breaths:

"There's some trees over there -to the right—a little—make for them—cover!"

The Butcher swerved automatically in the direction indicated.

"Curse you!" he wheezed out. "This is all your infernal, nosey work! What did you want to butt in for to-night—you fool—you couldn't have got that gold, anyway!"

"You close your face!" snapped back the Hawk. "I'm running my own show! There was a little cash—forty thousand bucks along with that gold, that maybe you didn't know about. That's what I was after—see? And that's what I got—see?"

"Yes"—the Butcher's voice broke in infuriated passion—"yes, and you got them all pinched, every last one of them—blast you! I——"

"You save your breath, and put it into running," retorted the Hawk savagely, "or else maybe you'll get pinched yourself! It's their lookout! I don't owe any of you any candy, do I!"

MacVightie himself was evidently one of those in pursuit behind, for again the Hawk recognised the other's voice:

"Spread out there to the right! And try and shoot a little straighter—before they get into that belt of trees!"

A renewed outburst of firing came in response—and the Hawk measured grimly the few yards that still separated him from the trees, as a bullet, drumming the air venomously, seemed to miss his cheek by but the fraction of an inch. MacVightie's presence was evidence that the detective was so well satisfied that the gang penned up in the car could not escape, that he obviously counted his temporary absence from the scene well warranted if thereby the clean-up were made complete in the capture of ———— The Hawk's mental soliloquy came to an abrupt end. There was a low cry from the Butcher, and the man, as they ran shoulder to shoulder, lurched against him.

"What's wrong?" flung out the Hawk sharply.

"They got me!" gasped the Butcher—and lurched again. "They got me—in the leg."

The Hawk glanced backward again. They were still those fifty yards behind, those dark, flitting, oncoming forms, those vicious yellow stabs of flame in the blackness—it had been a dead heat so far, here to the fringe of the trees.

The Butcher stumbled. The Hawk swung his free arm around the other's waist, and plunged in amongst the trees. It was slower work now, desperately slow. He clutched at the package of banknotes beneath his coat, and with his other hand tightened his grip upon the Butcher. The man was evidently badly hit, and was beginning to sag limply. Came the thrashing and branches, and the rush of feet behind them. The fifty yards was ten now—the Hawk, with his burden, struggled on—and then there came a cry again from the Butcher—they had gained the edge of the clearing, and the old farmhouse and its outbuildings loomed up before them.

"It's—it's——" the Butcher's voice choked weakly. "I—I know where we are—my God, *quick!* They'll search the house! I got to warn him now—quick!"

The man, as though under a stimulant, with new strength, had sprung forward alone into the clear, making for the farmhouse door. It was only a few yards, but halfway there he stumbled again—and again the Hawk pulled him to his feet.

A yell went up behind them. MacVightie and his men, too, were now in the clearing, and the ten yards' lead was cut to five, to three—and then the door before them was flung suddenly open, and a voice challenged hoarsely from within:

"Who's there? What's——"

The Butcher pitched across the threshold, dragging the Hawk down with him in his fall.

"The door, Jim—quick—slam it!" screamed the Butcher. "We're done—the cellar!"

The Hawk had leaped to his feet. The room was dark, unlighted, but from across it came, as there had come that other night, the faint glow from the open door of the cellarway. The Butcher had staggered up again, and was making in that direction—and then the Hawk, too, was across the room—but the next instant, turning to meet the rush from without, as the front door, evidently before the man whom the Butcher had addressed as Jim could fasten it, burst inward and crashed against the wall, he was borne backward, and, losing his balance, half pitched, half rolled down the cellar stairs.

The fall must have stunned him for a moment. He realised that as he struggled to his feet—to find himself staring into the muzzle of MacVightie's revolver, and to find that the bulging package of banknotes was gone from under his coat, as, too, were his automatic, his jimmy and the baggageman's revolver that had been in the side pockets of his coat. He raised his hand dazedly toward his eyes—and Mac-Vightie, reaching out, knocked his hand away.

"I'll do that for you—we were just getting around to it!" said MacVightie roughly—and jerked the Hawk's mask from his face. And then MacVightie leaned sharply forward. "O-ho!" he exclaimed grimly. "So it's *you*—is it? I guess you put it over me the night that ten thousand was lifted at the station—but I've got you now!"

The Hawk made no answer. He was staring, still in an apparently dazed way, about him. The cellar was a veritable maze of work benches and elaborate equipment—for counterfeiting work. A printing press stood over in one corner; on the benches, plates and engravers' tools of all descriptions were scattered about; and, near the wall by the stairway, he made out a telegraph set. But the Hawk's glance did not linger on any of these things —it fastened on a bent and twisted form that craned its neck forward from a rubber-tired wheel chair; on a livid face, out of which the coal-black eyes, narrowed to slits, smouldered in deadly menace, and from whose thin lips, that scarcely moved, there poured forth now a torrent of hideous blasphemy in that soft, silken voice that had earned the Ladybird his name; on the hand, crooked into a claw, that, pushing away the man who stood guard over him, reached out toward where the Butcher lay upon the floor.

"You ape, you gnat, you brainless pig! And you led them here—here—*here!*"

"I didn't know where I was until I was right on the house," mumbled the Butcher miserably. "I——"

"Shut up—both of you!" ordered MacVightie gruffly. "What do you say, Lanson? Is this the Hawk?"

The Hawk had not seen the superintendent, and he turned now quickly. Lanson's steel-grey eyes were boring into him coldly.

"Yes," said Lanson evenly, "I think I could swear he was the man who held us up in the private car the other night—but it's easily proved. If he is the Hawk, he has got a wound in his right side. I saw him clap his hand there when the pistol went off in his fight with Meridan."

"Well, we'll soon see!" snapped MacVightie.

The Hawk licked his lips.

"You needn't look," he said morosely. "It's there."

"So you admit it, do you?" MacVightie's smile was unpleasant. "Well, then, since you seem to be so thick with that pack of curs back there in the train, perhaps you'll admit to a hand in this little counterfeiting plant as well?"

"No; I won't!" said the Hawk shortly. "I never had anything to do with this! I don't admit anything of the kind! Ask him!"—the Hawk jerked his hand toward the Ladybird.

"Oh, all right!" MacVightie smiled unpleasantly again. "Let it go at that for now, if you like it that way. It doesn't much matter. You're birds of a feather, anyway, and there's enough on all of you to go around!" He reached behind him, and picked up the package of banknotes from where he had evidently laid it on the nearest bench. "How did you know this was on the train, and how did you know where it was in the car—and tell the truth about it!"

"I heard you and Mr. Lanson talking about it tonight," said the Hawk.

"Where?"

"In the roundhouse. I was outside the window. And"—the Hawk's voice thinned in a sudden snarl —"you go to the devil with your questions!"

The Ladybird was craned forward again in the wheel chair listening intently, he sank back now and scowled murderously at the Hawk. MacVightie shrugged his shoulders, handed the package to one of his three men who were with him in the cellar, and drew a pair of handcuffs from his pocket.

"Get that cash down to the train, and put it back with the gold where it will be under guard, Mac-Gregor!" he ordered brusquely. "And you two carry this fellow"—he rattled his handcuffs in the Butcher's direction—"down there, too. Tell Marston to let you have three or four more men. The chap that Williams has got upstairs there will have to be carried, too, I guess; and our friend here, in the invalid buggy, with the thanksgiving expression on his face, will have to have somebody to push him along over the ruts. Yes, and I'll want a couple to put in the night here—tell Marston to make it four. And now, beat it! You run ahead, MacGregor, and get back as soon as you can—we don't want to tie up the traffic all night!"

The two men picked up the Butcher, and, preceded by their companion with the package of banknotes, went up the stairs. MacVightie caught the Hawk's arm roughly, snapped one link of the steel cuffs over the Hawk's right wrist, and yanked the Hawk ungently over to a position beside the wheel chair.

He snapped the other link over the Ladybird's left wrist, and smiled menacingly.

"I guess there's dead weight enough there to anchor you for a few minutes while I take a look around here!" he said curtly—and turned to Lanson.

The Hawk was licking at his lips again. Upstairs, the tramp of feet was dying away. There would be no one there now but the other member of the gang who, it seemed, had been hurt when the house was rushed, and the one man who was guarding the prisoner. The Ladybird's cultured voice at the Hawk's side poured out an uninterrupted stream of abandoned oaths that were like a shudder in the nonchalant, conversational tones in which they fell from the twitching lips. MacVightie and Lanson were moving here and there about the place. Snatches of their conversation reached the Hawk:

". . . Well, I reckon I called the turn, all right, when I said it was the same crowd that was turning out the phony stuff, eh? . . . Yes, the telegraph set. . . . Can't trace the wires until daylight, of course. . . . Sure, a clean-up. . . ."

The Hawk's eyes travelled furtively around the cellar. They rested hungrily on a spot in front of him, where, in the centre of the floor, but partially hidden by one of the workbenches, was the bolted trapdoor of the underground passage that led out to the wagon shed. He circled his lips with his tongue again, and furtively again, his glance travelled on— to the door at the head of the cellar stairs that had a massive bolt, and that, evidently swinging back of its own accord after the men had passed through, now hung just ajar—to a long, narrow window, most tantalising of all because it was wide open, that was shoulder high, just above the stonework of the cellar and evidently on a level with the ground outside.

And then suddenly the Hawk's lids drooped—to hide a quick flash and gleam that lighted the dark eyes. MacVightie had stooped, and throwing back the bolt, had lifted up the trapdoor.

"Hello!" he ejaculated. "What's this? Here, Lanson! It looks like a passage of some sort." He was leaning down into the opening. "Yes, so help me, that's what it is!" He lowered himself hurriedly through the trapdoor, and his voice came back muffled into the cellar. "Come down here a minute, Lanson; they certainly had things worked out to a fine point!"

Lanson's back, as, following MacVightie, he lowered himself through the opening, was turned to the Hawk—and in a flash the Hawk's free hand had swept behind him under his coat to the concealed pocket in the back lining, and his eyes were thrust within an inch of the Ladybird's as he lowered his head.

"You understand?"—the Hawk's lips did not move, he was breathing his words, while a skeleton key worked swiftly at the handcuff on his wrist— "you understand? It's you or me! You make a sound to queer me, and I'll get you—*first!*"

The livid face was contorted, working with impotent fury, but, perhaps for the first time that it had ever been there, there was fear in the Ladybird's burning eyes. The Hawk's hand was free now. Lanson's shoulders were just disappearing through the opening, and with a lightning spring the Hawk reached the trapdoor, swung it down, bolted it, and, running without a sound, gained the head of the cellar stairs, pulled the door gently shut, slid the bolt silently into place—and the next moment the Hawk, returning, darted to the window, swung himself up to the ledge, and vanished.

"CONFIDENTIAL" CORRESPONDENCE

TWO days later MacVightie received a letter that had been posted the day before from a city quite a number of miles nearer the East than Selkirk was. In the left-hand, lower corner of the envelope, heavily underscored, was the word: "Confidential." What MacVightie read, when he opened the letter, was this:

"Dear Mr. MacVightie:—

"I feel that you are entitled to an explanation—I will not call it an apology, for I am sure you will recognise with me the unavoidable nature of the circumstances existing at the time —of my somewhat informal leave-taking of you two evenings ago; and I am afraid that my actions on that occasion have not enhanced your opinion of—the Hawk. I shall try and redeem myself. You have, I make no doubt, already searched that room where I first had the pleasure of making your acquaintance—and have found nothing. Let me begin, then, by saying that the diamond necklace belonging to His Excellency the Governor's wife, a certain well-known shipment of unset stones, and cash in varying amounts derived from sources with which you are acquainted, are in a black valise which you will find in the parcel room of the Selkirk station—and for which I enclose herewith the parcel-room check.

"I imagine that you are sceptical. I wonder, then, if it would also occasion you surprise to know that Birks of the Secret Service was, after all, 'on deck' the night that the Wire Devils fell into your hospitable hands? Yes, it is quite true—I am Birks. The newspaper biographies of the Hawk, the apparent authenticity of his prison record and release from Sing Sing was but 'inspired' fiction supplied from 'authoritative' sources. The East was being swamped with one of the cleverest counterfeit notes that the Federal authorities, popularly called the Secret Service, had ever had to deal with; and it was evident at once that the gang at work possessed an organisation against which ordinary methods would be of no avail. Facts in the possession of the Federal authorities indicated that the headquarters of the gang was in the West, and, indeed, as you later concluded yourself, that the so-called Wire Devils, who were just beginning to operate over the wires around Selkirk, were the men we wanted. That, because of my knowledge of telegraphy, I was detailed to the case, and how, almost at the outset, I was fortunate enough to secure the key to their cipher, need not be gone into here. Knowing their code, then, it would have been a simple enough matter to have run one or two of them to earth at almost any time, but that was not enough; it was necessary that the entire organisation, and especially its head, should be caught. The rôle of the Hawk furnished the solution to the problem. It enabled me to frustrate their plans, while at the same time I was working on the case, and it enabled me to do this without arousing their suspicions that the Secret Service was on the track of their counterfeiting plant. 'Birds of a feather,' you called us, Mr. Mac-Vightie; and 'birds of a feather' I am going to ask you to allow us, in the public's eyes, and particularly in the eyes of those you now have behind the bars, to remain.

"I am sure you will readily acquiesce in this. You will instantly see that my usefulness would be destroyed if the Hawk became known and recognised as Birks of the Secret Service by every crook in the country, as would result if he now figured in the case in his proper person. And this leads to a word of explanation in reference to the final act in our little drama of two nights ago. I had discovered the headquarters of the gang, and I had found that cleverest of unhung crooks, the Ladybird, to be in command. The plan outlined to you from Washington was at my suggestion, and was simply a

trap to collect them *all* into one net; a trap, I
might add, which they walked into, as they believed, with their eyes wide open, for they were
well aware of every move *you* had made. The
purpose of the money in banknotes accompanying the gold shipment was to supply the Hawk
with a *reason* for his appearance on the scene.
It was not altogether a question of coincidence
that the train was stopped just outside Conmore; nor that the chase led you to the farmhouse and the Ladybird. The rest you know.
It was necessary that I should be captured and
arrested in their presence, be caught in fact with
the 'goods,' and also that my escape should in
their eyes appear equally genuine, if I was to
preserve the Hawk's identity. As for this last
point, things turned out a little differently than
I had planned, for I had expected to be taken to
jail with the common herd, and there had intended to arrange some sort of an escape to
keep up appearances. As it turned out, however, I am sure you will agree with me that there
are worse things at times than a trapdoor in a
cellar floor!

"I think that is all—save for one little detail. I would suggest that you account for the
recovery of the 'swag' and the black valise
through the fact that, dissatisfied with your first
search of that room over our friend Seidelberger's saloon, you searched it again more
minutely, found a parcel-room check ingenious-

ly hidden, say, behind the wall bracket of the electric-light fixture—and by so doing permit me to remain,

"Ever and most sincerely yours,
"THE HAWK."

THE END

FRANK L. PACKARD (1877–1942) was a popular writer of crime fiction. Born in Montreal, Quebec, his early years were spent working as a civil engineer for the Canadian Pacific Railway. Between 1914 and 1938 he authored nearly thirty books, including the popular Jimmie Dale series. Many of his short stories and novels were made into motion pictures during the silent era, including *The Miracle Man* (1919), starring Thomas Meighan, Betty Compson, and Lon Chaney.

ROBERT MACDOUGALL is associate professor of history and associate director of the Centre for American Studies at the University of Western Ontario.